'Fans of PG Wodehouse and Aga[tha Christie] ... [a]
madcap comedy whodunnit ... O[ne of the funniest books,]
a perfect antidote to all real-[life worries]'
Daily M[ail]

'I couldn't put it down'
Santa Montefiore

'Sharp, funny and just the right amount of farcical – the best
sort of murder mystery'
Tatler

'An irresistible champagne bubble of pleasure and laughter'
Rachel Johnson

'What a triumph! It gave me enormous pleasure to read, plus
of course a few appropriate shudders. [*In the Crypt with a
Candlestick*] lightens the darkness in a way that is both
dark and light'
Antonia Fraser

'Fizzles, crackles and sparkles'
Elizabeth Buchan

'Agatha Christie but with a bit of Julian Fellowes's *Snobs* and
Downtown Abbey thrown in ... A masterclass in how to write
a rollicking good read'
Sarah Vine

Daisy Waugh is an author and Tarot reader. She has written several sad, historical novels, several contemporary, comic novels, a couple of non-fiction books, and a lot of newspaper articles and columns. She lives a quiet life with her family, not far from the River Thames in Barnes, South West London.

To find out more, visit her website at: daisywaugh.com.

DAISY WAUGH

IN THE
CRYPT
WITH A
CANDLESTICK

PIATKUS

PIATKUS

First published in Great Britain in 2020 by Piatkus
This paperback edition published in 2020 by Piatkus

1 3 5 7 9 10 8 6 4 2

Lyrics from 'Common People' on p. 164 by Candida Mary Doyle, Jarvis
Branson Cocker, Nick Banks, Russell Senior and Stephen Patrick Mackey. Lyrics
copyright © Universal Music Publishing Corp, Kobalt Music Publishing Ltd,
BMG Rights Management

A CIP catalogue record for this book is available from the British Library.

ISBN 978-0-349-42247-3

Typeset in Galliard by M Rules
Printed and bound in Great Britain by Clays Ltd, Elcograf S.p.A

Papers used by Piatkus are from well-managed forests
and other responsible sources.

MIX
Paper from
responsible sources
FSC
www.fsc.org   FSC® C104740

Piatkus
An imprint of
Little, Brown Book Group
Carmelite House
50 Victoria Embankment
London EC4Y 0DZ

An Hachette UK Company
www.hachette.co.uk

www.littlebrown.co.uk

In memory of my dashing grandparents,
Pamela, Arthur, Evelyn and Laura.

Alium Dime in Jukebox Pone

CHAPTER I

THE TODES OF TODE HALL

Lady Tode stood by the Great North Door of her important house, a vision of slimness and grief as she watched her husband take leave of the building for the last time. It was raining, as it always was, and Sir Ecgbert was dead. At the far end of the park, its huge, high dome obscured by mist, the Tode family mausoleum stood waiting, as it always had, to swallow his grim remains.

The mausoleum had been swallowing dead Sir Ecgberts for ten generations already, and had been waiting to swallow this one since the day of his birth ninety-three years ago. Which fact seemed, at his extended deathbed, to be a source of great comfort to him. Long after he could no longer recognise his wife or go to the lavatory unaided, he remained coherent and agitated about his final resting place. Was it ready for him? Had everyone understood which shelf he wanted? He didn't want to be anywhere near his Uncle Gilbert (a homosexualist) nor – God forbid – anywhere near 'the American'. Had they mowed the path across the park for the hearse? Would they remember to remove the cows from the field along the route? He didn't want the hearse getting butted by the bullocks ... Over and again, Lady Tode had to promise him that all was in order. *Yes, my Eggie-Peg*, she had to say. *We know which shelf you want! Everything is ready! You mustn't worry!* But he could never hear it enough. It was as if the mausoleum's mere presence, still standing where his ancestors had plopped it all those years ago, was proof that he had done his bit. The Tode mausoleum still belonged to the Todes. He could rest in peace.

It was in lousy shape, mind you. Non family members had to wear hard hats and sign waiver forms before they were allowed anywhere near it. There were cracks in the walls and missing tiles on the roof, and dry rot, and damp rot, and, in one of the four underground chambers (each with twenty or more shelves), a disgusting infestation of termites. There were stones that had come loose, and crypt fronts that had come off, and everywhere, signs warning tourists to Keep Out; not to mention the addition, in 1995, of a Missouri millionaire, 'the American', who'd paid the Tode Hall estate £35,000 for permission to rest his plebeian bones in an empty crypt beside Sir Ecgbert's great, great, great, great grandfather.

But no matter what state it was in, or whose bones rested inside, there was no denying the Tode mausoleum was something to behold. It was vast. It was preposterous. A building of such staggering importance and beauty that students of architecture came to admire it from all around the world. The name Tode meant 'death' in German. (As the late Sir Ecgbert often liked to remind his guests: it was his single joke. 'Welcome to

2

Death Hall,' he would say.) Perhaps this is why the Todes of Tode Hall invested so much in the family tomb. Maybe they'd always had an unhealthy preoccupation with the end.

In any case, Lady Tode could hardly bring herself to look at the wretched thing. She had hated it from the day she mistakenly became Sir Ecgbert's bride, fifty-four years ago, when, stepping out of the private chapel from which Sir Ecgbert's coffin was just now being removed, she had happened to glance at the mausoleum, its magnificent dome looming through the mist and the rain – and realised that, unless she did something radical and very brave, which was unlikely, the bloody thing would be looming at her until the day it was her turn to be slipped onto one of its shelves.

All things being equal, that wouldn't be for a while yet. Emma Tode was twenty-one years younger than the husband she was burying today. Still fit and fragrant and very much alive, and after fifty-four years of dutiful wifedom, longing to hand responsibility for the estate to the next generation, and spend more time at her lovely villa in Capri.

There were only three clouds on the horizon: Nicola, Ecgbert and Esmé, none of whom was prepared for the duties that lay ahead. It was too bad, because somebody had to do it. Lady Tode had served her time. She had waited long enough.

There was going to be an almighty row after the wake.

CHAPTER 2

B ut first, the funeral.

Ecgbert and Emma Tode's children, Nicola, Ecgbert and Esmé (fifty-three, fifty-one and forty-nine years, respectively), had not stayed together under the Tode Hall roof for many years, now. There were plenty of reasons for this. Nicola was a passionate socialist. She believed all property was theft and was bitterly ashamed of the house she grew up in, and consequently stayed away. Ecgbert – now Sir Ecgbert, of course: 12th Baronet – was a voluntary 'guest' in a nearby, privately owned luxury care home, from which he didn't like to spend many nights away, and Esmé lived with wife and family in Australia. So there were geographical reasons. Mostly though, they didn't see each other here, or under any other roof, because they didn't like each other much.

They had a lot of arguing to catch up on. In the past week, as their father's body lay in state in the chapel at the far end of the house, they had argued without pause: through every meal and all the boring bits in between. They argued about politics, religion, the name of Nicola's second pony, what Mrs Carfizzi would be cooking them for dinner, and above all, over every minuscule detail of their father's interment.

It turned out, despite Lady Tode's deathbed assurances, that the new style of hearse wouldn't be able to make it across the wet park without skidding, so the family eventually agreed they would load the coffin (eco-cardboard – over which, unimaginable squabbling) onto a trailer: and attach the trailer (still more squabbling) not onto Lady Tode's perfectly functional and more appropriate black Range Rover, but onto the estate tractor, which was orange.

Orange tractor, dirty trailer and cardboard coffin would then lead a stately cortège the traditional quarter-mile route across the park, starting at the Great North Door where Lady Tode, family and guests now stood waiting, past the lake, up towards Africa Folly (a slight detour, and quite a climb, but grand and picturesque) and then on down through the field usually occupied by bullocks, to the gates of the mausoleum.

Lady Tode would walk immediately behind the trailer, accompanied by her children and followed by everyone else: well wishers, of which there were a few, estate workers, domestic staff and tenants, of which there were many, and grievers, of which there were none.

Given the length of the walk from Hall to mausoleum, and (it being early autumn in Yorkshire) the almost-guaranteed horrible weather, Lady Tode had thought it might be practical to suggest a less formal dress code. Her children, for once united, could not have disagreed with her more. They insisted on everyone dressing smartly because it was 'what Father would have wanted'. Which was a bit rich.

This morning Lady Tode couldn't help but notice that all three had chosen to ignore the dress code themselves, each one having pitched up in mud-spattered coats grabbed from the boot room at the last minute. Nicola was also wearing a Che Guevara-style red woollen beret, to reflect the importance to herself of her politics. Her oldest brother, affectionately known as 'Mad Ecgbert', was wearing a pair of boots that weren't even a pair. And Esmé, who had small feet, was wearing a women's pair also grabbed from the boot room at the last minute, which were bright pink.

In any case, here they were: Lady Tode and her difficult children, amid a crowd of two hundred and fifty or so respectfully dressed, bitterly cold funeral guests. The tractor was rumbling toward them, and behind it, the coffin, balanced on eight damp bales of hay and adorned with a single wreath of lilies. The message on the card, covered in plastic to stop the ink from smudging, read:

For Father
Jolly good luck!
From the family

Not very loving. But then, neither was Sir Ecgbert. You reap what you sow.

The tractor drew up. Driving it, as had been debated and agreed upon beforehand, was the estate's handsome gamekeeper, Oliver Mellors. He looked magnificent.

However, when Mad Ecgbert saw Oliver Mellors at the tractor's wheel he was disconcerted: it was different from the way he had imagined it, and somehow he didn't like it. He stamped his foot. As the oldest son, not to mention heir to the ancient title, he should be the one doing the driving. It would be more appropriate – that's what he said to his mother, in a loud voice. 'Also,' he added, 'I know how to do it and it's fun.'

Lady Tode had never been able to manage Ecgbert. Least of all, when he stamped his foot. She was a meticulously correct woman, and easily embarrassed, and the last thing she wanted right now was a scene. She glanced apologetically at Oliver Mellors, who at that point was thirty-four years old and had been working for the estate for seventeen years. Lady Tode had always had a soft spot for him. He put the gear in neutral and climbed down from the driving seat.

'Thank you,' Ecgbert said. It sounded faintly self righteous. Then he seemed to hear himself and smiled at Oliver apologetically. As if it were those two – Oliver and Ecgbert – against the world.

Oliver said, 'You've driven it before, haven't you? I mean – with the trailer on the back?'

'Of course,' said Ecgbert.

'Just beware the back left wheel. When there's not much of a load on, like now, it can feel like it's going off on—'

'I know, I know all that,' interrupted Ecgbert. 'Shall we push on? These poor people are standing in the rain, freezing to death. Let's get the old man packed away!'

'Right-oh,' said Mellors.

'Father's been looking forward to this for ages, hasn't he Mother?' Ecgbert yelled as he climbed into his seat. He sent everyone a warm, mad smile, and accelerated off, cackling, and deliberately steering for a puddle.

Esmé and Nicola shouted after him to slow down but he couldn't hear; or he chose to ignore them. Off he drove, into the distance, and no one had much choice but to do their best to catch up. They walked as fast as they could, puffing and panting, while pretending nothing about the situation was amiss. And then, inevitably, disaster struck.

Half way across the park, near the top of the slope that crested somewhere by the Folly, so far away that the walkers could barely make out his figure, Mad Ecgbert's tractor veered to one side. He cried out and the tractor juddered to a halt. An almighty revving of engine echoed through the park, followed by another, angrier shout – and then the trailer did what trailers do when driven erratically by excitable amateurs on a steep slope and without sufficient load to ground them. The left back wheel had hit against a rock, and now the entire trailer was tipping.

... *One ... two ... three* ... The trailer recovered its balance too late to save its load. First the lilies fell, then the coffin, and then the hay bales. The coffin landed upside down and buckled under the weight of the bales as they landed on top.

Among the walkers, a horrified silence fell, and then Nicola started giggling. Esmé shot her a vicious look and broke into a run, his small, pink boots speeding to the disaster. No matter how mad or how irritating Esmé found his brother, Ecgbert was family, and he needed help.

By the time Esmé reached the tractor, Ecgbert had climbed down from the driving seat and was scrabbling among the wreckage, lifting hay bales off the coffin and dumping them onto the trailer as quickly as he could. He glanced across at Esmé, and then at the mourners, 150 or so yards away still, but coming closer every second.

'Not to worry!' he shouted. 'All under control!' He laughed, but Esmé could see that his brother was crying.

'*Idiot!*' Esmé said. Of all the things he'd called his brother in the past week, it was by far the mildest.

Ecgbert lifted another hay bale, 'Oh Christ, is that his arm, Es? Is his arm sticking out? Es! It's his skinny little arm – look! Disgusting ... It's Father's *arm*.'

'Get it back in,' said Esmé.

'It's his arm, Es! It's his fucking arm! I'm not touching—'

Esmé pushed his brother aside, grabbed the arm (stiff as board, light as feather), shoved it back into the coffin, and slammed the box shut. 'Coffin's upside down,' he said. 'Help me turn it over. Quick. We can get it back up before they come. Forget the bales, Ecgbert. *Hurry!*'

Ecgbert did as he was told, tears streaming down his face. 'We should never have got this ridiculous coffin!' he panted.

'Hurry!'

'If we'd got a decent coffin ...'

They plonked it back onto the trailer. Esmé picked up the wreath, still in pretty good shape all things considered, dusted it down and arranged it on top of the damaged coffin. By the time the guests had arrived, everything was more or less back in place. Ecgbert and Esmé had arranged the last two bales into an ad hoc seating area, and were perched one on each, chatting as if nothing were amiss. Except Ecgbert was shaking.

'Goodness, this rain!' said Lady Tode as she drew up before them. 'It really is *sheeting down*!'

'Oh, Emma, isn't it just!' said her friend, Veronica Snell of Snell Manor. 'Wretched weather!'

Nicola arrived, personality-defining hat bobbing as she jogged along.

'Your stupid coffin broke,' Ecgbert snarled, before she had time to gloat. 'I told you it wouldn't work. Father's arm fell out. Es had to stuff it back in.'

'*Goodness*,' exclaimed Lady Tode. 'That's a rather nice "seating area" you've got arranged there, Ecgbie! What an absolutely brilliant idea! I should think some of us would be grateful for a sit down, after that climb. Oof! Or shall we keep going?'

It was decided they should keep going.

Ecgbert looked at Oliver Mellors, who smiled back at him in a gentle, sympathetic, sexy, handsome, understanding, reassuring, confident manner. Nicola didn't go for cis men, so she wouldn't have noticed. Everyone else was still trying to catch their breath. Ecgbert returned the smile, a little ruefully. 'On second thoughts,' he said, 'you should probably take it from here, Oliver. If you don't mind.'

Order now restored, Sir Ecgbert's cortège continued on its solemn path.

CHAPTER 3

Things went relatively smoothly after that. The guests did not wear hard hats during the service. Esmé had asked them to sign waiver forms while signing the condolence book, but it proved to be an unnecessary precaution, as nobody tripped or slipped during the service, and no loose tiles fell on their heads. After a brief ceremony in the domed room above the chambers, immediate family members followed the cardboard coffin downstairs into the crypt for the committal. Mr Carfizzi, Tode Hall's long-standing caretaker/self-styled 'butler', came too. In fact he led the way, bearing a sweet-smelling candle in a silver candlestick. Nobody had invited him, but of all the people present, he was the only one even close to snivelling, and for that (for all sorts of reasons: they would have been quite lost without him) the family was grateful. In any case his presence diluted the intimacy of the atmosphere a bit, reducing any potential for embarrassment. Small talk continued nicely, as the body was shunted into its slot. Lady Tode said something about how smart everything looked, and thanked Mr Carfizzi for organising 'things so well', and after that, after a few moments of still quite embarrassing, but basically unavoidable silence, they made their way out into the daylight again.

The walk back to the Hall was always a pleasant one, having been designed to be so by the Tode ancestors three hundred years ago. It showed the house to its greatest advantage: the two long wings, the vast central dome – Tode Hall was the size of a village – looked perfectly symmetrical from this elevated angle. The house reclined in its landscape like an enormous, ancient spaceship, defiantly grand and ludicrously large (the bigness cannot be emphasised enough). It looked a little absurd. It looked beautiful *and* a little absurd. At any rate, the sight of it had always made Mad Ecgbert giggle.

House and grounds were closed to the public on this day of days, but in the normal run of things, even on a rainy one like this, the park would have been crawling with barbarians (who could buy tickets at the gates). There was an adventure playground somewhere down by the old Boathouse, now a café, and the old stable block, half way up the drive, had been converted into a tasteful retail centre selling fine teas and weirdly expensive trinkets to visitors. To be clear, Tode Hall wasn't just any old stately home – it was among the most famous in the country. And this fame had as much to do with its remarkable Vanbrugh-designed dome, 140-foot ballroom et cetera, as it did with one of the most popular novels of the twentieth century, *Prance to the Music in Time*.

Its author, the brilliant Lesley Piece, had dropped in for tea at Tode Hall between the Wars, so legend has it: and found herself so inspired by the grandeur of the place that she wrote a novel. *Prance to the Music* is a story about the aristocratic

12

owners of said massive house, with especial focus on the family's alcoholic youngest son, an amateur detective with possible homosexual leanings, named Tintin. To be sure, most of Tode Hall's visitors wouldn't have read the famous book, but they certainly would have heard of it, and they would have seen at least one of its glossy screen dramatisations. There had been a couple: an extravagant multi-part TV series twenty or so years back, with a stirring theme tune that still played on call-waiting systems all over the world; and more recently a Hollywood movie, starring an actor who went on to play James Bond! According to Esmé Tode, who was by far the most clued up of his siblings (he owned a small chain of luxury gyms around Melbourne), the BBC were in discussions about filming yet another dramatisation, this time with a huge emphasis on the LBGTQ angle which, due to changing times, had only been hinted at in Mrs Piece's original book.

All of which was good news for the Tode family coffers, but simultaneously quite irritating for the late Sir Ecgbert, who felt the house should be remembered for much more than 'one ruddy homosexualist novel' which he had never read. Sir Ecgbert felt acutely that 'people' – guests, tourists, utility facilitators – on glimpsing the house, shouldn't immediately start humming the *Prance to the Music* theme tune. He used to say it was impertinent. Which was all very well, but 'people' couldn't help themselves. The tune was catchy.

In any case, for all his antipathy to the book he had never read, Sir Ecgbert didn't hesitate to exploit the connection. There was a whole section of the house dedicated to *Prance*, with the theme music piped in, and pictures of the future James Bond, holding his famous teddy, Dogmatix, while chatting with his co-stars between takes.

13

Perhaps Lady Tode overheard a couple of the guests singing, very quietly, after the committal, because she was humming it herself on the way back to the house. People aren't supposed to hum at their husband's funerals, least of all the tune their husband most disliked. Her daughter, walking beside her, told her she was being 'gross'. Lady Tode apologised and stopped at once. They trudged along in silence – snatches of the theme tune reaching them from the ranks, as the 'people' intermittently, inadvertently, broke into song.

The aristocratic family in the novel was glamorous, elegant, winsome, impossibly charming – and in the TV show (where the title was abbreviated to a more manageable *Prance*) the house was always bathed in golden sunlight, it was full of people being witty and having picnics from hampers. And there were servants in uniforms and shiny, old-fashioned cars and—

'Shame, though, isn't it?' said Mad Ecgbert, walking between his mother and sister. 'We're a lot frumpier than they were in the show.'

'Nonsense, Ecgbie,' said Lady Tode. 'Don't run yourself down.'

They reached the house eventually. Mrs Carfizzi had made some little canapés and laid them out in the Yellow Drawing Room before the service. She and her husband, Mr Carfizzi, had ridden back to the Hall on Mellors's trailer, so they were there in time to welcome the guests – rather, Mrs Carfizzi, who was the cook, could get back to the kitchen, and Mr Carfizzi, who was the caretaker/butler, could stand at the door looking sombre, and take the coats.

Like everything in Emma Tode's life to date, her husband's wake passed in a haze of small talk and pointlessness. It was held in the (aforementioned) Yellow Drawing Room, which was normally laid out for public goggling, with a red rope preventing anyone from touching objects or sitting in seats. It was very grand. There was a Stubbs and a Reynolds on one wall, and a gaping hole on the other where, normally, there hung a large Gainsborough. However, due to a complicated deal with the government involving death tax avoidance, the painting was currently hanging in one of the public rooms at 10 Downing Street, and nobody knew quite when, or if, it would ever be returned.

Guests sipped on cheap white wine and nibbled on Mrs Carfizzi's disgusting canapés, and felt intimidated by their surroundings. Everyone agreed it had been a lovely service and that Sir Ecgbert had lived to an impressive age. Then they went home, leaving the Carfizzis, who lived in a flat in the cellar, to clear up.

By then it was four o'clock. Emma Tode retired to her room for a snooze, and the children retired to the Long Gallery to watch separate TV shows on their iPhones.

And then there was dinner.

CHAPTER 4

Lady Tode didn't know her children very well. After a busy life of dutiful delightfulness, she hardly knew herself. She assumed, quite rightly, that her children would be cross with the news she was due to share with them, but she hadn't considered quite how cross, or even, with any seriousness, their reasons why. They always seemed to be a bit cross with her in any case, for their own inexplicable reasons. So in a way it wouldn't make much difference.

Dinner was due to be served at 8 p.m., as usual, in the Red Dining Room (Tode Hall had three dining rooms: this was the smallest), and everyone knew it was inconsiderate to the staff to be late. After a pleasant snooze and a long, hot Floris-infused bath, Lady Tode combed her hair, dabbed a few understated colours here and there on her still-handsome face, and in such an orderly manner prepared herself for the night ahead. With luck there wouldn't be too much of a scene.

A knock on her door. It was Mr Carfizzi. As always, he

16

breathed in deep, inhaling the scent of her bedroom as she pulled back the door. Always the same smell. So feminine. So light and exquisite. So understated. So Lady Tode. After all these years, she was still his idea of a perfect woman: aloof, untouchable, delicious smelling. His poor, innocent wife of forty years had yet to realise, but when it came to matters touchable, Mr Carfizzi much preferred men.

He apologised to Lady Tode for disturbing her. Mrs Camer was downstairs, he said, insisting on a meeting.

'Mrs Camer? What, now? But it's almost dinner,' replied Lady Tode. 'Can't it wait until tomorrow?'

'Unfortunately she says this isn't possible.'

Mr Carfizzi left his childhood home in Calabria more than fifty years ago, but he had never lost his strong Italian accent. (His Italian wife, who left Italy at about the same time, spoke English so badly it was impossible to understand a word she said. The Todes had always suspected she made herself incomprehensible on purpose but – inasmuch as they had ever bothered to wonder about it at all – nobody could work out *why*.)

'Not possible? Is she all right?'

'She is perfectly all right . . . ' Mr Carfizzi was ready to burst with the news.

'Well – why is she still here? I thought everyone left hours ago. She wasn't working, was she? She works too hard, poor thing . . . Really, on a day like this she should allow herself a little time off. Don't you think?'

Mrs Camer, forty-eight, divorced and often lonely, had her own office in the East Wing of the house, in the Estate Offices courtyard. She lived in an estate-owned cottage and was also provided with an estate-owned car. Her official title was

'House and Grounds Manager, Tode Hall Estates', although she would have preferred something that sounded more executive. Unfortunately Sir Ecgbert, who'd come up with the job title when he took her on, ten years previously, thought she was being impertinent when she suggested it, and wouldn't entertain that idea. Mrs Camer had borne a grudge against her employers ever since. It was unfair. Lady Tode had never been anything but polite to her, and had even supported her in the argument about the job title. It didn't make any difference. Mrs Camer had always been jealous of Lady Tode and disliked her specifically.

'I think,' said Mr Carfizzi, who could no longer contain the news, 'she has a train she wants to catch. She's *leaving* us, Lady Tode. She says she's found a gentleman who wants to marry her, but I don't think it's possible, do you?'

'What?'

Mr Carfizzi shuddered. 'Some poor man has proposed marriage to her, so she says. And now she's going to make his life a misery by moving in with him in ...' He paused. 'She told me where she was going but I don't remember. She wants to say goodbye. She's leaving us tonight.'

Lady Tode took a moment to ponder this. 'It's a bit sudden,' she said.

Mr Carfizzi shrugged. Indeed it was.

'Well ... well, I suppose I had better go and say goodbye, then.' Lady Tode sighed. 'She might have waited a day or two, really. Never mind. We'll have to replace her ... put an advertisement in somewhere ... Does *The Lady* still exist?' Emma Tode followed Mr Carfizzi out of her extravagant bedroom (her bed had once been slept in by George II) leaving her Slovakian housekeeper, Kveta, to switch off lights and restore

18

the order while she was gone. 'Thank you, Mr Carfizzi. I'd better go and deal with her. Will you tell the children I'll catch up with them? They should start dinner without me. I won't be long. We don't want to keep Mrs Carfizzi waiting.'

In the time it took for Lady Tode to leave her bedroom, travel the long corridor and arrive in the Great Hall (two minutes of solid walking) she was feeling a teeny bit cross with Mrs Camer, because really – to do this just before dinner, following Sir Ecgbert's funeral was beyond bad form. It was shocking.

She didn't invite Mrs Camer to have a drink. By the look on Mrs Camer's face she probably wouldn't have accepted it anyway. For a moment they stood, one in front of the other, before the roaring fire, beneath the echoing seventy-foot dome, two small women in an insanely large room, waiting for the other to begin. Then they both began at once.

—'I'm ever so sorry to disturb you, Lady Tode . . . ' began Mrs Camer (suddenly nervous) and fell silent.

—'Carfizzi tells me you're leaving us,' began Lady Tode, in her frostiest voice. (It was of course Lady Tode who continued.) 'I'm so sorry to hear it.'

'I'm ever so sorry too,' said Mrs Camer again. She'd been looking forward to this moment since the day she ever arrived at the job. And then she burst into tears.

Lady Tode comforted her and sent her packing in the time it took for her children to finish the first course (toasted cheese on white sliced bread, cut into soldiers), argue about the moon landing, and ring the bell for Mrs Carfizzi to clear the plates.

CHAPTER 5

Cottage pie for mains. Ecgbert's favourite.

Her children wanted to know what had been the cause of the delay. When she told them the news, they cheered: united on this. None of them had ever taken to Mrs Camer. 'Plus,' said Mad Ecgbert, 'she hated us.'

'Of course she didn't,' said Lady Tode.

'Yes she did,' said Esmé.

'How could she possibly?' asked Lady Tode.

'How could she not?' snarled Nicola from beneath the hat. 'Our family literally owned her – we "owned" her house, her car, the food she put on her table—'

'As usual Nicola,' Esmé answered, 'you're being ridiculous. We didn't own the food she put on her table. She paid for her food out her income.'

'Which we paid her.'

'Well, obviously. She had this funny thing called "a job". Perhaps I should explain how it works?'

'You disgust me,' Nicola said. 'This family made its fortune out of slavery.'

'No it didn't, darling,' Lady Tode corrected her. 'Actually, we made our money out of agriculture. Which is not—'

'We made our money out of the exploitation of workers. I don't care what you call it, but I call that slavery.'

'Call it whatever you like, you mad cow,' said Mad Ecgbert. 'Call it salsa dancing, for all I care. Only pass the ketchup.'

She passed the ketchup, and they fell silent a while. Lady Tode cleared her throat.

'It was a lovely service, I thought,' she said.

'Absolutely,' Esmé replied. 'If you ignore the bit where Father fell out of his coffin. A splendid service.'

'And by the way Nicola, that was your fault,' said Ecgbert. 'It would have been perfectly OK if it hadn't been for you forcing us to send poor Father off in a bloody fag packet. You should be ashamed of yourself. Our family will probably never live it down.'

'*You* should be ashamed, not me. I wasn't the one who treated my own father's funeral like a funfair ride and tipped the poor sod out of the box.'

Once again, Lady Tode cleared her throat. 'But anyway . . . ' she said.

'I agree with you, Mother!' Ecgbert cried. '"*But anyway.*" Good for you. For God's sake, let's move on. Esmé, you're a twat. Nicola, words don't even cover what low regard I have for you. But never mind that. I think we should toast the future. Father had a very long life . . . *indeed* . . . And obviously we're all very sorry he's gone. That being said I, for one, look forward to seeing a few changes around here. Mother – are you going to jazz things up now the old man's out the way? I certainly hope so.'

21

Again, Lady Tode cleared her throat. Third time lucky. 'It's a good question, Ecgbie, and I'm very happy you've asked it . . . '

Something about her tone made the three junior Todes pause in their feasting, for just a moment. Their mother looked the same. Elegant and neat, detached and unruffled. But she sounded serious. Nervous. Until that moment, it had not much occurred to any of them that anything would actually change. Not really. Lady Tode was still young, after all: to all intents she'd been running the estate for years. Their father had only been wheeled out for ceremonies – to shake hands and open fetes, etc; but he hadn't even learned how to switch on a computer. He'd not had the faintest comprehension of how the business ran, because his young wife oversaw everything. So why would anything change?

Across the shimmering expanse of silver and mahogany, Mad Ecgbert gazed at his dreadful mother, and voiced the question that was on all their lips: 'What's up, Doc?'

'Well Ecgbie . . . ' she began, 'I think you may be going to be a teeny bit cross.'

'With you, Ma? Never!'

'I think you may. Esmé – Nicola. This concerns all of you, and I'm afraid you're *all* going to be a teeny bit cross. But the thing is, darlings, I feel . . . ' She seemed to cast around for the right words. 'I really do *feel* as if I've done my bit. For the Todes and Tode Hall.'

They stared at her, still not clear what she was trying to say, or rather, in what way whatever it was she was trying to say might possibly impact on them.

'You've done an awful lot,' said Esmé. 'Everyone knows it, Mother. You've been an absolute brick. If it weren't for your amazing efforts, this house would been have sold off to an oligarch years ago.'

'I don't think even an oligarch would have been willing to take on a place as large as this,' sighed Lady Tode.

'Well. Or even worse,' Esmé shuddered. 'We would have handed it over to the National Trust.'

'Yuk!' said Mad Ecgbert. 'Nicola, are you actually planning to hog those peas for the rest of your life? *What is wrong with you?*'

'There's nothing wrong with me. Why didn't you just ask me to pass them?'

Lady Tode didn't often raise her voice but on this occasion she needed to be heard. 'The fact is,' she said – almost, very nearly shouted, 'Ecgbert, Nicola, Esmé – I don't want to continue running things here any longer. Not without your father. I have been so fortunate. To be surrounded by so much beauty for so long. But really – that's enough now. I'm rather tired. It's time I passed all this on to the next generation . . . Of course I'm ready to stay on for another few months or so – even a year, if I must – to help with the transition. But after that, I have decided . . . Children, as you know I love my little house in Capri so very much, and I've never spent as much time there as I would like. My plan is, next week, to move out of the Hall and into the Gardener's House. So I'll still be around for a while, and I will still have a base here. But I'll be spending a lot more time in Capri.'

'Don't be ridiculous,' said Esmé. 'That's ridiculous.' There was panic in his voice. 'Ecgbert can't possibly run this place without you, Mummy. You know that.'

'Yes I bloody well can!' Ecgbert snapped back. But there was, beneath the outrage, a hint of panic in his voice, too.

'And Nicola can't do it. She'd turn it into some sort of twinkie WOOF hold out. Or she'd hand it over to a radical

Islam lesbian fucking support group to grow organic tofu, given half a chance. Mother, I don't actually think you've thought this through. And by the way *I* can't do it. In case you're thinking I can. *I'm* not bloody well doing it. Jesus Christ ... '

Esmé was growing increasingly agitated. He knew what was coming – from the look on his mother's face, he knew what she was about to ask. And it was out of the question. Even thinking about it made him want to cry – everything about England made Esmé want to cry: this family, this house, this mother sitting there, waiting calmly to ask the unaskable, that father, falling out his cardboard coffin, the shelf that awaited him in the mausoleum ... Esmé imagined returning to Australia and breaking the news to his wife, Chelsea: she would laugh in his face! She would tell him to shove his ancestral duties up his fat English arse (because that was how she spoke, unlike Lady Tode: it was one of the reasons he loved her). She'd take Piper and Kyle with her, because they wouldn't come back with him. His children hated it here. And for the rest of his lonely life he'd be stuck in the middle of Yorkshire with no wife and no children, in a house the size of a fucking town, talking to people like Mrs Camer about the cost of Keep off the Grass signs.

He was hyperventilating.

'Sit down, darling,' said Lady Tode. 'Breathe deeply.'

'I'm not doing it, Mother. Don't ask me.'

'Cool your boots, Es,' said Ecgbert, whacking him, not unkindly, on the back. 'No one's asking you. Mother, if you need me to step up, you only have to say. I'd be delighted!' But nobody paid any attention.

Lady Tode took a moment. She considered her children, staring at her angrily across the shiny silverware. For fifty-four years, she had dedicated herself to the glory of their inheritance ... (This is what ran through her mind.) ... And now it was their turn. Ecgbert couldn't do it, obviously. But Esmé could. And if he refused to do it, she would have to find somebody else.

'Esmé,' she said. It sounded very sombre. 'You disappoint me.'

'What? Why? Why me? There are three children in this family. I'm the only one who's actually made a success of my life. Why would you ask me to wreck it all now? Ask one of these two jokers. For God's sake, they have nothing to lose. I have a wife, kids, a successful business—'

'This house,' she said, 'has been in your family for over three hundred years. Can you imagine how hard each generation has had to fight to keep it that way?'

'I didn't see Father fighting that hard,' said Nicola. 'Everything fell into his lap.'

'You didn't see,' said Lady Tode, 'because you chose not to look. He dedicated his life to keeping this house in the family. Now it's your turn. And yes, Esmé – you're right. I think you would do a brilliant job if—'

'Well that's too bad.'

'Mother, I just told you,' interrupted Ecgbert, 'I can do it. Why does nobody have any faith in me around here? It's outrageous. And by the way, in case you'd forgotten, I am in fact the oldest.'

'No you're not,' said Nicola.

He rolled his eyes. 'Obviously, I mean the oldest son. Don't be stupid Nicola. I don't know why we're even having this conversation.'

Just then Mrs Carfizzi came in to clear the cottage pie,

25

and despite all the emotion around the table, their lifetime of good training kicked in. They fell silent. Lady Tode, as Mrs Carfizzi lifted her plate, smiled politely and said, 'That was delicious, Mrs Carfizzi, as usual! Thank you so much.' Esmé said, 'Nothing like good old home cooking, Mrs Car Fizzy. I'm going to miss you back in Aussie!' Ecgbert said, 'Scrumptious as ever!'

Nicola was the only one to say nothing. Mrs Carfizzi had never acknowledged a single one of her dietary stances. (She was a vegan currently, but had been all sorts of things over the years: she had a bad relationship with food.) And so, though she always gobbled the food when she was home, Nicola refused to acknowledge either Mrs Carfizzi or her cooking. They hadn't exchanged a word since Nicola was seventeen.

Mrs Carfizzi replied to the others, something smiley but incomprehensible, and left the room. The moment she closed the door, the family struck up again.

'Well *I'm* willing to step up,' Nicola said. 'I don't know why you don't ask me. I'd do a brilliant job. And as the eldest, I think—'

Lady Tode said: 'Don't be silly, darling.'

She said she wasn't being silly.

Her mother said: 'But you don't have any experience – not of anything, really, darling. Which isn't to say you're not a terrific artist. You're a *wonderful* artist . . .'

She was a lousy artist. Had barely picked up a pencil since she finished her foundation course back in 1987. It wasn't the point. Nicola took the moment to remind her family, in an angry monotone (she'd said it many times before) that 'salaried work' wasn't the only measure of a person's value, and that she happened to spend a lot of time working with

26

underprivileged kids, also offering counselling at an LBGTQ beauty care through arts-and-crafts support group in one of the poorest parts of Edinburgh, the sort of place her family probably couldn't even imagine existed, and that if she could do that, which they couldn't, she could certainly organise ...

But by then everyone had stopped listening. Esmé was on his feet again, shouting about his love of Australia. Ecgbert was close to tears, lamenting his mother's lack of love for him. Which was, in fact, his perennial cry. None of the children felt loved by her, and never had, but only Mad Ecgbert seemed to sense the lack of it. Or at least he was the only one who ever voiced his feelings on the matter. 'You may not love me, Ma,' he was saying. 'I can't force you to love me. But I can force you to hand over what is rightfully mine!' It was a matter of family honour, he said. He was the oldest son. He was the 12th Baronet. He *was* Tode Hall. It was his to inherit.

All in all, the conversation was going even less smoothly than Lady Tode had imagined it would. It simply hadn't occurred to her that Ecgbert could ever have imagined he might be fit to inherit: or that Nicola, who despised everything her family was and stood for, would suddenly decide to throw her (silly) hat in the ring. Above all, it hadn't occurred to her that Esmé would be so violently averse to coming home and doing his duty. Even if he hadn't been expecting the move to be so imminent, he must have known that at some point he was going to be called upon ... She was taken aback.

A silence fell. Lady Tode, at the head of the table, gazed implacably at her three unruly children, and they gazed angrily back. It was a stalemate. Except that Lady Tode had no intention whatever of sticking around. If the worst came to the worst, she would leave it all to Oliver Mellors. (She'd always

27

had a very soft spot for Oliver Mellors.) In any case, one way or another a solution would have to be found.

'Are we ready for pudding?' she said.

They were.

It was chocolate mousse. Mad Ecgbert's favourite. When Mrs Carfizzi carried it in Ecgbert, still emotional, stood up and gave her a hug.

'I wish *you* were my mother, Mrs Car Fizzy,' he said.

Mrs Carfizzi told him not to be silly. But she had no children of her own, and a husband who gave every impression he loved the Todes of Tode Hall far more than he had ever loved his wife. So she took the compliment, buried it deep in her broad bosom, to be basked in and gloated over when the dinner was done.

CHAPTER 6

A week later, Lady Tode had booked herself onto a train to London. Esmé was back with his family in Sydney, Nicola was back doing good works in Edinburgh, happily reunited with her gender non-specified lover, Bone, and Ecgbert had returned to his computer game, his model army, and the long-suffering care of his keepers at Todeister House, where he lived with a small collection of similarly well-born loose cannons, out of harm's way and without credit cards. The family had parted company without referring to the inheritance row again. This was to be expected. It was a long-held family convention never to resolve an argument, but to sweep it under the massive Tode Hall carpets, and move on.

What the Tode children hoped – assumed even, inasmuch as they considered it at all – was that life would continue as before, amen. They failed to notice the unusual strength of their mother's feelings on the matter.

They couldn't know it, because in all her years of duty and

delight, she had never let it slip, never once lifted the mask. But Emma Tode had been looking forward to leaving Tode Hall since her wedding day, fifty-four years, three months and one week ago. Sir Ecgbert (11th) had been old when they married. He might have done her the service of popping his clogs at any point, but he'd taken *until he was ninety-three*. And this, despite there having been encouraging signs of decrepitude from about seventy. It had been a long wait. Lady Tode could not – would not – wait any longer.

So, having taken note of Esmé's disgraceful refusal to do his duty, she had turned her attention to her nephew by marriage, the young Egbert Tode. Egbert, NB, without the 'c'. Lady Tode hardly knew him. The last time she'd seen him was at his christening, thirty-five years ago. He was the only son of the late Hon. Esmé Tode who was the younger brother (and only sibling) of her dead husband.

Her children had never laid eyes on their only first cousin. Their father had fallen out with his father, over the spelling of Egbert's name. By deliberately dropping the 'c', the late Hon. Esmé had turned his back on centuries of family tradition. To his older brother, Ecgbert (11th) this seemed to be an act of the most grotesque betrayal. He never confronted Esmé about it, but he never forgave him either. After Egbert's christening, the two brothers never spoke again. Which may offer a clue as to why Ecgbert (11th) was so little mourned at his own funeral. He was an awful man. His wife had more than earned her time in Capri.

In any case, Sir Ecgbert was dead at last, and Tode Hall needed a custodian, preferably with the family name. It wasn't hard for Lady Tode to track Egbert down. He was working at the Wandsworth branch of Savills estate agent, and had recently been promoted to Lettings Manager.

When she rang to ask for a meeting, he was polite but wary. Egbert's mother-in-law, (Lady) Mary Percy, had read in *The Times* that his uncle Ecgbert (11th) was dead. So he was aware of it, and he remarked to Lady Tode that he was sorry for her loss, which could not possibly have been the case. He also told her, by way of conversation, that he had two small children, named Ludo, four, and Passion, three; and a wife called India. (Actually Lady Tode knew this. She had once been friends with India's aunt, Beatrice Percy, and knew several people who knew India's mother.)

Egbert wondered why Lady Tode was calling him, but he was too polite to ask. So they chatted about this and that for several minutes. Esmé was in Australia, she told Egbert, 'doing awfully well', and (Mad) Ecgbert was 'really, really happy, just tootling about' at Todeister House, outside Todeister. And Nicola meanwhile was 'doing marvellous things with her art, living in a sweet little flat in Edinburgh'.

'Good, good!' said Egbert, while mouthing apologetically at a colleague to start the meeting without him. 'That's terrific news. I'm so pleased everyone's doing so well.'

'We're very lucky,' agreed Lady Tode. 'Obviously the death of their papa was a bit of a shock. But they've all taken it terribly well. And it was such a lovely service. I'm sorry you couldn't have been there.'

'Next time!' said Egbert. He wasn't concentrating. He needed to be at the meeting, and she wasn't getting to the point.

'Well but Egbert ... ' she said, a little confused. 'I don't think there'll be a "next time".'

'Of course not. I'm so sorry ... Anyway – it really is so lovely to catch up ...'

31

Finally she told him why she was calling. She 'happened to be' in London, she said, and she needed very much to have a word with him and his wife, India. Could she drop round for a drink this evening? It was important.

He told her the address and got her off the line as quickly as possible. It was only after he hung up that it occurred to him to wonder what, after all these years, she could possibly have to talk to him about. He felt, as he said to India later, 'a tingle of serious excitement' for the rest of the afternoon.

CHAPTER 7

Egbert and India's house in Wandsworth was an estate agent's dream: the sort of house that is snapped up by buyers even in dismal markets. Egbert sometimes wished his clients could take a leaf out of his prudent book: present their houses as smartly as he and India presented theirs. It was modern, tasteful, luxurious, pastel and mostly open-plan. They had bought it five years earlier, soon after they married, just before India got pregnant with Ludo. As her belly grew, India, who'd spent a short time, before she was married, answering the phone at her godmother's interior design office just off Sloane Street, dedicated her expertise to its lavish refurbishment. They'd spent a fortune remodelling the kitchen, especially. There was a 'chiller cabinet' with a glass door, for storing champagne and wine. There was a coffee machine built into the wall, and two little extra taps beside the sink; one for filtered water, the other for water kept permanently at boiling point, thereby eliminating the need for a kettle. There was also a kettle. There were pull out, pull in recycling bins, and cupboards that slid and shelves that popped, and every space was sleek and designated, and every little object had a designated space.

'I got a teeny bit obsessed!' India would generally chortle, when showing it off to her friends. 'Couldn't help myself! Preggers brain!'

India could blame 'preggers brain' as much as she liked – but the truth is there had never been a time when she *could* 'help herself', pregnant or not. India Tode (as Lady Tode was about to discover) may have looked like a conventional, wholesome, amenable, well-born beauty. She looked ideal. But – as her parents used to say – somewhere along the line, there had always been 'a bit of a chink missing'. India lived, for better or worse, by instinct and whim. She and Lady Tode may have been born of similar stock but temperamentally they couldn't have been further apart.

In the meantime … the kitchen looked like a tasteful oak'n'chrome spaceship. It had cost the young Todes £375,000 to install.

Lady Tode thought it was a bit common: but of course she didn't say so. In any case pretty much every square inch of Tode Hall was Grade 1 listed. They wouldn't be allowed to turn the place into a space station, whether they liked to or not.

'What a stunning house!' she said. 'And what an incredible kitchen! Goodness, you young people are inventive! All these funny drawers and clever lights! What fun!'

India and the au pair were putting the children to bed when Lady Tode arrived. This was a mammoth operation, often taking well over two hours, the tail end of which usually also required Egbert who, on his return from work, would help with the final push. This evening, however, he was on small talk and drink-mixing duty. He took Lady Tode into the sitting room; a padded cell, or so it felt to Lady Tode, of thick carpet and thickly interlined curtain. On the shelves, where books might otherwise have been, there were dozens of photographs of India in bridal wear, Egbert in sportswear, Ludo and Passion, in various states of undress.

Lady Tode gasped at the loveliness. And there really was plenty of loveliness to gasp at. The children looked cuddlesome and golden in their nakedness; and India was a blonde, shiny-toothed angel. Outrageously pretty. An English rose with a sporty Californian edge. There were pictures of her not only in bridal wear, but arm-in-arm with Egbert, in matching biking Lycra, their healthy, grinning faces spattered in English mud.

'What a beautiful family!' exclaimed Lady Tode. 'What a lucky man you are, Egbert!'

Egbert wasn't so bad looking himself, to be fair. He looked rather like her own Esmé, Lady Tode realised – except taller: dark and solid, with broad shoulders and a manly jaw. (Mad Ecgbert was handsome in a completely different way. He was very tall, like his father: six foot three at least. And there was nothing broad or solid about him. He looked lanky and chiselled, *delicate* and *poetic*. Of her two sons, Emma Tode much preferred him.)

Egbert and Emma talked about nothing much until India arrived. Emma asked about their wedding, and Egbert sipped his lager and told her that it had been a special day. The best day of his life. She asked him about the property business in south-west London, and he said it had been sticky for a while, what with the raised stamp tax and then of course Brexit.

'Yes *Brexit*,' said Lady Tode. They nodded solemnly, neither offering an opinion.

'But you know,' he said, 'things are really picking up now. Especially in Wandsworth. It's such a great area for families. And that is something which is literally never going to change. Plus we have amazing schools down here, independent and state. And they really do seem to be getting on top of the transport situation. It's definitely improving. Whereas eighteen months ago ...' Lady Tode zoned out. She was good at it. Egbert would never have guessed.

And then, at last, the beautiful, charming, warm, unpredictable India *whooshed* in.

CHAPTER 8

'Sorry I took so long,' she said, wrapping the widow, Lady Tode, in a lovely cashmere hug. 'Ludo's been playing up *like mad*. I think he's got a bit of a tummy bug tbh, because it's so unlike him. And now of course naughty little Passion thinks he's terribly funny, so she's saying, "Mummy, Mummy, I've got a tummy bug", and then literally ...' – Lady Tode zoned out again – '... creasing up with little giggly laughter. She's such a monkey! Is that a G&T, I see there, Egg, darling?' India interrupted herself. She was peering into Lady Tode's glass. 'Yes *please*! Lots of ice for me! And lots of gin!'

She collapsed onto the big white sofa, a flurry of sunlight and flowery smells. She leaned in towards Lady Tode and said: 'We meet at last! How intriguing! You didn't tell Egg what you wanted to see us about, did you?'

Lady Tode didn't like her. Not that she realised it herself, and not that it really mattered at this point. But the thing about Lady Tode; she didn't like any women. She especially didn't like women who were beautiful and confident and carefree and cheerful and young. They did something to her insides, similar to the effect of salt on slug skin. She smiled her sphinx-like smile: 'I haven't told Egbert anything yet, no, India. I thought—'

India giggled. 'I'm going to take a wild guess.'

'Are you really?' said Lady Tode, with the smile still on her face.

'Well it hardly takes Einstein to work it out,' replied India. '... Gosh I wish Egg'd hurry with my drink! It's been a long day, Lady Tode – Emma. I can call you Emma, can't I?'

'I should think you must be exhausted,' agreed Lady Tode (deftly ignoring the question). 'I remember when my children were small, they—'

'I'm pretty sure you want Egbert and me to take over at Tode Hall. Am I right?'

Lady Tode said: ' ... I ... '

India grinned, her theory confirmed: 'You're probably ready to move on, aren't you? I know I would be. After fifty years, or however long you've been there. I'd be *longing* for the next adventure. And from what I've read in the *Daily Mail* about Egg's cousins, I get the impression your wonderful amazing kids just don't feel that passionate about taking up the reins, am I right? Which means, short of selling the place, or worse case, handing it over to the National Trust—'

Lady Tode shuddered.

'Which absolutely nobody wants,' India agreed. 'You should have seen what they did to my Great Uncle Siegfried's house ... before they burned it to the ground.'

'Yes. I was so sorry about that.'

India waved it aside. 'So if the options are A) selling up

38

to some crazy oligarch or B) surrendering everything to the boneheaded National Trust – well then, my darling husband is probably the best – the only possible choice! Am I right Emma?'

India saw the look of astonishment on Lady Tode's face, and chortled with pleasure at her own cleverness. She gave a little bounce on her fatly upholstered sofa. 'I knew it! I knew it, *I knew it*! Ha ha ha – Egg! EGG!' she shouted through to him. 'I told you! I was *right*!'

'Well, look—' Lady Tode sensed the conversation slipping out of her control. Not a sense she ever enjoyed. 'We mustn't jump the gun, India . . . I was simply wondering . . .'

Egbert appeared, still in his work suit, carrying a small bowl of olives and a perfect gin and tonic for his wife. There were tiny spots of colour on his cheekbones.

'*See?*' cried India triumphantly, taking the glass. 'Thank you, darling. See that, Emma? Those little pink spots? He's excited, aren't you sweetheart?' India grinned.

'I really – are you? I don't know,' Lady Tode sounded flustered. Smiling unhappily, she looked up at Egbert, now standing between them with the pink spots at his cheekbones. She gave a little shrug. The conversation had accelerated to a speed well beyond her preferred pace and she wasn't sure how to pull it back again. Added to which, of course, India was quite right. Spot on. She said, 'Well, I don't know quite what to say. I mean, obviously, I have a great deal to say. But in principle . . . *yes*. Of course the house and contents are very much tied up in all sorts of family trusts, as you may imagine, and could never be sold – not that you would want to—'

'Certainly not!' Egbert agreed.

'Nothing could be sold without the say-so of the trustees – and they are myself, obviously; and my children Ecgbert,

Nicola, Esmé. But the running of the estate, and the income from the estate is really . . .' Lady Tode paused.

'Up for grabs!' cried India, and giggled. 'What fun!'

'Well,' Lady Tode would have put it another way, and did. 'It's at the disposal, obviously, of whomever is at the helm, living at the Hall and overseeing its many businesses. Of which, you may not be aware . . .'

'Oh I'm aware it's very large,' said Egbert.

Again, India giggled. 'Funnily enough I was looking up the public accounts the other day, wasn't I Egg—'

'No you weren't,' said Egbert, blushing furiously.

'*I was!* When Mummy told me Sir Ecgbert had died, she and I were wondering who would inherit everything, given – you know. Your kids having minds of their own. I wanted to remind myself of what my Egbert was missing out on, because of the "c". I said to him – didn't I Egg? We were laughing about it! – I said, maybe you should think about putting the "c" back in!'

'No,' said Egbert, 'I don't really remember.'

'It's not just a missing "c",' Lady Tode said, still smiling but now really quite irritated. 'With or without the "c", your husband is the son of the younger son. That was the reason.'

'But not anymore!' cried India. 'Anyway, who cares? I'm up for it. What about you Egg? I think it could be absolutely good fun. A brilliant adventure. The kids can have ponies. And those adorable little electric cars. *Everything*. They can have *everything*! God, they're going to love it! Who wants another drink?'

Egbert looked embarrassed. Emma Tode hadn't yet made a formal offer – and really, there was so much to discuss. Not least, how his disinherited cousins might feel about their usurpation. Also, Egbert enjoyed his life in London. They had only just finished doing up the house, he had friends nearby, he'd just been given a promotion. Life was pretty good.

'India,' he muttered, 'I think you may be jumping the gun ...'

Lady Tode smiled. 'The fact is, the house desperately needs someone young and enthusiastic to bring in new ideas ... Really it's a constant – I won't say "battle" but it's certainly a challenge to ...' she took a breath and started again. 'For one reason or another, my children, who in any case really aren't that young anymore, are – how does one explain it? – they are wonderful people. I am tremendously proud of their achievements. However they are none of them in a position to take on the responsibilities of a house like Tode Hall. It's my duty to find someone who is. Which leads one, as your wife guesses correctly, to *you* Egbert, and to your delightful family. I am happy to stay on at the Hall for a while, to help oversee the transition. In fact—' she glanced at India, 'I think that would be essential ... But India is quite right. I would like to hand over responsibility while I am still young enough to enjoy my life ... I can't live forever, after all!'

'Yes you can, Emma!' interjected India, warmly. 'Never say die!'

Lady Tode nodded. She turned to Egbert.

Egbert said, 'What do the others think about the idea?'

Lady Tode looked blank. 'Who?'

'The children.'

'Your children?'

'No – *yours*. What do my cousins think about India and me coming in and taking over? Are they happy with the idea?'

Lady Tode didn't flinch. 'Trust me,' she said at once, 'they'll be delighted.'

41

Egbert smiled. 'Well in that case . . . Obviously India and I need to think about it. Look into schools and so on. Consider the financial implications. It's a big move.'

'Of course it is,' agreed Lady Tode. 'I'll put you in touch with our finance man. He can talk you through all the ins and outs. He's based in Darlington, but he works for us most of the week – perhaps you and he—'

'And *me*,' said India.

'Absolutely,' Lady Tode agreed quickly. 'You and Egbert and our money chap should get together over lunch. And then you can come up for a weekend and we can show you around – I know you'll fall in love with the place. Everybody does . . . '

'I bet,' Egbert said.

Lady Tode thought a moment, felt a spark of life inside her frosty little heart: a flicker of light at the end of a long, dark tunnel. She could almost smell the Tyrrhenian Sea. 'In fact,' she added, with something quite like openness, 'we're looking for a new household manager. Our last one gave in her notice – can you believe this? – on the day of my husband's funeral.'

'That's a bit much,' Egbert agreed.

'So, if you're interested, and I hope you are, because I think you would both be very happy at Tode Hall – I think you would be perfect for it – perhaps you could help me sift through the applicants? Since, ultimately, I very much hope, whomever we choose will be working, not for me but for you.'

'Oh, what *fun*!' said India.

They persuaded Lady Tode to stay for supper. She didn't want to stay, and they didn't really want to have her – but it seemed unavoidable. She was offering them a home in one of the largest, most beautiful houses in the country; and the income from an estate whose annual turnover, when you took into account the two cafés, the trinket shop, the organic grocer, the tourist entry tickets, the film and TV locations fees, the farming subsidies, the farming income, the holiday cottages . . . came in at nearly £10 million.

In exchange for which they would submit to life in a house they could never alter or call their own, which for half the year was full of tour guides and red ropes and goggling tourists; a house surrounded by grounds that were open to the public 365 days a year. They would never again be able to look out of their own window without fear of being confronted by a coach-load of barbarians goggling in.

Oh, and the paperwork!

And the lack of privacy.

And the unrelenting demand for gracious manners.

And the lack of privacy.

And the lack of privacy.

And the lack of privacy.

For fifty-four years, beneath that serene, close-lipped smile, Lady Tode had been suffocating. Now, it seemed, there was an end in sight.

And Egbert and India would be able to leave London and all the irritations of urban life: they would buy ponies and little electric cars for their lucky children, and instead of being just one of thousands of rich couples in the rich Wandsworth crowd, they would be King and Queen of their own castle.

So everyone was happy, really. More or less.

Of course it couldn't last.

CHAPTER 9

I n an overheated one-bed flat at an assisted care home in Clapham, London, meanwhile, ninety-six-year-old Violet Dean was attempting, slowly and clumsily, to dial her grand-daughter's landline. Balanced on her lap, she had the most recent issue of *The Lady*, and she was so excited with what she'd read inside it she kept botching the number and having to start again.

But she cracked it eventually. The call went directly to voicemail, which meant Alice was *in* – and on the line. Her grandmother pressed redial once, twice, seven times. She had nothing else to do with her time. She would keep at it until she got through.

Alice Liddell, only three hundred yards up the road, and on the phone to a friend, could hear beeps on the line and knew exactly who was calling. Her grandmother, Violet Dean, whom she loved better than anyone (after her sons, obviously), could be quite annoying. And although Alice had every intention of ignoring the beeps and finishing her call in her own good time, that soon became impossible, so she said goodbye to her friend and then, calmly, unplugged the phone.

The house was a mess. She wanted a glass of wine and her end-of-day spliff and a hot bath. Unfortunately not all of this would be possible at once. Upstairs, she could hear one of her sons taking a shower in the only bathroom. She looked up at the ceiling. Sure enough, drips of water were leaking through the light fitting again. She muttered something under her breath, and headed out to the hallway.

'Jacko! You're flooding the kitchen again. Jacko – you're FLOODING the kitchen! ... Drez – can you tell him? Drez? *Tell your brother he's flooding the kitchen!* ... Can anyone hear me?'

A long pause. Water thundering from the bathroom. Music thumping from the boys' bedroom. And then, 'What's that, Mum?'

'Drez can you tell your brother he's flooding the kitchen! And tell him not to take all the hot water. I want a bath.'

Another long pause.

'Drez?'

'Drez's gone out, Mum. This is Morman. Shall I tell him?'

'Yes!'

And yet somehow, between Morman's good intentions and the incredibly short journey from his shared bedroom to the landing outside the bathroom, the message went astray. And the shower kept running, and the water kept dripping through into the kitchen – and Alice Liddell lost interest in the battle. Jacko would come out of the bathroom eventually. And the ceiling had been dripping through the light fixture for months. Aside from the damp patch, which was definitely growing, it didn't seem to be doing any harm.

45

Alice thought she should probably find out what her grandmother had been calling about, in case it was important. (This was unlikely. Violet called Alice approximately twice a day.) The hot bath would have to wait.

The grandmother, the spliff and the glass of wine, on the other hand, could easily be dealt with simultaneously.

That's how Alice first heard about the job at Tode Hall.

But first – rewind (very briefly) to the year 1946, when Alice's grandmother, Violet Dean, arrived at Tode Hall with a small child in her arms, looking for a job. The child was Alice's mother, born of a brief fling with an American soldier, since killed in combat, or so Violet claimed. Alice's mother never laid eyes on her father, and Violet, so far as we know, never heard from him again.

Tode Hall was struggling, like all the great houses, under the post-war financial strain of a high tax government; not to mention, after so many had been killed, a shortage of available servants. The incumbent Sir Ecgbert (10th Baronet 1900–1947) and his wife, Geraldine (1907–1971), were so desperate for staff that they set aside their usual concern for the morality of the lower classes, and opened a sort of 'crèche' for babies of any female servants who had somehow mislaid their spouses in the war. The crèche wouldn't have passed today's health and safety requirements, but there was a room, just off the kitchen, where servants' bastards and orphans could be dumped and sometimes attended to, during their mothers' long working day.

Violet was employed as a maid. When she left Tode Hall, thirty-four years later, she was the Hall housekeeper. She would never have left – she loved it there. But in 1980, her wayward daughter (Alice's mother) died of an overdose-induced heart attack, after a lifetime of drink, drugs, and gentle hopelessness. In her beautiful youth she'd been drawn into a world that hit the headlines with the Profumo affair; a few years later she'd hooked up with a fashion photographer, also a junkie, who had fathered Alice and then disappeared.

In her short life, Alice's mother had not been good at much. With her sweet nature, her open heart and her unusual beauty, she had lurched from one badly thought-out love affair to the next. But through it all, to the best of her limited ability, she had loved and cared for her daughter. Alice was fourteen when her mother died. She had never met her father, had no siblings, and no cousins. Her grandmother Violet was the only relative left. Violet, at that point, was living in a pretty cottage on the Tode Hall estate, and could have moved Alice up to Yorkshire to live with her there. It might have been preferable.

But in grief we do not always make the wisest choices. Violet felt terribly that she had let down her daughter. She wanted to make it up to Alice. So instead of moving Alice to Yorkshire, she moved herself to London.

Years passed and Alice grew up; and in due course, like mother and grandmother, bred with a man who failed to hang around to deal with the consequences.

In one respect, she fared better than either of them, because by the time the man abandoned ship, Britain's laws had changed. Also he was reasonably well off. He left Alice with the house that she and her children now shared. In another respect, she fared less well: where the previous generations had been abandoned to look after only one child, Alice had produced triplets.

Jacko, Drez and Morman were twenty years old, delightful, handsome and sweet natured. They loved their mother, believed wholeheartedly in equality, inclusiveness, diversity and tolerance, and studied just hard enough to keep their places at their various colleges. And they all still lived at home.

When the boys were about ten, Alice, in need of money, had started a cookery school. That is, she offered one-on-one cooking tutorials from her Clapham kitchen, and for a while the classes did well. London being full of rich insecure people, and Alice being full of careless bohemian charm (not to mention an excellent cook), she had, without much effort, managed to attract a fairly solid stream of clients who liked the cut of her jib, and wanted to be a tiny, safe bit like her. But these days it was getting harder. Her kitchen (her entire house) had grown just too tatty. Added to which her sons, who were barely house trained, never seemed to attend any lectures and consequently spent their lives loafing agreeably around the kitchen, making toast and leaving marmalade blobs exactly where Alice wanted to teach people about puff pastry.

Her boys went to bed at the time Alice got up, and each morning when she came downstairs, she would be met with a fresh carpet of beer cans and ashtrays and pizza boxes and dirty socks. When there were clients due to arrive she had to rush around Hoovering and opening windows. Even so – the house always smelled of beer and cigarettes and cannabis. It looked old and dirty. Where once it might have appeared, to the Clapham bankers' wives, thrillingly bohemian, now it looked slutty: a breeding ground for salmonella and botulism. Not a place where rich people would dream of wanting to learn to cook. Bad reviews had appeared online. Clients had started complaining to her face: the last had taken one look at the kitchen and demanded her money back.

Short of throwing her children onto the street, which was out of the question, or persuading them to behave like responsible adults – also impossible – it seemed to Alice there wasn't much she could do about the situation. Or maybe she didn't care enough. Truth be told, she was bored. Bored of cooking. Bored of rich housewives. Bored of clearing up after her agreeable children. Bored of London. *Bored of life*. The time was ripe for a new adventure.

And now, here was this.

'Don't be ridiculous, Granny!' she said. 'I'm nowhere near qualified. Anyway I've got my cooking school . . .'

'Hardly,' said Violet Dean.

Alice had lived in London all her life. The thought of leaving it filled her with a sticky, lazy kind of dread. Add to that the prospect of applying for a job; putting together a non-existent CV, turning up in clean clothes, at the right time and in the right place – all of it seemed to Alice, as she puffed on her spliff in her leaking kitchen, to be beyond all realms of achievability.

Nevertheless, as her grandmother talked, Alice's gaze moved from the dripping light fitting, to Morman, just then rummaging through the fridge, dumping half its contents onto a nearby pile of clean laundry, pulling out a chicken leg, shoving it in his mouth and wandering away, leaving everything where he'd dumped it . . . Her business was dying and her children didn't really need her anymore . . .

'The job comes with a cottage,' Violet Dean was telling her. 'Doesn't say which one . . . but it's a good job, Alice, so I expect it'll be one of the better ones. You'd be HOUSEHOLD

MANAGER, Alice! And have you forgotten how big the house is? That's like being Town Manager. It's like being Mayor, Alice! Imagine that! Imagine being Mayor of the most beautiful town in the entire world. And you get a free house ... And a free car. And it pays ... says here ... "salary negotiable" ...'

Alice, puffing quietly on her joint, listened intently.

'Salary negotiable... What do you suppose that means, Alice?'

'Don't know, Gran,' she said. 'I haven't really had a job before. Not a real one ... Why would they want to give it to me?'

'I should think it means that if they like you, you could charge whatever you wanted! That's what I think it means. And they'll like you, Alice. I know they will. Everybody always likes you.' The last remark sounded dismissive. Not everybody liked Violet. For that matter, there weren't many people that Violet liked. So it evened out. She had a Northerner's baldness about her, and a Londoner's sharpness, and the two combined tended to frighten most people off. She'd not made many friends since leaving Tode Hall.

'Mmmm,' said Alice, thinking.

'Never mind "Mmmm",' snapped her grandmother. '"*Mmmm*" doesn't get you on the train to Todeister in time for an interview, does it? What are you doing?'

'What, now?'

'That's right.'

'Well I was going to have a bath ...'

'You can have a bath later. Come round. I'll get dinner in. We can do an application. And I'll send my own letter in with it, Alice. They'll remember me. Lady Tode and me used to get along well, in a manner of speaking. We did. She'll be happy to hear from me.'

'Can I think about it, Gran?'

'No you can't. And before you say again that you're not qualified, I'll tell you this, Alice – you've been running your own *extremely* successful business these past however many years . . .'

Alice didn't correct her.

' . . . Whilst also looking after your old granny and those three naughty boys. Keeping everything shipshape. If that doesn't qualify you for being boss of the most beautiful house in the country, *nothing* does. And it's not like you had the easiest of starts in life either. So. You've got a lot to be proud of Alice Liddell. And I'll tell her – I'll tell Lady Tode, because it's true – that you already know your way round the Hall upside down and backwards. Plus you know all about the history, don't you Alice? I've talked enough about it all these years.'

'I do,' Alice agreed. She had many happy memories of the place. In fact, all the happiest memories of her childhood were at Tode Hall, far away from her mother and the mayhem at home. She and (Mad) Ecgbert were the same age exactly – to the day – and for years they'd used to be inseparable: More than that (this was something she would never tell her grandmother) on their fourteenth birthday, they had shared a stolen spliff and kissed each other, up by Africa Folly. It was the last time she stayed at Tode Hall, and the last time she and Ecgbert ever laid eyes on each other. Not that it mattered. But it was funny. The memory made Alice smile.

'So buck up and get your bum round here, Alice my love. I'll be expecting you in ten minutes.'

'But Granny—'

'What's that?'

'I can't just *move to Tode Hall*. Even if they wanted me to and

51

I don't know why they would! I'm not leaving you. I wouldn't want to. Not in a million years.'

'I never thought you would, Alice my love,' she said.

'Well then—'

'But I can't last much longer, can I? We both know that.'

'Yes you can!'

'I bloody hope not, Alice. I'm ninety-six and ready to go. With luck I'll be dead by winter. And if I can die back at Tode Hall, believe me, I'd be the happiest corpse in Yorkshire. So. Don't you go worrying about *that*, my love. If you get the job, which you will, I'll be coming along with you.'

CHAPTER 10

Some time needed to pass before any of these plans could become reality.

For Alice there was a question of remembering to post her reply to the job advertisement, which she and her grandmother had spent several evenings putting together. A week after she claimed to have done so, Violet spotted the envelope, along with her own handwritten letter to Lady Tode, folded away at the bottom of Alice's handbag. Alice would have claimed the oversight was unintended: a simple failure to remember to buy the correct stamp. But Violet knew better. She said nothing about it. She just took the envelopes back from Alice's bag and posted them herself.

Egbert and India Tode were much more efficient. It took them only two months to pack up, find tenants for the house, find a nursery school for the children, say goodbye to their friends and move their lives to Yorkshire.

On their last day in London, with the children farmed out

to India's parents in Pimlico, the young couple gazed out of their bedroom window, onto the convoy of tightly packed removal trucks below. It was astonishing, as Egbert observed, how they'd managed to accumulate quite so much stuff in quite such a short married life together. Especially considering they must have dumped at the least two trucks' worth of junk at the local charity shop during the pack-up.

'How did we fit it all into this little house?' he exclaimed.

India grinned. 'Amazing isn't it?' she said.

'Actually, *you're* amazing,' Egbert said. 'That's what's amazing.' He kissed her.

'We packed the bikes, Egg, didn't we?' she said.

'You bet!'

Then he turned around, rummaged under his jacket, which was lying folded on the floor, and produced with one hand – 'Te-dar!' – proudly and a little shyly, a bottle of India's favourite champagne, and with the other hand – 'Te-dar!' – two of their finest wedding present champagne glasses. 'I think we should drink,' he said, popping the cork, 'to a new chapter.'

'To our smart new status!' India said. They clinked glasses. (Lady Tode would have thought it was common.) 'Isn't it *hilarious*?' she said.

Egbert didn't quite agree with that. He thought it was pretty serious. He said, 'To all the amazing challenges ahead!'

India said, 'And to us. Being so posh.'

'To us,' he said.

'Being so posh,' she said again.

He smiled. 'If you insist. To us being so posh.'

And that was the end of their life in Wandsworth.

CHAPTER II

Another month passed before Alice was at last able to make it to Tode Hall for her interview. It had been difficult to finalise the date, because Lady Tode was always busy. She had also already arranged to spend November and December in Capri. In the end it proved impossible for her to squeeze in a meeting before leaving for Italy, so, sometime in early-mid November, knowing they would only be meeting Egbert and India, Alice and her grandmother headed North. Violet was bitterly disappointed she wouldn't be seeing her old employer again. Lady Tode indicated that she was bitterly disappointed, too, although not enough to alter the date of her departure.

It was almost forty years since either Alice or Violet had been back to Tode Hall and as they pulled in to Todeister station that morning, both, in their own ways, were struggling to manage their emotions. Violet would not stop talking. Alice, on the other hand, preferred not to speak at all. She was regretting very much indeed having been cajoled into coming back here. She realised – too late – that it was likely to awaken memories she'd spent most of her adult life learning to avoid. Returning to Tode Hall, Alice realised – too late – reminded her of the death of her mother; not because she had ever been here with her mother (on the contrary, she'd always been sent here to escape her) but because her mother and Tode Hall had both been expunged from her young life at the same time. They were inextricably linked. Alice kept this uncomfortable realisation to herself, just as she kept most things, and focused her mind on getting her grandmother's wheelchair off the train.

Mr Carfizzi, smiling warmly, was waiting on the platform to greet them. A short man, chubby and swarthy, he gleamed, among the Todeister anoraks, with continental elegance and self-care. He smelled good too. Violet and Alice caught a whiff of him even as they stepped down from the train.

'Meessis Violet Dean!' he cried, with his Italian accent. 'After so many years! You don't look a day younger!'

Violet, who was adamant she remembered every small detail of her old life at Tode Hall, claimed not to remember Mr Carfizzi, and was quite rude (Alice thought) in her insistence that they'd never met. Nevertheless, he seemed to remember her. It was thanks to Violet Dean, he told her, as he wrapped two stout arms and a fog of cologne around her frail, wheel-chaired body, that he had accepted the job at Tode Hall, so many years ago. He reminded her (she remained unconvinced) that he had joined the staff as butler/caretaker just a few months before Violet herself had left. He said he would never forget how welcome she'd made him feel, how much trouble she had taken to show him the ropes.

'Is that so?' she said stiffly.

Violet Dean didn't like men who wore aftershave. She didn't like men who hugged her. And she didn't like men who wore yellow sweaters.

'Yes that is so!' he laughed. The haughtiness of the English never ceased to tickle him. 'You were very kind to me,' he said. 'Whether you don't like to remember or not.'

It was a blustery afternoon. He had offered to help with the wheelchair, but she insisted on Alice pushing it so, with what Violet considered to be a flashy Johnnie-foreigner shrug, Mr Carfizzi led the way to Lady Tode's Range Rover. He'd chosen it over his own little Fiat, the better to fit in Violet's chair. He'd brought a blanket for the journey, too, in case she got cold; and a Thermos of tea with sugar.

'How am I going to drink that?' she said. 'It'll spill all over the seat.'

Mr Carfizzi laughed.

'But I suppose I should thank you,' Violet added.

'*Prego*, Mrs Dean,' he said, smelling of cologne, and carefully, ignoring her protestations, he arranged the blanket over her knees.

Climbing into the back seat behind them both, Alice thanked him loudly. She was embarrassed by her grandmother's rudeness, not that Mr Carfizzi seemed to care. He gave another of his flashy shrugs, and started the engine.

'Everyone ready?' he said. 'Are you comfortable, Mrs Dean?'

Violet, having talked incessantly from the moment their train pulled out of King's Cross to the moment she smelled Mr

57

Carfizzi's aftershave, had welded her mouth into a thin, mean line and would not reply.

'Are you comfortable?' he asked again, laughing merrily.

She nodded, waved her skinny hand beneath her nose and opened the window.

'I used to come up here a lot,' Alice said, still trying to cover for her. 'Every holiday. I used to love it so much. I don't think we ever met?'

But his attention was focused on Violet.

'Mrs Dean,' he said, 'your daughter had just passed at that time, and you were in no state for new friends. But I am telling you, Mrs Dean, I have always remembered how kind you were to me. I will never forget it . . .'

'Very nice of you to say,' said Violet. 'Maybe I do remember you a little bit . . .'

'Ah ha ha, you see?' Mr Carfizzi grinned at her, waggled his finger playfully.

The car fell silent. Alice and Violet gazed out at the passing suburbs of Todeister: the new roads and new roundabouts, new little Lego-style houses . . . Nothing was quite as either remembered it.

'Everything changes outside the Hall,' Mr Carfizzi said, reading their thoughts. 'But you will see – nothing changes inside! Or not so much. You will be happy, Mrs Dean, when you see. It is still so beautiful.'

Violet nodded. The view outside the window grew prettier, less cluttered and more familiar. It wasn't very long before Violet's curiosity won out. There was so much news to catch up on she couldn't sustain her disapproval of his warm Italian manner and nice aftershave any longer.

'And how is the family?' she asked, stiffly.

Mr Carfizzi said, 'Of course you know the tragic news of Sir Ecgbert passing?'

'I was aware of that. Yes, indeed.'

'The household – everyone – we are only just beginning on our recovery. Such a shock. Such a terrible shock . . .'

'But wasn't he into his nineties?' asked Alice, politely, poking her head between the two seats.

'A dreadful shock,' Mr Carfizzi said, and kept driving.

'And how is Lady Tode coping?' Violet wanted to know. 'I should think she's pleased to see the back of him, is she?'

Mr Carfizzi pursed his lips, but he didn't, Alice thought, look entirely displeased.

' . . . And young Ecgbert,' Violet continued. 'I read in the *Mail* he's been a tad under the weather. Not quite "all there" in the top storey as it were. He never was, mind. But I was sorry when I read that. I always had a soft spot for that boy . . .'

'Ah, Ecgbert – *Sir* Ecgbert, of course, as he is now. The Twelfth Baronet Sir Ecgbert Tode. He is *very* well! He is currently engaged in writing a marvellous game for the computer, he tells me. It's a children's fairytale story. I look forward to playing it one day.'

'That's nice,' said Violet. 'How long's he been working on that for then?'

'Ah! Many years, Mrs Dean! *E un perfezionista, quello.*'

'And the other two? – I was never so fond of them,' she added unnecessarily.

Carfizzi didn't answer.

' . . . Esmé's gone to Australia, I read in the *Mail*,' she continued, happy to answer for herself. 'He's done very well for himself. Turned into quite an Aussie. I should think he's got a pet kangaroo in the garden, has he?' Violet rocked with delight at her own funny joke. But Mr Carfizzi wasn't amused. He stared at the road ahead, stony-faced.

'... And *Nicola*,' continued Violet, 'I don't tend to read much about her in the newspapers. She was always a tricky one. Very "argumentative" is my opinion. I don't know what *she's* up to now. She seems to keep a bit of a quiet profile?'

Still, Carfizzi said nothing.

'... What's she up to now, Mr Car Fizzy?' Violet asked him. 'I saw a photo once, and I wondered, maybe she's one of these "lesbians" ...?' Violet chuckled again. 'You never know these days, do you?'

'Nicola and Esmé are both very well,' Carfizzi replied at last. 'Unfortunately they do not make her ladyship's life easy. Lady Tode has many burdens in her family life. She is a brave lady. A lady of exceptional courage and grace, do you agree Mrs Dean?'

Violet said, 'I don't know about that. I always thought she should stand up to that husband of hers more than she did ... but then again you never can be sure what goes on between two people, behind closed doors.'

Mr Carfizzi fell back into angry silence.

Not that Violet minded. She was warmed up now. She had plenty to say and the less anyone interrupted, the better.

'You know I've not been back here since they did the big TV show, Mr Car Fizzy. But you must have been here for all the filming, were you? What a laugh! We used to watch it, didn't we Alice? Every Sunday night. We *loved* it. I must have watched it a hundred times. What did the family think?'

Mr Carfizzi said (as if there could have been any doubt): 'You are talking about *Prance*?'

'Of course I am talking about *Prance*! What else would I be talking about? I used to say to Alice, didn't I Alice?, I used to say, "Shame the real-life Todes aren't a bit more dashing, like that Tintin chap with the teddy bear." By comparison I used to say the Todes were a bit *ordinary*, didn't I say that, Alice?'

'Yes, you did,' said Alice.

'Ord-in-ary?' repeated Mr Carfizzi.

'So I missed all the fun of the filming. But it must have been very special, Mr Car Fizzy. Was it special? Being surrounded by all the stars? That's something I regret. If I regret anything, and I don't, then I suppose I *do* regret not being here when they were doing the filming. What was it like, Mr Car Fizzy? Meeting all the stars? Laurence Olivier ... Did you meet him? ... I *adored* that chap. What was he like then? I expect he was a dreadful disappointment, was he?'

'Lord Olivier was a remarkable man. Very, very gracious,' Mr Carfizzi replied. 'Not a disappointment in any way. The most gracious and generous gentleman I have ever been fortunate to meet. And so natural! The most natural gentleman I ever met. We got along very well. He used to call me "Mr Car Fixy".' Mr Carfizzi chuckled richly at the memory. 'A lovely, special man,' he said. 'Lord Olivier would have been happy to stay with us at the Hall. But you may remember Sir Ecgbert wasn't *entusiasto* about the actors.'

'Miserable old sod,' said Violet.

Carfizzi didn't respond.

A longer silence fell: Violet, brooding on her missed chances with Olivier, Carfizzi brooding on Violet's inappropriate attitude and language, Alice wondering whether Carfizzi was slightly insane, and then thinking, *probably not*. She'd been mixing with the drab, well-behaved home-owners of Clapham for far too long.

Mr Carfizzi, his bald head barely peeking above the

dashboard, his back ramrod straight, and his speedometer never moving above twenty, looked, it occurred to Alice, like a small, angry undertaker. 'What about the other actors, then?' she asked for the sake of it, to break the silence. 'Did any of the stars ever stay in the house? The one who played Tintin? I always fancied him. Did he stay at the house? I bet everyone adored him.'

But her innocent question seemed only to push Carfizzi further into his dark mood. He said: 'No.'

Which wasn't strictly true. But Violet and Alice didn't know that.

Alice tried again: 'So – I understand Sir Ecgbert's widow – Lady Tode – has moved into the cottage in the Rose Garden?'

'That is correct. The Gardener's House,' agreed Mr Carfizzi. He seemed to prefer this line of questioning. He chuckled. 'She has always used it as her own little hideaway, but now she is making it her home. When she is not in Capri, of course ... But your grandmother will tell you – it is not quite a "cottage", is it Mrs Dean?'

'Certainly not!' chuckled Violet. 'Alice, don't you remember the Gardener's House? Oh it's beautiful! Like a little toy mansion. The prettiest, most miniature mansion you'll ever see. And with a rose garden laid all around it. I used to dream of that house, you know. Long after I left, I used to dream about that house. It was perfect. Alice, how can you not remember it?'

'Well I think I do—'

'It's only across the grass from the Hall. You and young Sir Ecgbert, as he is now, you must have played together in the Rose Garden a hundred times.' She sighed with contentment. 'Oh! I must say, it's good to be back!'

The temperature in the car warmed considerably after that.

Violet and Mr Carfizzi chatted quickly and happily about changes in the household, who still lived or worked at the Hall, who was alive and who was dead . . .

There was Oliver Mellors (son of the previous gamekeeper Brian Mellors, now dead) whom Lady Tode seemed to think walked on water, but Carfizzi thought was a 'nasty conceited little man'. There was Mrs Danvers, the office manager, whom Carfizzi was certain had been at the Hall when he started in 1983, and Mr Friday, who—

Alice poked her head between the two front seats to join in. 'So what about the new people?' she asked.

She felt Mr Carfizzi bristling. 'What "new" people?' he said.

'The new Todes, of course. India and Egbert Tode, who'll be interviewing me. What are they like to work for? Quite a change, is it?'

Mr Carfizzi was approaching a junction. He slowed down (even further), changed gear, checked his mirror, indicated, eased left. It became apparent that he was never going to answer.

'. . . You don't like them?' Alice tried again.

He said: 'Of course I "like" them.'

Violet chuckled. 'Doesn't sound like you do, Mr Car Fizzy.'

'Well of course I "like" them. But of course, it would be strange if we weren't with any problems.'

'Teething problems,' Violet nodded knowingly.

'They are from *London*,' he explained. (As was Alice.) 'They have arrived here, full of their London ideas, very certain about how things should be done, when – of course – we've been doing things at Tode Hall *very well without them*, you know, for more than three hundred years. So—'

'A bit of in-fighting,' Violet said. 'Only to be expected.'

'She insulted Mrs Carfizzi's cooking on the first day they arrived here! Lady Tode was very kind, as always. Mrs Carfizzi was crying and weeping and sobbing. Terrible! Lady Tode had to have a little word.'

'With Mrs Carfizzi?' Alice asked.

'With Mrs Tode. *India* Tode, as she says we must call her. Why must we call her "India"? We're not friends.'

Violet said, 'So you're not happy with her. What about the husband? Is he any better?'

'I didn't say I wasn't happy with her! What I said was— Ah! Now, here we are at the house. Never mind. You will see for yourselves. In any case Lady Tode is away now, so "India" will be the boss today. Which is just as she likes it . . . ' He let that sink in. 'You will see for yourself. But now . . . ' The funereal drive was reaching its climax. Slowly (so slowly) the car turned in to the long West drive. And there, at last, a quarter-mile distant and framed by a giant arch, loomed the great house. It was a view designed to take the breath away; to end all previous conversations, and so it did, thankfully. Mr Carfizzi had been on the point of losing his temper.

CHAPTER 12

They continued along the drive in silence, interspersed by the occasional, barely audible whimper from Violet, who was clutching her heart and fighting back tears. The car rolled on, past the Old Stable Yard and its retail outlets, and on, past the car park for coaches, and the Garden Centre, the adventure playground, the Boathouse Café . . .

'I never believed,' Violet said at last, 'the day would come when I would be back here.'

The house was closed to the public for the winter, it being November. But the gardens were open every day of the year, and on this misty morning, as ever, the grounds were strewn with tourists. Today was a weekday, which meant the majority of visitors were on international coach tours. Tode Hall (and its retail outlets) had, in the last five or so years, become especially fashionable in China.

Carfizzi weaved carefully and slowly between the milling tourists, along the front of the house, past the chapel, past the

Great North Door, and on to the Estate Offices at the back end of the East Wing. Alice hummed the theme tune. Her heart was beating. It felt neither good nor bad to be back, but she was aware of blood pumping too fast around her body and she didn't like it.

'Funny,' she said, as the car drew up, 'You know how most places get smaller when you revisit them as an adult. I think this place may have grown.'

'It is a large house,' Mr Carfizzi agreed proudly. He glanced at his watch. His instructions had been to bring his passengers to the café in the basement, but first, he needed to show them their bedrooms.

Alice and Violet had been invited to stay the night. This was mostly in honour of Violet's great age and former position in the household. Alice had made it clear she wasn't coming without bringing her grandmother, and everyone agreed she probably wasn't up to making the return journey in a single day.

The invitation also worked well for the young Todes, who wanted, more than anything, to charm Alice into taking the job. They were desperate for help. The running of Tode Hall was proving to be a massive operation – and far more political than, in their innocence, they had ever imagined. They felt isolated. In a household long stuck in its ways, whose allegiance to the outgoing Lady Tode was overt and quite oppressive, India, especially, needed a friend: someone even newer to the situation than she was, and yet also unquestionably connected to the past. Alice Liddell could not have been more perfect.

Alice didn't know this. She also didn't know that there had, in fact, only ever been three applicants for the job – despite running the advertisement twice. India had already rejected the other two applicants. The first, a Manchester-based NHS manager, had wanted to leave her stressful job, the better to take care of an ailing husband, and was well equipped for the position, but had been dismissed as 'boring'. The other one, young Egbert and Lady Tode had both been ready to employ. She was a qualified accountant with a master's degree in business, a single mother, currently based in London and looking for a better place to raise her two young children. India had rejected her for being 'gross'.

'"Gross" in what way, Munchkin?' young Egbert had asked.

When pushed for more detail, it transpired that India didn't like her wardrobe – 'very power-suity'; nor her exaggerated levels of efficiency; 'she'll make us all feel hopeless'; nor her apparent total absence of humour. 'I'm going to have to spend a lot of time with this person,' India said. 'After half an hour with that woman I wanted to throw myself off a cliff.'

Alice wasn't boring, or gross, or remotely efficient; was unlikely to make anyone feel hopeless, being fairly hopeless herself, and she had an excellent sense of humour. Add that to the fact that she knew the house, had spent much of her childhood here – it was a shoo-in. Assuming she wanted the job.

Violet Dean was mortified when Alice told her she'd arranged for them to be staying a night as guests in Tode Hall. She would have far preferred to stay in a B&B. But it was too late, Alice had already accepted the invitation. 'After all those years looking after the place, you should spend a night in one of those big four-poster beds, anyway,' Alice said. 'It might be fun.'

'It'll be weird, more likely . . .' A terrible thought occurred to her. 'We won't have to *eat* with them in the dining room, will we?'

'I should think we will,' replied Alice. 'Unless they give us sandwiches to eat in the bedroom? But that really would be a bit weird – wouldn't it? They wouldn't do that, would they?'

'Don't ask me,' Violet snapped. 'You're the bloody fool who accepted the invitation.'

In any case, here they were, each with their overnight bag, not knowing what to expect with regard to sandwiches, but as ready as they ever would be for the adventure ahead. Mr Carfizzi lifted Violet out of the car and into her wheelchair. There was a cold wind blowing. He wanted to tuck her under the blanket again, but she waved it away.

Not all the rooms in the house could get a wheelchair into them very easily. The rooms with the most obvious wheelchair access happened, as Violet knew well, also to be the best rooms in the house. To reach them, they would need to wheel all the way back along the front of the house, past the Great North Door to the entrance in the west, beneath the Chapel.

'Feels more like Peking than Yorkshire,' Violet said, as they barrelled along.

'Not really, Granny,' said Alice. 'Don't be like that.'

'I'm just *saying*,' said Violet. ' . . . It's not like it was.'

'I agree with you, Mrs Dean. But even here at Tode Hall we must move with the times,' said Carfizzi. 'Our Chinese visitors spend a lot of money in the gift shops. They are very welcome here.'

'I'm sure they are if you say so,' she said.

He put the guests in the Queen Charlotte Suite (so named because in June 1782 a pregnant Queen Charlotte, formerly Her Serene Highness Princess Sophia Charlotte of Mecklenburg, had used the rooms to rest and change, en route, it was believed, to a shooting and shopping trip in Edinburgh). The rooms were adjoining: built as bedroom and dressing room to the first Baronet's wife, Rosalind (1686–1734), they were as grand as it is possible for two rooms to be. Each one was dominated by an ancient four-poster, upholstered in suffocating damask, and on every wall, paintings of long-dead, waxy-faced Todes in powdered wigs glowered down at them.

'My goodness,' muttered Alice, feeling slightly overwhelmed. She glanced at her grandmother.

But Violet was beaming. There were tears in her eyes. Alice had never seen her look so happy. ' . . . Mr Car Fizzy, I didn't dare to hope,' she was saying. 'But I *was* hoping, I was *hoping* . . . because of the wheelchair, see. But I didn't *know*, I was only *hoping* . . . These are the most beautiful rooms in the Hall. I've always thought so, Mr Car Fizzy. Do you agree?'

Mr Carfizzi beamed back at her. He waggled a finger in the air. 'Ah-ha!' he cried. 'I think you know why the rooms are so special!'

'Know what? I don't know anything . . . ' But she was blushing like a maiden.

Carfizzi explained to Alice that, in *Prance to the Music*, these were the rooms where Tintin's father's long drawn death scenes had been recorded.

'That's quite special, eh?' Carfizzi chuckled. He knew why she was blushing.

'I think I could die now, Mr Car Fizzy!' she said. 'Quite happily!'

He laughed. 'No need for that, Mrs Dean. Just enjoy this special night.'

'It's certainly a beautiful room,' Alice said. 'Are you all right, Granny?'

Mr Carfizzi, still grinning, patted the bed: 'You can imagine his Lordship, the Lord Olivier, right there on the pillow beside you, Mrs Dean!'

Her smile died. 'No thank you,' she said. 'There's no need to be disgusting.'

CHAPTER 13

The basement restaurant, cannily designed by Lady Tode to look and feel no different from a John Lewis coffee shop, was heated to a pleasant room temperature. There was a food bar along one side of the room displaying a selection of nice-looking salads, some involving feta; also a hell of a lot of cakes. Interspersed between tables of slim and serious Chinese, there were fatter, plainer English folk, many with pushchairs. As young Egbert would explain shortly, Tode Hall offered Annual House & Grounds Membership Cards, which were popular with local young families, who liked to take advantage of the adventure playground below the Boathouse, and who appreciated the John Lewis style restaurant, especially the cakes.

Carfizzi was meant to stay with the women until India and Egbert arrived, but he didn't want to do that: he said he was too busy to stand around waiting, and that India was always late. He left them alone in the restaurant.

Violet said to Alice: 'Go on then, love. Go and get me one

of those flapjacky things.' Alice was delving in her purse for the money when Egbert and India rolled in.

There could be no mistaking them. They shone with good health, and good diet, and good looks, and good nature, and good bank balances. It wasn't that they wanted to attract attention to themselves: they couldn't help it. The two of them paused at the door, side by side, smiling expectantly – scanning the tables for their guests – and a shimmy of glamour passed through the room. Even the Chinese tourists, not attuned to the subtleties of British class, could feel a change in the vibe. Everyone sat up a little straighter.

'Forget the flapjack,' said Violet, too loudly. 'They're here. And my goodness, she's a beauty, isn't she? Mr Car Fizzy didn't mention *that*. I tell you what though,' she added, 'I *suspect* our Mr Car Fizzy's more into the gentlemen. Don't you?'

'Maybe,' Alice said. 'You may be right there ... Shall I go over and introduce myself?'

'Coo-ee!' Violet shouted: 'Over here!'

India and Egbert spotted her, waved and smiled, and made their way over.

'Hello, hello, HELLO!' Egbert boomed, but not on purpose. It was just the way he spoke. His voice carried across the restaurant, its loudness ruffling English and Chinese airwaves alike. Only the toddlers thought it was normal. 'Mrs Dean! You must be Mrs Dean! Well done, getting here!' he bellowed, giving her frail hand a hearty shake. 'Was it a dreadful journey? I hope Mr Car Fizzy was on time? I must say it's an absolute honour to meet you! – And you,' he said, turning toward Alice, 'you must be Mrs Liddell? I'm Egbert, and this is my wife India and we are *absolutely thrilled* to meet you both! Aren't we India?'

'You bet we are!' said India, with her big beautiful smile.

'Especially you Mrs Dean, if I may say,' continued Egbert. 'Super impressed you made it! How does it feel to be back here, after all these years? Does it feel strange? I bet it does. My aunt, Lady Tode – unfortunately she's not here today, as you know, but she wanted me to tell you *specially* how very, very sorry she was to miss you ... She was so looking forward to seeing you again after so many years. She was terribly upset. But that's the trouble with these cheapo airlines, isn't it? She'd booked the ticket and there was absolutely no way they were going to let her change the date! So.'

'Never mind,' said Violet. 'I was looking forward to seeing her again too. But not to worry. It's just smashing to be back.'

'Yes, I bet!' boomed Egbert. 'And Mrs Liddell – for you too, I imagine? I understand you spent many of your school holidays here, is that right?'

'It is, yes—'

'Well, well!' Egbert smiled. 'I should think you two know this place a hell of a lot better than we do! I'm not certain whether you should give us a tour, or the other way round!'

Everyone laughed. And then there was a kerfuffle while they settled themselves at a table. Egbert, with enormous politeness, asked a waitress to bring cakes and tea. India, elegantly cocooned in oatmeal cashmere and loose, expensive jeans (she learned of the label via an actress friend in LA), plopped herself onto the metal seat opposite Alice, and beamed.

'I can tell already that I'm going to like you!' she said.

Alice didn't reply at once. It was, she thought, a nice thing to say. A very positive way to start a job interview. Not the usual way, she assumed (not that she would know, having never been interviewed for a job before). It occurred to her fuzzily that the

73

feeling might even be reciprocated. She liked the look of India. There was a lively look about her: a promise of mischief which Alice found attractive.

'I think I'm going to like you, too,' Alice said at last.

Again, it was an odd way for the interview to begin. But the two of them were simply stating facts.

Egbert rubbed his hands together and laughed very merrily. 'Well then,' he said, 'that's settled! When can you start?'

Ha ha ha, they all agreed.

But he wasn't really joking.

In the meantime, they ate cakes and listened to Violet talking about the old days. Alice wanted to know what the job of Tode Hall House and Grounds Manager actually entailed, but nobody seemed able to tell her. Egbert said: 'Look, it's a jolly hard job, I'll tell you that much.'

India said: 'But you get a car and a house and virtually everything you need, paid for. Doesn't she Egg? A phone, heating. Your whole life would be for free really. Everyone gets free veg from the kitchen garden – literally. I don't think anyone on the estate has paid for a single vegetable in three hundred years ...'

'Wow,' Alice said.

'The fact is ... ' India leaned forward, directing her saucer blue eyes directly at Alice. 'I just need someone to *help*. You know what I mean? Someone I can whinge to – that sort of thing.'

'Oh *well*,' said Violet. 'She's been listening to me whingeing for God knows how long, haven't you Alice? She's a good listener.'

'I bet she is!' Egbert said. He'd eaten a doughnut and there was jam on his jacket cuff. He was a bit distracted, trying to scrape it off. 'I think alongside that,' he said, 'I'll be honest with you Alice – I think there's probably quite a lot of *organisational* stuff that needs doing. The Estate Offices already have a couple of wonderful PAs and an office manager, of course. So nothing too terrible. Just sort of – what do you think Munchkin? It's more a PR-y sort of type job really, isn't it Munch?'

'Yup,' said Munch. She was getting restless. The coffee shop reminded her of boring school holidays. Buying school uniforms with her mother. She grinned. 'Are we done here? Shall we show each other round?'

Alice was about to stand up. Instead, she said, ' . . . India, I hope you don't mind me saying. Only I really hate it when people don't tell me and I just wander around for ages not knowing. You've got something caught in your teeth.'

There was a pause. Egbert looked alarmed. ' . . . She's right Munch,' he said gingerly.

India, straight faced, her eyes locked on Alice's, stuck a ringed finger into her mouth. 'Where?'

'Just – just there,' said Alice, staring at it. ' . . . That's it. You've got it . . . '

'Oh. My. God,' said India. '*Thank you*. I think I love you, Alice. I swear, if you don't come and work for us now, I'm going to throw myself off a bridge. I'm going to kill myself. I'm going to throw myself off the gallery in the Great Hall. And I'll do it while you're watching so you'll feel guilty for the rest of your life . . . ' She was laughing. Egbert laughed along too.

'Bit much, Munchkin! Slow down – you'll scare the poor girl off.'

India giggled. 'I'm not scaring you off, am I?'

'Not really,' Alice said. 'I presume you're not serious.'

Ha ha ha! More laughter. No one was being serious. On

75

the other hand it was clear that India loved Alice. And if India loved Alice then obviously so did Egbert. Only one question remained: did Alice love India – and her grandmother – enough to uproot both their lives and move North? Not even Violet could have answered that. Alice was never an easy woman to read.

CHAPTER 14

India wanted to pick up the children from their riding lesson, and so it was left to Egbert to give the guided tour. He could hardly get a word in, though, because Violet seemed to know everything about the place already, and gave a running commentary, from her wheelchair, on the myriad ways in which the place had deteriorated since last she was here. She was upset, above all, by the number of safety notices everywhere.

'Don't go here, don't tread there, step this way, don't touch that! It's not like a home anymore, Mr Tode. I hope you and your wife can make it more like a home again.'

'We'd like to try ... The problem is of course—'

'It's like going on the London Underground, isn't it Alice? Remember? When we went on the Underground in summer? I couldn't believe it, could I Alice? You'll be telling us to "stay hydrated" next.'

Egbert laughed. 'The problem is, when you have as many

people as we do coming through the gates ... We can't afford to have them suing us.'

Violet scoffed. 'What are they going to sue you for? Having a lovely house?'

'People will sue, I am discovering, for just about anything, if they think there's a bit of cash to be made... For example, Mrs Dean, there's a case we've just had to settle – somebody broke their toe climbing into the fountain. Well. They're not actually *allowed* in the fountain, as they perfectly well know. There's a *very* large sign prohibiting it. But you see, they said they hadn't seen the sign, because they approached the fountain from an angle where it wasn't immediately visible, and somehow, believe it or not, that leaves us coughing up £1700 in damages. I'm not keen on the signs, either, Mrs Dean. But we have to have them, or we'd be liable every time someone's dog took a leak on the lawn.'

'A leak on the lawn?' repeated Mrs Dean, who (unlike Alice) was not a good listener. 'What are you talking about?'

Alice would have liked to see the cottage which came with the job, but Egbert didn't want to show it to her yet, for fear of putting her off. It was in the village, and very nice, he assured her – or it would be. It had belonged to her predecessor, Mrs Camer, whose job Alice would be filling, but she'd left it looking like a tip. Nobody had been into the house for years, and the state of it, after she left, revealed a side to Mrs Camer's character nobody had guessed at.

'Fact is,' said Egbert, 'she scrawled all over the walls. I'm not sure if they were meant to be paintings ... They were religious – pictures of devils and so on. Plus she'd smashed things up – it looked very much as if she'd gone at the place with a sledge hammer. So – we think she may have had a screw loose.

78

It was rather upsetting ... My aunt, Lady Tode, was very upset when she heard about it. In any case. The point is, it's a super house. Or it will be. We've got the estate carpenter licking it into shape literally as I speak. But honestly at the moment, it's not in a fit state ... As I say, we don't want to put you off!'

The cottage was a mile or so from the Hall, in a hamlet the entirety of which belonged to the Tode estate. Violet knew the hamlet very well, and asked Egbert if they couldn't at least drive by and look at the outside of their future home. 'And since we'll be in the car,' she added, 'would you mind very much driving us up to Africa Folly and down to the mausoleum on the other side? I should love that so much, just for the view of the house. I used to walk up there every Sunday, on my day off. Could we do that, Mr Tode?'

He didn't much want to do that. It would involve using his aunt's Range Rover again, which would involve dealing with Carfizzi, who would be bound to find a reason to obstruct things, since he always did. Aside from which Egbert had a lot to do this afternoon and had been hoping to leave Violet and Alice to wander about on their own for a few hours before dinner. This, it appeared, was not going to be possible. India had whispered strict instructions into his ear as she left, reminding him that he must do 'whatever it takes and whatever they ask' to persuade Alice to come and work for them.

So he said, 'What a brilliant idea, Mrs Dean, and by the way I do wish you'd call me Egbert.'

Half an hour later they were travelling the same bumpy path that Sir Ecgbert (11th) had taken in his cardboard coffin only a few months earlier. Violet kept up a running commentary. She was fairly certain the path had deteriorated since her day. 'It was never so bumpy back then,' she said.

'Well Granny, you weren't ninety-six the last time you came here. Things feel bumpier when you're ninety-six.'

'Is that right, Alice Liddell? And how would you know?'

Alice didn't bother to reply.

They drew up in front of Africa Folly. There was a gate across the path that led on to the mausoleum and it was locked, as all gates on the estate had to be, due to the problem of tourists forgetting to close them and leaving the livestock to escape. Egbert had grown accustomed to travelling everywhere with a giant collection of keys. (Often the wrong ones. People deliberately, Egbert sometimes suspected, put them back on the wrong hooks.) In any case he had a bunch of them with him now. He was hoping Violet wouldn't ask to travel beyond the Folly, and that maybe they could admire the view of house and mausoleum, from here – from inside the car – and then head back to the house. He waited.

'Well, are you going to open it?' Violet asked.

'Trouble is, it's locked,' he said weakly.

'Well you've got all those keys there. Can't you unlock it?'

'I could certainly try ... If you're sure. I always think this is the best view you get – south to the house, north to the mausoleum. Not sure we can top it! Also I don't want to disturb the cows ... Apparently quite a few of them are pregnant.'

'Pah!' said Violet. 'There's no cows in there, Mr Tode! Can't you tell the difference?'

'What? Oh—' He was embarrassed. She was right – the field was full of grazing sheep. He hadn't bothered to look. 'What a dope I am! Usually we keep cows in there – I think. Still a bit new to me, all this! Wait there – I'll go and unlock the gate.'

The padlock was fiddly – rusty from the Yorkshire rain. Plus it took him ages to find the right key. By the time he turned back to the car, Violet was seated in her wheelchair, a blanket on her knees, and Alice was standing to attention behind her, waiting to push.

'Oh!' he said. 'I thought we might drive down ...'

But Violet wanted to breathe the air. She wanted to go down to the mausoleum and touch the stones, and remember what her life was like when she was young. So they set off down the path together, *bump bump bump*.

There was a smell of sheep in the air. Egbert, who'd grown up in a large house in South Kensington, didn't like it much.

'Sorry about the whiff,' he said. 'Sheep. Eat grass and live in the fresh air their entire lives – and yet manage to give off the most almighty pong. Funny old world, isn't it?'

'They are quite stinky,' said Alice, who'd grown up in Acton.

'Nonsense,' Violet said, because she was argumentative. Egbert and Alice were right though. There was a nasty sheep-smell in the air.

Violet's eyes were old and weak but as they drew closer to the mausoleum she saw for the first time the state of the place: the rusty gate, the broken balustrades, the cracks in the long, high walls, the signposts.

'My goodness!' she said. 'Well you've certainly let this run to rack and ruin!'

Egbert nodded: 'Yes it's definitely in need of a bit of maintenance, currently. But the sad truth is, these things are *cataclysmically* expensive, Mrs Dean. Plus the entire building is Grade 1 listed, so we're not really allowed to do anything. It's all a teeny bit of a nightmare, if I'm honest with you ... But so beautiful,' he added quickly. 'So beautiful ...' They paused to gaze at it. For a brief moment the sun – what was left of it – found a gap in the Yorkshire cloud and the mausoleum's huge, domed roof shone blinding white.

Egbert broke the silence. He said: ' . . . Trying to get my head round the idea of being buried in there one day . . . India doesn't want it at all. Not sure I do either, tbh. Teeny bit *grisly*, really . . . In this day and age . . . '

'It's death that's grisly,' said Alice, who hadn't spoken for some time. 'Not where you put the body once it's finished with. You have to put it somewhere, don't you?'

Egbert sent her an odd look. Reminded himself how much India wanted to employ her. 'Well yes I suppose,' he said politely. 'I hadn't really thought about it like that.'

Violet asked if they could go inside the crypt. She said she'd been in the room above, but she'd never in the crypt before.

But Egbert thought that *really was* a bit much. They were meant to be conducting a job interview, after all, not wandering around peering at his dead relations. In any case, he hadn't brought the key with him. Couldn't have, fortunately. It was one of the many keys in the key cupboard that, as usual, had not been returned to its correct hook. He suspected Car Fizzy of purposely confusing the system to maintain control . . . But that was for another day. Egbert said: 'Sorry, Mrs Dean. *Really sorry*. Of course I would've loved to show you inside, but I left the key back at the house . . . Shall we head back? You must be freezing.'

She said she wasn't freezing. But at that point, Egbert really felt he had had enough. The feelings that came upon him when confronted by the mausoleum were, though he couldn't have known it, very similar to the feelings of his aunt, Lady Tode. The sight of it made him miserable. Added to which the smell of sheep seemed to be getting stronger. One way and another the situation was beginning to make him feel sick.

Alice said: 'Smells like when a mouse has died under the sofa, doesn't it?'

'Only if you don't clean under your sofa,' Violet replied.

'Well I do clean under the sofa,' said Alice. 'Of course I do, especially when there's a dead mouse ...'

A gust of wind sent them all an even stronger whiff. 'It *is* rather pungent,' said Egbert. 'Maybe you and I are just a pair of feeble townies, Alice, but I might send someone up here to investigate. If it's a dead animal we don't want the tourists complaining.'

They returned to the house. It was 4.30 p.m., and Egbert had work to catch up on. Dinner, he said, would be at eight o'clock sharp in the Red Dining Room, 'which is the one—'

'I know which one it is,' interrupted Violet. 'Thank you very much.'

CHAPTER 15

There were just the four of them at dinner. Mrs Carfizzi served up Yorkshire pudding, mushy peas and brown roast beef. India beamed at her: 'Thank you *so much* Mrs Carfizzi . . . So delicious. Maybe one day you'll treat us to some of your amazing *Italian* cooking?' Mrs Carfizzi beamed back, but didn't reply. 'I can smell it, you know, coming out of your flat downstairs . . . Smells *so good* . . .'

'*Inglesi* non like.'

'But Mrs Car Fizzy,' Egbert laughed, 'we like Italian food *very much*!'

She shook her head, put the dish on the side table and left the room.

'It's crazy,' India confided to Alice. 'Something's got to be done. She's an amazing cook. I know it. But she refuses to cook anything for us except Mad Ecgbert's favourites. I swear, I'll be joining him in the Funny House, if I have to eat much more of this.' She left everything on her plate.

Violet ate it all, but also drank too much, due to her intense discomfort at being waited on, and as the short evening wore on, she became vaguely abusive. Egbert and India were too good natured to take offence. India, especially, was sweet. She said to Violet, with her usual frankness:

'Gosh, it must be strange for you, being on this side of that kitchen door. Is it? I suppose you would have been one of the people waiting on people, last time you were in this room? How weird must that be?'

'Not at all,' Violet said. 'When I left Tode Hall, young lady, I was the housekeeper. Previous to that I was Emma, Lady Tode's lady's maid. And previous to *that*, I was of course the late Geraldine, Lady Tode's lady's maid. I certainly wasn't waiting in the dining room. And of course, in my day, when the house was running *properly*, there would have been Mr Jeeves, the butler – no. Wait a bit, was it Mr Jeeves? Am I confusing myself with the character on the telly? That would have been – oh goodness – Well, there were *two* footmen after the War, of course. We had Mr . . . Mr . . . '

Bedtime.

Alice and her grandmother were booked onto a train that left Todeister at 11.30 the following morning, but India begged them to stay on until the end of the day. She said she would pay for the new tickets, and for a taxi from King's Cross to take them back home. 'Alice, we need you!' she said. 'It's Tintin & Dogmatix Day and Emma Tode's buggered off to Capri. And Dominic's not picking up his phone and I've honestly not the foggiest idea what's going on. It's going to be mayhem. Also, by the way, I desperately want you to meet Dominic before you go. It's so important you two get along. And I know you will. He's incredibly handsome.'

'Bit much, Munch,' said Egbert. 'He's not *that* handsome.'

She stretched across the dining table and patted Egbert's hand. 'Not as handsome as you, don't worry Egg! Too old for me anyway,' she added. 'But I think he's *just right* for you, Alice. If you happen to be on the lookout for a new man. You're so gorgeous and so's he. So it's a perfect match. Plus he's an actor. You'll recognise him. He does coffee commercials on TV – the ones where you put the capsule in? Very debonair! I swear you're going to love him. He's our resident "celebrity".'

'Actually Munch – I think strictly speaking Dominic's our archivist. Not sure he'd appreciate being called the "resident celebrity"! Yes, he's an actor, or was. Indeed, a rather successful actor. He's also a very learned, very impressive man. Knows absolutely everything about everything we have here at Tode.'

'*Yawn*,' India said.

'Well you *say* that, Munchkin. But someone has to know it.'

'Do they?' India turned to Alice. 'He keeps records on every little watercolour, every little water jug, every loose button in the entire house. But it's just an excuse – don't say I said so – so he can stay in his cottage. And by the way *whatever you do*,' she looked earnestly at Alice, 'DO NOT get him on the subject of Tode Hall and its history. He'll literally never shut up. Get him to talk about the TV show. And what it's like being famous. He likes that. And he *is* famous, you know! Whatever Egg may say. People still recognise him ... Anyway you'll see for yourself. He'll be back in time to do the teddy tour tomorrow. He'd better be – I don't know what we'll do if he isn't.'

Violet spoke up: fully emerged from her alcoholic funk. So excited she was shaking.

'Dominic on the coffee ads – you don't mean *Dominic Rathbone*?'

'That's right,' said Egbert. 'He has a cottage in the village – actually it's the one next door to what we hope is going to be yours, Alice. Fingers crossed.'

'*Dominic Rathbone?*' Violet looked from Egbert to Alice and back again. As if the world were spinning upside down (which it may have been). '*Tintin?*' she said. 'Alice – they're talking about Tintin! Off the TV show, Alice! For goodness sake, wake up! Tintin lives at Tode Hall!'

'Well, he lives in the village,' Egbert corrected her.

'He's going to be our neighbour, Alice!'

'Fingers crossed!' Egbert laughed.

'So you'll stay 'til a bit later?' India asked her.

'You bet we will!' said Violet.

The following day was a Saturday, and the forecast was good, and it was, as India had mentioned, a popular day with the tourists: Tintin & Dogmatix day had become an annual tradition, instigated by Lady Tode and the late Sir Ecgbert fifteen years previously, as yet another way to cash in on the famous novel.

In the show (and the book) Tintin had always carried a teddy with him, Dogmatix, named after the well-known Italian druid. It was one of the things, aside from Tintin's handsomeness and wit, that made his character so delightful to TV audiences. The Old Stable Yard did a good trade in Dogmatixs, identical to the one on the show, which they sold for £56 a pop. This being Tintin & Dogmatix day (in which tourists could dress up and compete to look most like Tintin or his bear) they were likely to do a roaring trade.

CHAPTER 16

The day got off to a bumpy start due to Mad Ecgbert making one of his unannounced visitations to the Hall. He tended to drop in about once a week, arriving in a minicab (leaving Mr Carfizzi to deal with the bill). He'd roam around the house, picking things up and making a nuisance of himself. Over the past few months, Egbert and India had grown accustomed to this pattern, and despite Mad Ecgbert's relentless hostility, they greeted him with equanimity. He came with the house, after all, and – as young Egbert often pointed out, in his reasonable manner, if his cousin Mad Ecgbert weren't so mad, they would never have been offered Tode Hall in the first place. The very least he and India could do, therefore, was to put up with his little visits, and to pay the minicab bills without a fuss.

On that day, he turned up at 6 a.m., before anyone in the house was awake. He knew the alarm code to the family's private entrance, which accessed the part of the house never open to tourists – and when his more sensible cousin Egbert surfaced, in Lycra biking gear, at a quarter to seven, Mad Ecgbert was sitting at the breakfast table in the Red Dining Room, munching his way through a pile of burnt toast.

Egbert said: 'Ecgbert! You're up with the lark! What a lovely surprise! Would you like some coffee?'

To which his mad cousin replied: 'What the fuck are you wearing?'

Young Egbert grinned: 'Bit much at breakfast, is it? I'm squeezing in a bike ride before Tintin & Dogmatix Day. Looks like we're going to be lucky with the weather ... How are you?'

To which Mad Ecgbert, crunching on his burnt toast, had replied: 'You look ridiculous. By the way ...' he indicated a large oil painting on the wall; a distant grandfather, wearing tight white breeches, high boots and a wig: 'I need that painting. Tell Car Fizzy to send it over, will you?' And then he threw his burnt toast onto his plate and stood up. 'Or you'll be hearing from my lawyers.'

Egbert said: 'Are you sure you wouldn't like some coffee, Coz?'

Mad Ecgbert replied: 'I can't eat breakfast with a fucking bumblebee. You look like a bumblebee, Egbert.'

Egbert shrugged and settled down to breakfast on his own. Car Fizzy normally took charge in these situations ... He didn't start work for another fifteen minutes but Egbert assumed he would take care of said situation soon enough: he would probably organise for a car to take Ecgbert back home – without the painting, obviously.

In the meantime, young Egbert had more pressing concerns. Tintin & Dogmatix day was traditionally a great favourite with the tourists, and in his first year in charge at Tode Hall, it was important to him that he didn't disappoint.

Later, while Egbert was in his post bike-ride shower, and Mr Carfizzi was putting Mad Ecgbert back into his minicab, India called on her guests in the Queen Charlotte Suite. Violet was still luxuriating in Lord Olivier's bed, so it was Alice who answered the door. She found India dressed in sexy-maid uniform, stilettos and fishnets, carrying a breakfast tray and laughing so her shoulders shook, making the breakfast slide around the tray.

'Surprise for your grandmother!' she whispered. 'Thought it was time the tables were turned . . . ' She looked at Alice's face (always hard to read). ' . . . *Funny*?' India asked her, suddenly doubtful. '*Not* funny? Oh *God*. I thought it would be nice for her to have breakfast in bed. About time, really. To thank her for all the times she brought Emma and Geraldine Tode their breakfasts in bed – and I bet she did, you know, every single day . . . Should I not have done it?'

On the tray, most beautifully laid out, with silver toast rack and silver marmalade bowl was a breakfast fit for a Queen . . . It was a sweet gesture. Alice was only concerned about the sexy maid get-up. Her grandmother, who could be quite touchy, might think India was laughing at her.

However, in the time it took for Alice to form these thoughts, India had grown impatient. She'd made all the effort. She was going to see it through.

'Come on,' she whispered to Alice. 'She'll *love* it! Let's do it!'

Alice stepped aside, India delivered the tray. It turned out Violet was too old and blind to notice the details of India's get-up in any case. But the laden breakfast tray, in all its elegance and grandeur, reduced her to tears.

'Bless you,' she said to India, tucking into the kippers. 'It's the best morning of my life.'

CHAPTER 17

Tintin day went very smoothly until about three o'clock. Visitors to the John Lewis style café in the basement were offered Tintin & Dogmatix themed cakes, and India had also arranged a miniature teddy-themed treasure hunt around the adventure playground for the children.

Dominic Rathbone was meant to announce the winner of the dressing-up contest at 3 p.m. sharp. (India and Egbert had passed the decision wholly over to him.) But at 3.20 p.m. Alice, Violet, the Todes and about fifty idiotic-looking tourists, dressed as teddy bears, were milling around on the lawn by the lake, still waiting for Dominic to begin. It was getting quite boring.

India kept telling him to buck up, because it was cold and 'nobody was that interested'. But he wouldn't be hurried. Sunkissed and fit, post his European tennis holiday, and looking at least a decade younger than his sixty-three years, Dominic appeared to be taking the decision very seriously. He had a clipboard. He was examining each teddy costume slowly and carefully, and making notes. Even the competitors, toasty in their stupid outfits, were beginning to voice some impatience.

But there was nothing to be done. The spotlight was on Dominic, and that didn't happen often enough these days. His acting career had peaked in *Prance*. The coffee ad currently running was a happy aberration and – as Dominic liked to say when in his cups: 'You can take the man out of the theatre but you can't take the theatre out of the man.' This afternoon, he was playing the role of Celebrity Judge at the annual Tode Hall Tintin & Dogmatix Costume Contest, and he intended to milk it for as long as he could.

Carfizzi ruined everything. (On purpose, Dominic assumed at the time. He and Carfizzi enjoyed a complicated love–hate relationship. Rather, Carfizzi love–hated Dominic. Dominic's feelings were less intense.) In any case, just as Dominic was clearing his throat, just as he was about to announce the winner – Carfizzi sidled slap into the centre of the action and whispered something into Egbert's ear. It was off putting. More off putting still, the expression on Egbert's face as he received Carfizzi's news.

Not a happy face.

'*Are you certain?*' Egbert asked him.

Carfizzi nodded. He looked terrible.

'*It can't be true . . .*'

India, standing beside her husband, but focusing on Dominic, was unaware of Carfizzi and Egbert's whispered exchange. She had noticed Dominic clearing his throat, preparing to start – *and then bloody well stopping* again. 'Come on, you old thesp,' she shouted at him, 'get on with it! You can't string this out forever!'

Egbert tapped her on the shoulder. Carfizzi, his swarthy

face bereft of its usual health and colour, stood quietly, waiting. It was as if (Dominic thought later) the entire scene had been played out in theatrical slow-motion. When Egbert finally spoke, his words sounded distorted. Dominic wasn't sure if he'd heard them right.

'... *The smell* ...' Egbert said.

'What's up?' India asked, coming to stand beside him.

Egbert put a finger to his lips. He glanced across at Alice, caught her eye – seemed to hesitate, and then beckoned her over. Alice left her place behind her grandmother's wheelchair and went to join him.

Someone's died, she thought. She knew. She could see it from the look on their faces – Dominic, India, Egbert, Carfizzi. Someone had died.

Egbert said to India, very quietly – 'Munchkin, I want you to stay calm.'

India said, 'Egbert, what the fuck has happened? Can we please just get this crapshow over and done with and go back inside?'

'*Shhhh*,' he said. (Mustn't alarm the tourists.)

'Well, what is it?'

'The smell,' Egbert said again. 'Alice – the smell we noticed up by the mausoleum ...'

Egbert put a hand on India's shoulder, but continued directing his words to Alice. 'It wasn't sheep. It was – Carfizzi's found ... He found ... *a body* ... in the mausoleum. Dead.'

'Human?' India laughed. It was too loud, all wrong. 'I should hope so, Egg! There are lots of bodies in the mausoleum. That's what it's for!'

He shook his head. 'No. She shouldn't have been in there ... She was meant to be in Capri.'

India's eyes goggled. '*Oh my God*,' she said. And then: 'I think I'm going to be sick.'

Carfizzi nodded. 'Lady Tode. She must have been lying there all this time . . .'

India's eyes swivelled. Through the throng of teddy bears, she sought out Dominic, who was staring back at her, making his way over. India turned back to Alice, to Carfizzi, to Egbert. '*Dead?*' she said. 'Since when? I thought she went to Capri?'

'*Shhh!*' said Egbert.

Dominic joined them. 'What's happened? What's going on?'

Carfizzi laughed: not a funny laugh, full of bitterness. 'You're saying you don't already know?' he said.

'Know what?' Dominic said. 'What are you talking about? What have you done, Carfizzi? What have you done this time?'

India took hold of Dominic's arm. 'They've found her,' she mumbled, and burst into tears.

'Found who? What have you done, Carfizzi?' Dominic asked again. 'What the hell is going on? Somebody tell me!' He was talking far too loudly. It was the last thing anyone needed.

Egbert held up a hand. 'Everyone, keep calm. India, Munchkin. Try not to cry. First and foremost, let's not create a drama. *First and foremost*, we've got to finish this Tintin show. Get the tourists out of the area. Car Fizzy, have you called the police?'

Mr Carfizzi shook his head. His eyes shifted again to Dominic. 'I thought it would be prudent to wait,' he said.

'Of course you did,' muttered Dominic.

'*Excellent*,' Egbert said. 'Good thinking. The last thing we want is to make a fuss. Munchkin, how are you feeling? Are you feeling better?'

India nodded.

'Good girl! Now then, Munchie, can you *face* carrying on here? Carry on as if nothing has happened. That's what we have to do – Dominic, you too.'

'I still don't know what you're all talking about. What's happened?'

'I want you both to carry on as if everything was *quite normal*. All right? Dominic, announce the winner. Don't rush it. Make an event of it! These people are counting on you. They've gone to a lot of trouble, getting their costumes right. Whoever's won today will want to feel special. Let's not take that away from them . . .'

'Egg,' said India, wiping her eyes. 'You're amazing. I love it when you take control.'

Egbert nodded. Businesslike in this crisis. His eyes turned to Alice, who was standing there, calmly and quietly, observing events. 'Alice, I know it's a bit much. You haven't even officially started yet . . . But could you bear to come with me? I'm going to have to head up there and check it out, and I have a feeling your calm presence would really help. Mr Car Fizzy – shall you come with us? It's entirely up to you. But I must say, I'd be awfully grateful if you did . . .'

CHAPTER 18

It wasn't the first time Alice had seen a dead body. She found her mother, post overdose. She came back from school and found her dead in her bed, covered in vomit. Nothing, ever, would compare to that. Maybe Alice was already a little shut-down. Maybe a childhood spent with a fragile, alcoholic, junkie mother had taken its toll on her already. But ever since that day – that was the amazing thing about Alice – nothing rocked her anymore. Not since then.

So she followed Egbert and Carfizzi into the mausoleum with no more than curiosity – and distaste, of course: the smell was bad.

'How long's she been there?' she asked Egbert, as they climbed into the car together.

Egbert didn't know. Neither he, nor India, nor apparently Carfizzi, had seen or spoken to Lady Tode for almost a fortnight. Not since the day she was due to leave for Capri. Relations had grown so sour between her and India it had been a tremendous relief for all parties that she left when she did. There would have been no reason for either of the young Todes to get in touch with her.

Looking down onto her two-week-old corpse, Egbert could feel bad about that now.

The crypt was arranged around a central, circular hallway, with four small rooms branching off it, each one lit with a single window, high in the wall, at ground level. There was no electricity down there. What remained of the daylight landed in soft beams from the four high windows, meeting in the crypt's centre, where Lady Tode now lay, a silver candlestick and a broken candle half-clasped in her hand. She'd been hit on the head. That much seemed to be obvious. Her hair was matted like wire, and she was surrounded by a dark brown pool of her own blood.

'Even in death, she is elegant,' muttered Carfizzi.

It wasn't strictly true. Her right leg had twisted unnaturally beneath her, and her skirt had hoiked up revealing thick winter stockings and expensive silky pants. There was something especially shocking about seeing Lady Tode's pants: a violent reminder to Egbert and Carfizzi that she must, in life, have had – a bottom. This was gross. And now she was dead.

'So true,' sighed Egbert. 'Always elegant. D'you think we should cover her up?'

The three of them gazed at the body in silence. Lying beside her, just beyond her dead hand was an old-fashioned key, the Tode family crest engraved on its handle: the key, Alice presumed, to the mausoleum.

'You think someone did this to her?' asked Alice, thinking aloud. It was tactless.

'Absolutely not!' Egbert replied quickly. 'You've been reading too many penny dreadfuls, Alice Liddell! My goodness! Aunt Emma obviously came to say a fond farewell to Uncle Ecgbert before leaving for Capri, and then obviously fell over, hit her head ... poor old thing. And the problem is, of course, no one would have heard her down here, except the sheep ...' He shuddered. 'Awful way to go, I must say. We have to hope she didn't cling on for too long. I expect she lost consciousness the moment she landed, don't you, Car Fizzy? Otherwise she could have raised the alarm – somehow. Walked home ...'

'Unless she was locked in,' said Alice.

Carfizzi pointed angrily at the key, lying in the blood beside her corpse. He had gone to some length (though Alice couldn't have known this) to position the key just so, as it lay, specifically to prevent nosy parkers from making these sort of unhelpful suggestions. His pointing finger, packed with so much energy, reminded Alice of God's finger on the ceiling of the Sistine Chapel. But maybe that was because Carfizzi was Italian. Her sons would probably tell her she was being racist. In the meantime, he was glaring at Alice. 'You don't see the key?' he said. 'Can't you see the key, lying there? Of course she wasn't locked in ... Anyway the door was unlocked. That is why nobody ever suspected something. The door was closed but it wasn't locked. Why would she lock herself into the place? It doesn't make any sense, what you're saying.'

Alice bent inwards, the better to see the key in question. 'It's very clean though, isn't it?' she observed. 'Like it's just been placed there, after the event. I mean – considering everything else is covered in blood.'

'And is that my fault?' Carfizzi snapped.

'No, of course not,' said Alice. 'I don't suppose so. I was just mentioning ...'

Egbert said: 'I think we should call the police. I'll wait for them at the West arch, and maybe I can lead them in round via the Home Farm entrance.' He checked his watch. 'The gardens close in twenty minutes, but we don't want to risk … You know. We don't want to make a fuss.'

'In any case,' Carfizzi said, still glaring at Alice, 'the door wasn't even locked. So I don't know why you want to say that Lady Tode was locked into this disgusting place … I don't know why you want to think something so horrible.' His lower lip was trembling. He was very emotional.

Egbert patted him on the shoulder. 'Easy does it, Car Fizzy. You're obviously upset. We're all upset. I don't think Alice meant badly, did you Alice?'

Alice shrugged. 'I was just observing.'

They had been down there long enough. Egbert led Alice out into the fresh air again. They sat together in the Range Rover while Carfizzi locked up. It was time to call the police.

CHAPTER 19

Egbert drove Alice and Violet to the train station late the following morning. Between dealing with police, undertakers, and scores of grief-stricken estate employees (India seemed, as usual, to have wandered off) Egbert had formally offered Alice a position, and she had accepted it. The job didn't pay excessively well, nevertheless she would be earning more than she ever had before: not to mention the free car, free house, free utility bills, free phone, free vegetables, six weeks a year holiday and, for her triplets, should they wish to visit her (which they would), five train fares to and from London each, per year. Egbert only bridled when Violet, also present during negotiations, tried to push for the tickets to be first class. He said:

'Oh come on, Mrs Dean. They're only youngsters. I don't even travel first class. Seems a bit much.'

Other than that, he agreed to everything they asked for. In return, Egbert asked Alice to make the move North as soon as she possibly could. Alice thought about it. Assuming the cottage was ready (and able to accommodate Violet's wheel-chair) there was nothing much to prevent her from moving up here right away.

She imagined a life without the triplets and felt a wave of tremendous sadness. But then she imagined a life without the triplets' dirty socks, empty pizza boxes, overflowing ash-trays, their constant stealing of her hash and emptying of the fridge. She thought of living in a house that didn't leak from the kitchen ceiling and didn't thud from night until morning to the sound of mindless rap. She imagined all that. And at that instant, despite the hideousness of the scene in the mausoleum, she felt, for the first time in many, many years, like dancing a jig of joy. She agreed to start work within a fortnight.

On the train back to London Violet was unusually quiet. When Alice asked her if there was something wrong, she denied it, though there obviously was. Alice opened her Agatha Christie novel and started to read, confident that her grandmother was unlikely to keep her concerns to herself for long.

After five minutes, Violet said, irritably, 'I would've thought you'd have read all the Agatha Christies by now. Why don't you read something else for a change?'

'I like her,' said Alice.

'There are a lot of other books out there, you know . . .'

Alice read on.

'Alice, I don't know how you can sit there reading that rot, so carefree, like you haven't got a care in the wide world.

You must think it's a bit strange, don't you? It's just like you. Pretending everything's OK, just so you don't have to *do* anything. It's your life in a nutshell isn't it, Alice? You're lazy. That's what you are. *Lazy, lazy, lazy.*'

With a sigh, Alice closed her book. 'What's up, Granny?'

'You know exactly what's up. You know as well as I do.' Violet leaned forward in her wheelchair, and whispered loudly across the table, so that everyone within three rows could hear it quite clearly. 'If that woman "slipped and fell", then I'm the Queen of Sheba. Somebody killed her!'

The thought had of course occurred to Alice. She had observed as much to Carfizzi. She said, calmly: 'What makes you say so, Granny?'

'What makes me say so?' Violet rapped the arm of her wheelchair in frustration. 'What makes me *not* say so! That's what you should be asking. It's as clear as the nose on that face of yours.'

Alice kept that face of hers impassive. She waited to hear more. Her grandmother had a point. She couldn't quite put her finger on it. But there were bad vibes in the house: between India and Lady Tode, most obviously; between India and Mrs Carfizzi, between India and Mr Carfizzi, between Mr Carfizzi and Egbert, Mr Carfizzi and Dominic Rathbone, between Mad Ecgbert and Egbert . . .

'Lady Tode didn't even like her husband. Never did, never had. He was a dreadful man and everybody knew it. If you want to know,' Violet added, 'she was having it off with Brian Mellors the gamekeeper for several years, and then after that, there was the Nazi-looking chap . . . I forget his name. And of course the dog painter, what was *his* name? He was always staying at the Hall . . . And then, I shouldn't be surprised, from what Mr Carfizzi was saying – I have a feeling she had a good go with Brian Mellor's son. Everyone knew it. Lady Tode could never get enough sex!'

'Granny—'

'What? I'm *telling* you.'

Alice said, talking now in an ostentatiously quiet voice, in the hope her grandmother might be inspired to follow suit. 'I must say, Granny, I got the impression she was ultra-respectable.'

'Because she was,' yelled Violet. 'But only in *public*, d'you see? You couldn't expect her to be loyal to that husband of hers, not for all those years. Awful man.' She shuddered. '*Very* unattractive.'

'Well – that's interesting,' murmured Alice, as quietly as possible, 'I'm not sure it means she was murdered though. Lots of people have affairs. They don't get murdered.'

'I'm SAYING I don't see why she would have gone to visit his silly coffin when she didn't care two hoots about him, even when he was alive.'

Alice thought about this. Hardly compelling evidence. On the other hand ... 'Perhaps—' she began.

'Perhaps nothing ...' Violet settled, now she'd got the thing off her chest. She spoke more softly, adding: 'I can't help wondering about your young friend, Ecgbert, Alice ...'

'Ecgbert or Egbert?'

'Ecgbert, of course. Young Egbert wouldn't hurt a fly. A very nice young man.'

'You mean, crazy Ecgbert? Disinherited Ecgbert? He's not my friend.'

'He certainly used to be.'

Alice laughed. 'More than thirty-five years ago, Granny. I haven't laid eyes on him since we were fourteen.'

'You laid a lot more than eyes on each other then, if I remember rightly.'

This annoyed Alice. How did her grandmother know about *that*? It was nothing – a long forgotten nothing: a single summer evening up at Africa Folly, watching the sun go down … a bottle of disgusting sherry, stolen from the Tode cellar, a joint, stolen from Alice's mother, and the 'eternal snog', as they referred to it immediately afterwards; followed by dopey – happy – fourteen-year-old giggles … All of it long forgotten. Except, apparently, by her grandmother, who was looking at her now with an irritating, knowing expression. Alice, as ever, remained impassive.

Violet said: 'He must have been devastated when his mother gave the Hall to those two nincompoops. *Devastated*. He used to adore his mother – do you remember? Like a little puppy, he was. Dragging around behind her, just waiting for a nod or a smile. But she was a cold fish, Lady Tode. Chilly as you like.'

'I thought people loved her.'

'Well they did,' Violet said, gazing out on the passing landscape. 'Everybody loved Lady Tode. Just, she didn't love them back. It can drive people a bit mad, that, you know, Alice. If you love someone with all your heart and you can never get through their shell. It can be agony.' This was not the way Violet spoke, generally. This was unusual. Alice wondered if taking her grandmother to Tode Hall had been a mistake. Perhaps the journey had been too much for her.

Alice nodded kindly, as if she understood, which she didn't.

Violet laughed. 'But you wouldn't understand about that, would you Alice Liddell, my darling? You're a bit like Lady Tode yourself. *Impenetrable*. Not that I blame you.' She patted

Alice's hand, which was resting on the table between them, holding the book. 'You had a difficult childhood.'

Alice said: 'Would you like a cup of tea, Granny? I can go to the buffet.'

She chuckled. 'Did you see Mr Car Fizzy? I should think he was in love with her. He could hardly stand up, could he? . . . Why do you suppose he lied about Dominic Rathbone, then? He said none of the actors from the show had stayed at the Hall – he didn't mention Dominic, did he? Maybe *Mr Carfizzi* did her ladyship in. He might have done.'

Alice said: 'Do you think you should talk a bit more quietly?'

'Or – my heart doesn't like it, Alice, but my head keeps going back to Ecgbert. Poor, mad Ecgbert. He comes and goes, India said. Always hanging around the place. Very angry. Very disappointed and hurt. I wouldn't blame him, frankly. He probably lured her in there, and then bopped her on the head. I bet he did.'

'Well, I don't think that's very likely,' Alice snapped. 'And I think you should shut your cake-hole.'

Alice never snapped. It jolted Violet to silence. Absolute silence. She sent her granddaughter a wide-eyed, knowing look; and sulked for the rest of the way home.

CHAPTER 20

Alice delivered her still-sulking grandmother back to the flat, settled her in, and went home to break the news of her new job to the triplets. They would be pleased. For a long time now, it had been obvious to them (to everyone but Alice) that she was bored and listless, and needed to find something to fill the yawning gap that made up most of her waking life. The move to Yorkshire would also, of course, give them free run of the London house, and a place to hide out when city life became too expensive or tiring.

They weren't in when she got home, in any case. She wandered around the house, not quite sure what to do with herself. Should she start packing? But she had a fortnight to do that. Should she maybe call a friend, tell them the news? She couldn't think of anyone to tell.

In the bath, she tried to imagine her new life in Yorkshire, but couldn't. Images of Ecgbert in his care home, being told by housekeepers that his mother was dead, kept floating through her mind. But she didn't want to think about that. She thought about her grandmother instead: her peculiar openness on the train back home. Her titanic sulk, after Alice had snapped at her. The argument was still unresolved. *That* was the problem! Alice knew she couldn't end the day like this. What if Violet died in the night? What if she died, and she and Alice were still fighting?

The last thing Alice said to her mother, the morning she left for school and her mother died: she said, 'You shouldn't smoke in bed, Mum. You'll set the house on fire.' Her mother had not replied. And Alice, suddenly angry, said: 'Maybe it would be a good thing.' She'd slammed the bedroom door and gone to school. The end.

So after the bath, which was wonderful, very relaxing, Alice returned to her grandmother's flat to make peace. There was a security coded keypad at the main entrance (as there was at Tode Hall), and Alice had a key to Violet's studio flat. She let herself in.

It was only nine o'clock but Violet was already in bed. She looked frail, Alice thought. Her supper had been delivered to her room on a tray, but it lay untouched, half-congealed on the coffee table in front of the television. When Alice tiptoed into her grandmother's overheated bedroom, Violet turned her face to the wall.

'You all right, Granny?' Alice said, sitting herself by the bed. 'Sorry I snapped at you on the train.'

Violet sniffed. Still she wouldn't look at Alice. She said: 'You're very touchy, you know.'

'Not really,' said Alice. 'Just sometimes you have a way of getting under my skin, Granny. That's all it is. I think you know that, anyway.'

'You shouldn't talk to me like that. Telling me to "shut my cake-hole". You shouldn't talk to me like that.'

'I'm sorry, Granny. Really, I am. It was very, very rude of me. Can we be friends now? Please?'

Violet didn't say yes, but she didn't say no, either. Alice smiled. 'It was a good trip though, wasn't it?'

'Well – give or take the odd murder,' Violet said. At last, she turned to look at her granddaughter. 'A bloody good trip, yes it was,' she said. 'And you'll be happy there, Alice. With all them outcasts and peculiars. You'll feel like you came home at last. I know you will.'

'*We'll* feel it, Granny. Don't forget you're coming with me!'

Violet Dean smiled. She patted her granddaughter's hand. 'Been a difficult life for you, darling,' she said softly. 'But you'll be all right now . . .'

And then she closed her eyes and never opened them again.

CHAPTER 21

The police, their resources tied up detecting more manageable infringements, were keen not to be too drawn into the circumstances surrounding Lady Tode's death. Thankfully, an examination of the scene revealed a raised slab on the ground just a half metre from her feet. There was a little moss growing around it, and the damage to her skull looked as if it might have occurred when her head hit the stone floor. She was quite old. Her eyesight was imperfect. The central chamber was dark. And in any case – India and Egbert were charming, and the outgoing Sergeant enjoyed Tode Hall House & Grounds annual membership, and often took his grandchildren to the adventure playground by the Boathouse Café. On top of which it was well known in the area that everyone, everywhere, had loved the late Lady Tode. It was inconceivable that anyone might have wanted to kill her.

Even so, she clearly hadn't died of natural causes. It was an inconvenience, an embarrassment for everyone concerned, but there would still need to be an inquest. The law was the law, up to a point. Even at Tode Hall. In the meantime, as India so boldly put it, 'Life must go on!'

In London, Alice packed up her suitcase, bade farewell to her triplets, cancelled the only two bookings still pending on the cookery course – and buried her grandmother. It wasn't much. There wasn't much to Alice's life before she came North.

She felt an ache in her heart on the train journey back to Todeister. Last time she had made the journey it had been with her grandmother – and for her grandmother, too, really. Without Violet's bossy insistence, Alice would never have applied for the job.

But here she was: a suitcase hardly larger than the one she had brought with her for the interview, crammed, now, with everything she cared about, except her children: her floaty hippy clothes, her junk jewellery, her pack of yellow hair dye, her tobacco tin. A woman half numbed by the knocks life had dealt her, with a ropey wardrobe and hair too long and too blonde for her smoke-creased, once-lovely face: fifty-one years old and ready to start all over again.

India Tode didn't have much scheduled that day. The au pair had taken the children to the Boathouse for a picnic and wouldn't be back until dark. She told Egbert she would go to meet Alice's train.

She might easily have sent Mr Carfizzi, but she was looking forward to Alice's arrival. Also, she realised, Alice might be feeling a bit down in the dumps, given that her grandmother had died. India wanted to make Alice feel as welcome and happy at Tode Hall as possible.

'That's so sweet of you, Munch,' Egbert said to his wife, who was lying in bed. (A modern bed, their marital bed, brought from London. The old four-posters gave India the creeps.) He was already up and showered. 'I feel a bit bad we haven't cleared out the house for her,' he said, putting his trousers on. 'Do you think she'll mind organising it herself? There's not a great deal to do... Lottie and Lisa can help. And Kveta, if needs be ...'

'Oh she'll be fine,' India said. Now that Emma Tode had vacated it Alice had been allocated the far superior Gardener's House to live in. India thought, when Alice discovered this change of plan, she would be unlikely to resent the delay. In any case, India said, 'She's not employing me, I'm employing her, for God's sake. I'm not doing her housework for her.'

Egbert smiled at India. 'Alice is a very lucky lady,' he said. 'I wish I could come with you to the station but I really can't. I'm absolutely chocka ...'

He had meetings all day: with the local constabulary, about the need for more tasteful traffic cones on the South drive; with Basmich Safety Solutions, about the implications of hosting a three-day Vegan Food Festival on a couple of fields behind Harsmead Wood; with handsome Oliver Mellors, about the possibility of building an expanded pheasant hatchery on the land below Vallory Farm ... with a pushy friend of Dominic Rathbone, who was taking an exhibition of eighteenth-century dog paintings to Japan and wanted to borrow a couple from

112

Tode Hall ... on it went. 'Will you be all right, Munchie? I don't want you getting overtired. You've got so much on ...'

India said: 'I haven't really. Ludo and Passion spend literally all day playing down by the boats with Weronika – they're boat obsessed. They're so happy here, Egbert! Sometimes I just think it makes up for everything ... missing London, Carfizzi being such a pig, tourists peering in at the windows, stupid bloody Emma falling over in the mausoleum, wrecking Tintin & Dogmatix day ...'

'She did *not* wreck Tintin & Dogmatix day!' Egbert protested. 'You and Dominic did sterling work, keeping the show on the road. I was so proud of you. Actually I think Tintin & Dogmatix day was a tremendous success. Something you should be bloody proud of, India. Seriously.'

India shrugged.

'Also,' Egbert continued, 'on the Emma front ... It's all jolly horrid. Not pretending it wasn't. But honestly, I seriously think the best policy is not to think about it. Try to focus on all the *lovely* things about being here, darling.'

'Easy to say.'

'I know it is sweetheart. But we just have *to push on*. Be brave! It was a dreadful, awful, unfortunate, tragic accident. But I really do believe passionately that the best thing we can possibly do, under the circs, is to pretend it never happened. As much as we can. We certainly don't want to upset the littles, do we?'

She smiled her angelic smile, and Egbert was reminded, once again, of what a lucky man he was. 'They just love it here, don't they Egg?' she said again. 'Makes everything worthwhile.' He leaned across their luxurious modern bed and kissed her. He had a meeting to get to. Time to crack on.

India presented Alice with the keys to her new home with great fanfare. The house was only a hundred yards from the Hall, but it was set within its own walled garden, and neither building was visible from the other. This might have allowed for some privacy, but for the tourists who were always everywhere. The Gardener's House had a private back yard, at least, but its front looked directly onto the Rose Garden's lawn and a couple of benches which, Alice would soon learn, were a favourite spot among savvier tourists, for setting out their illicit picnics.

The Gardener's House was designed more as a garden ornament than a home. With its toy-town mansion front, it looked like something out of Wonderland, or possibly Disneyland. Either way, behind the eccentric exterior, it was coincidentally a warm and welcoming place to live. There were three bedrooms, a large kitchen with wood burning Aga, a sitting room with French doors that opened out onto the private yard, and a pleasant terrace. The place hadn't been done up since the seventies. Emma Tode had been planning a lavish refit, but in the end she'd barely had time to unpack. Her belongings were piled high in boxes and cases in every room. Obviously it had been a last minute decision to put Alice into the Gardener's House. Nobody had even got around to cleaning out Emma's kitchen cupboard. There was stale milk and a carton of orange juice in the fridge, and Emma's sheets were still on the bed.

'Bit gross,' India said, when she showed Alice round. 'Sorry about that. I definitely asked them to deal with it before you got here. They must have forgotten. Don't worry! Let's go and have lunch in the Old Stable Yard Café, and I'll get Carfizzi to send over the girls for a tidy up. Once they've got some of the junk out you can start making yourself at home. You can do whatever you like! Move stuff around. And if you want to order new curtains or anything – just say. Whatever you want. A new telly. A new bath. Whatever – we just want you to be happy.'

Alice followed her new employer back to the car, and they drove the distance to the Old Stable Yard, where India said they did really good bangers and mash and that everything was organic. Alice wondered when she might be expected to start work – or even what that work might entail. What with everything that happened last time she was here, and then her grandmother talking so much nobody else could get a word in, and Egbert being so keen to please, and India not being especially focused, the subject of her duties had never been very thoroughly covered. 'Don't worry!' India said. 'We'll talk about all that during lunch.'

Over the bangers and mash, between warm exchanges with café staff and sundry, passing employees, India said: 'So your job, Alice – don't laugh. I've thought about this a lot, because I know we left it a bit woolly . . . But here we are, stuck in the middle of nowhere, you know . . . in the middle of Yorkshire. And it's fantastic, and the kids are happy, and Egbert's happy and . . . all that . . . But I just think – I *love* my family. Obviously. But Egbert can be a bit serious, bless him. So the main point is – you and I have got to make sure we keep it *fun*.'

'Keep it fun,' repeated Alice. Should she be taking notes?

'It's only a bloody house, after all!' India said. 'And seriously, what's the point of living in a bloody great palace like this, and spending all day and all night worrying about the roof, and the taxman, and the bloody tourists – *sorry* – and not even having any fun? Don't you think?'

Alice tried not to laugh, but laughed anyway. She said: 'So. I'm the Fun Manager, am I?'

India clapped her hands together. 'Exactly!' she said. 'I knew you'd get it! We've got to think of lots and lots of ways of making money for the estate which do not involve – you know, boring meetings with boring people. And that's it! So. Let's brainstorm! Are you ready? Or do you want to settle into your lovely house first? I don't want to rush you. What we need, *obviously*, is another movie to be made at the Hall. And let's get some fashion shoots done here. Get lots of glamorous people up here, which is fun for us, great publicity for the house – *and* brings in lots of lolly, all at the same time. That's my idea. Question to you: How are we going to do it? I know a few *Voguey* types. But film ... I don't know. Do you know anyone in the film world, Alice? Let's invite them to stay with us, and then *blow them away* with ... you know. Everything. Get Carfizzi to dress up as a butler. He loves that. We can really ham it up! Don't you think? Hilarious. You look so rock'n'roll Alice. I just bet you know some of the coolest cats in town. Who do you know? Who can we invite up here to jolly the place up a bit?'

Alice did, in her ropey fashion, look quite rock'n'roll. But she didn't know anyone in that world. Or if she did, she wasn't aware of it, or couldn't remember, or wouldn't recognise them, or had no clear idea what it was they actually did. She thought about it for moment. 'I don't think it matters if you know them, India. I think you could invite pretty much anyone to stay here for the weekend, and they'd say yes. The question is, who do you want to invite?'

India loved that. At Alice's words, her beautiful face lit up with pleasure. 'That's what I *thought*!' she said. 'I knew it! I knew I was right to want you on board, Alice. I knew it! You know everything, and you just don't give a blue-arse buggery about any of it! Am I right?'

'Well I . . .'

'Don't answer! I know I'm right. I know it. And when I'm old, Alice – I hope you don't mind me saying this. But when I'm your age I want to be exactly like you. You are literally the coolest human being I have ever met.' She leaned across the bangers and mash and wrapped Alice in an unwanted hug. Alice pushed her back into her seat.

'Sorry!' India said. 'I see you don't like that. I won't hug you again. Got over excited! I'm so *so* happy you're here, Alice. We are going to have a *ball*.'

CHAPTER 22

Kveta, the Slovakian housekeeper, had been over to the Gardener's House with clean sheets and towels, and a bin bag to remove all the food in the fridge. She was annoyed about it, as she had enough on her plate, but she couldn't send over 'the girls', because as usual they'd both called in sick. Lottie and Lisa were twin sisters, shy, young, goofy, whose mother worked at the Old Stable Yard retail centre and whose father managed the Tode Hall livestock. There was no chance of firing them without upsetting the parents (who weren't at all goofy) and nobody wanted to do that. Unfortunately for Kveta, on top of being incompetent and immoveable, the girls were unusually susceptible to colds, and since one couldn't seem to come to work without the other, they rarely checked in for work at all. Which left Kveta to keep the Hall in order on her own. It was no wonder the Gardener's House clearout had been overlooked.

She'd left, without having done a particularly thorough job, by the time Alice returned, several hours later. Not that Alice cared or even noticed. Compared to the chaos of Clapham, the place looked like a Swiss science lab.

It had been a long day. Alice was tired. She ran herself a bath, smoked her evening joint – and then remembered she would need to make up a bed. India had muttered something about finding clean linen, but she hadn't mentioned where, so Alice set about searching through the cupboards. Not as easy a task as it might seem, because the cupboards were still stuffed with Lady Tode's belongings, also because of the peculiar number of cupboards – or so it seemed to Alice, who kept forgetting which ones she'd opened, and opening them again – and then getting distracted by the treasures she found inside: a pale gold Astrakhan coat, a signed first edition of Lesley Piece's novel, *Prance to the Music in Time*, an ivory mah-jong set; a foldable top hat; a mahogany walking stick with a silver sword hidden inside; and then, the thing that stopped her mind in its tracks: lying upside down on top of a locked cigar box, an old, silver sugar dispenser, shaped like a bowling skittle, with a loose, hinged lid. It was heavily tarnished, and at first glance, nothing much: certainly not in comparison with the other treasures she had unearthed. And yet, for some reason, it captured her attention. She picked it up. It needed a polish.

With the bed still unmade, and the clean sheets yet to be located, she wandered back to the kitchen. She looked under the sink for some silver polish, didn't find any, and decided instead to run the sugar pot under the hot tap. She used some of Lady Tode's Fairy Liquid to remove the worst of the tarnish and then, finding a clean tea cloth (Ah-ha! Kveta had left a pile of clean laundry on the kitchen counter all along – there were

119

bath towels, tea towels, bed sheets, everything she needed) Alice sat down at the kitchen table to polish.

The joint she'd rolled herself must have been stronger than usual: or perhaps it was the mix of cannabis, tiredness, solitude and fresh country air, but she polished that sugar dispenser with an other-world intensity – as if uncovering its shine was the only thing that mattered in her life: which, indeed, in that instant, it was.

And then at some point she resurfaced. She was back in the Gardener's House kitchen, exhausted from all the polishing, a little lonely, missing her triplets, missing London, missing her grandmother. She noticed that her efforts had produced minimal effect on the wretched pot, and abruptly abandoned the task. She took some of the fresh linen from the pile on the counter and rambled upstairs to make her bed.

CHAPTER 23

The house, in the middle of so much silence, turned out to be noisy at night. Things creaked. Alice woke a couple of times, thinking she'd heard a door opening downstairs. The third time she woke she was certain of it.

She heard the squeak of a hinge: a cupboard, perhaps?

And *footsteps*, dammit.

She thought she felt a cold breeze. (How could she feel it, up here in her bedroom?)

She heard the clink of glass, or china.

And then – someone breathing in the hallway.

Alice was not easily frightened. But this was alarming. She wondered if it was her own breathing she was listening to, and told herself that it was. Except she knew it wasn't. There was someone in the house.

She thought of the walking stick with the hidden sword inside. Which cupboard had she found it in? She couldn't remember. Her bedroom was pitch black – a level of darkness

Alice wasn't used to, after a life in London. She could hardly even remember where the door was.

... A creak from downstairs. It was quite loud this time ...
She couldn't just lie there ...

She pulled back the duvet and carefully, softly climbed out of bed. The floorboards creaked beneath her weight. She stopped. Whoever was downstairs, stopped too. A moment of intense silence filled the house– and then whoever it was, broke into a run. She heard a clatter – deafening, in the darkness – as something hard fell onto the stone hall floor. Alice found the light switch and stepped out onto the landing. Another blast of cold air. She stumbled down the stairs – but she was too late. As her feet touched the bottom step, she saw a figure, tall and slim, hurtling through the open back door.

She ran after him. 'HEY! YOU!' she shouted into the darkness. Her voice sounded muffled in the open space. 'Who are you?' But her only answer was the sound of his receding footsteps, sprinting. She tried to follow him, but it was pointless in her bare feet, and very painful. He was gone. She turned back towards the house and found, lying on the gravel, a shoe.

A brown lace-up from Church's of Jermyn Street, size twelve. The back heel was trodden down, the sole was worn through in patches. She picked it up and took it back inside – was gazing at it so intently that she tripped on the laptop lying, smashed, on the hall floor.

She scooped that up too. Looked around her. There was no sign of any break-in, or not that she could see. Whoever it was, must have simply walked through the front door. Or the back door. (In her fuzzy state the previous night, had she remembered to lock either? Probably not.)

She stood very still, feeling her heart beat, wondering whether to call the police.

And realised that even now she wasn't alone. Again from inside the house, she heard a sound. The clink of china. It was coming from the kitchen. Alice turned to open the kitchen door behind her. A tall slim woman sat at her table, in the darkness, drinking from a cup.

'For God's *sake*!' Alice said, and switched on the light.

The woman appeared undisturbed, and continued to sip daintily from her cup. She was elegant, in her late sixties, her dark grey hair pinned up into a fantastic chignon, wearing a flowing silk 1960s pantsuit. She had good deportment: the straightest back, the longest neck, the slimmest wrists Alice had ever seen. She looked, in fact, more like a dress mannequin than a living, breathing human – which, of course, she was not. Alice knew that at once. She knew it, without knowing it. Nothing much rocked Alice. She stared at the woman sipping her tea, and the woman stared haughtily back.

CHAPTER 24

'What are you doing in here?' demanded Alice. 'This is my house.'

'I beg to differ,' the woman replied, in a voice so grand, so languid it seemed miraculous to Alice that tongue and throat had submitted to the imposition of forming the words at all. 'On the contrary,' the woman continued, 'this house is mine. What are you doing in my kitchen, and why aren't you wearing any shoes?'

'It's the middle of the night,' Alice said. 'I've just got out of bed ... Who are you? Why are you here? Did you see that man? What the—'

The woman gave an infinitesimal shudder. (Too many questions.) 'My name,' she said, 'is, or I suppose, if we're to be literal, it *was* Geraldine, the Lady Tode. I am the mother of Sir Ecgbert Eleventh, who died earlier this year. His widow, Emma, Lady Tode, of whom I have come here to speak, was my daughter-in-law. I had understood that she would be living here. But now of course she's dead.'

Alice, standing in her pyjamas, peroxide hair in her face, hand still resting on the kitchen light switch, said: 'Well, but – so are you dead, Geraldine?'

Geraldine, Lady Tode closed her eyes. 'Please don't call me Geraldine.'

'The man who ran out of the house – did you see him?'

She opened them again. 'That was poor, Mad Ecgbert, of course. Come to fetch some of his mother's belongings, I presume. You'll have to change the locks, you realise. Of course it might help if you actually used the locks, too. But you weren't quite up to it, were you, when you stumbled off to bed last night?'

'You were here last night?' Alice said. 'I'm confused—'

Geraldine Tode held up a hand for quiet. Her large sapphire ring caught the light. 'I know exactly who you are, Alice Liddell. We've met before. But you won't remember it.'

'I don't think so.'

'You were very young. You used to come and stay with your grandmother, when your mother was ill. You were a dreadful nuisance, but you couldn't help it, I suppose . . .' She noted Alice's ongoing confusion. 'Your grandmother, Violet Dean, was for many years my lady's maid.'

' . . . Really? . . . '

'And actually, I was rather fond of her.' Geraldine Tode glanced at Alice, who was still looking confused. 'Oh do buck up,' she snapped. 'Sit down and have tea with me. We have information to trade.'

Alice didn't want tea. Nevertheless, clearly, there were a lot of questions hanging. She shuffled her bare feet across the cold wooden kitchen floor, and sat down at the table.

'Take some tea,' Geraldine ordered. Alice noticed an empty cup and saucer already laid out for her.

'I don't want any.'

Geraldine poured her some anyway. Steam rose from the cup as she tipped it in, but when Alice took the cup and drank from it, the liquid was stone cold. She choked a little on the shock. Geraldine watched, amused.

'I'm a ghost,' she said. 'What did you expect?'

Alice said: 'Am I the only one who can see you?'

The question seemed to irritate her. Most questions did. She said: 'How should I know? I'm not in people's skulls. Emma couldn't see me. Nor can that ghastly little man ... I think my darling grandson, poor Mad Ecgbert, sees me sometimes. But because everyone insists on telling him he's mad, he doesn't seem very willing to believe it ... He saw me just now, by the way.' She laughed. 'That's what made him skittle off like that. Not you. Don't flatter yourself! As far as he knows, this house is still his mother's home. Except of course she's dead.'

'Like you,' Alice said again: for her own clarification more than anything else. She would have liked Geraldine to acknowledge the fact, but Geraldine ignored the comment.

'As far as Mad Ecgbert is concerned, this house is still empty.'

'Do you think he recognised you?' Alice asked.

Geraldine, outraged, said: 'Well of course he bloody well recognised me. I'm his grandmother. What do you think?'

'I don't know,' said Alice. 'Depends when you died. Ecgbert's my age – my twin, actually ... How old was he when you died? What year was it?'

Geraldine drew herself up. There was something indefinable but very slightly impertinent, she felt, about Alice's tone. She chose to ignore the question. '... You do realise, Alice dear, that I am your elder and by some stretch?'

Alice laughed. 'I should hope so!' she said. 'Tell me, when did you die?'

'... I died ...' began Geraldine, Lady Tode – her face clouded, and her piercing blue eyes glazed, briefly. 'I "*died*", as you put it ...' she began again, 'since you so badly want to know, and by the way I think it's a remarkably insensitive question, in nineteen seventy-one.'

'Nineteen seventy-one. So Ecgbert would have been four years old. It would be quite surprising if he did recognise you,' Alice said.

Geraldine Tode dismissed the comment. She waved it aside with her delicate, sapphired hand. 'I'm his grandmother. He will have seen pictures. I was a great beauty in my day, Alice.'

'I can see.'

'I could have married anyone.'

'You didn't do so badly ...'

Geraldine Tode shook her head. 'You're quite wrong. He was a dreadful man. Queer as a nine-bob note. Like most men. The Todes, I'm afraid, make dreadful husbands.'

'They have a lovely house though.'

'Too big. Mother always said the Todes were vulgar, and she was absolutely right. There's no need for a house to be as large as this. Look at Chatsworth – perfectly large enough. A perfectly reasonable, *manageable* size. Whereas Tode Hall is silly. I always said so ...' She laughed, but she wasn't really talking to Alice anymore. 'It used to infuriate Sir Ecgbert.'

'I can imagine.'

'The Todes are ghastly. Always have been. Very vulgar, and actually *quite dim*. Land people, really. I should never have married into them ...'

'Well – all I know . . . is too many are called Ecgbert. I never know which one anyone is talking about.'

Geraldine looked at Alice with disappointment: Violet Dean's unfortunate granddaughter was obviously stupid. 'It's very simple,' she said slowly. 'We have young Egbert, without the "c". In our day we used to call men like that "chinless wonders", although Egbert has rather a manly chin. Young Egbert, *sans "c"*, is of course my youngest grandson. I call him the Young Buck from Wandsworth.' Geraldine smiled, pleased with that, took a deep breath and continued. 'He is the young man whom my quite wicked daughter-in-law chose to inherit over her own darling son, Sir Ecgbert Twelfth, otherwise known as Mad Ecgbert. Mad Ecgbert is the individual whom you just now spotted running into the night, having broken into this house in search of something by which to remember his wicked mother. We don't know what it was, and so far as I could tell, he left without it. Mad Ecgbert's father, my son, was of course also called Sir Ecgbert. He was married to Emma, recently found dead in the mausoleum, and he *really was* a dreadful man, if I say it myself as his mother . . . All of which goes some way to explaining Emma's numerous extramarital affairs. I must say it's always been a mystery to me quite how – or if – my son sired a single one of those three children. I don't believe for a second that Australian Esmé is a Tode. He's too short. Also . . . I mean, those meaty forearms . . . ' She considered it a moment. 'I should think he's Mellors's son. But that's neither here nor there. My husband was also a Sir Ecgbert of course. But he died years ago. He died playing polo, just after the War.' She paused, and seemed to run out of interest. 'And he was ghastly too,' she added. 'So. I hope that's clear. The question is,' Geraldine Tode leaned forward, and Alice noticed a cool breeze coming off her, as if she'd just stepped inside after a long winter walk, or perhaps, from a fridge: 'What I want to know is, *who killed my daughter-in-law*, Alice?'

'What?'

'You heard me. Who killed Emma?'

CHAPTER 25

'Well *I* don't know who killed her,' Alice replied, irritably. 'I'm not sure that anyone did.' She had come to Tode Hall as Fun Manager, not chief murder investigator. No matter what all the grandmothers in the world seemed to think, Emma Tode's death was none of her business. She didn't want to get involved. 'The police think she tripped over. She probably did. That's what Egbert and India think, and they should know. Mr Carfizzi actually found her. He told me the same . . .'

'Never mind *Car Fizzy*,' Geraldine Tode dismissed him. 'I wouldn't believe a word that cretin has to say on the matter. Queer as a coot, like all the rest of them. Infatuated with Emma. Like only a left footer could be.' She glanced at Alice, noted confusion: 'Catholic queers are the worst of all, Alice . . . They're *tortured* by it. Car Fizzy worshipped Emma. Enough to kill her, without a doubt . . . Although of course, as I assume you will have worked out by now, whom he really adores is Dominic. Car Fizzy loathes Dominic and yet adores him.

And they both adored Emma. Emma, bless her, never gave a damn about either of them. Nor anyone else, frankly. Nor anything . . .' She considered it. 'Well, she cared about being adored, obviously. And *sex*. She cared about sex and being adored . . . But they tend to be the same, don't they? With the female narcissist.'

'Well this is all very interesting,' Alice said wearily.

'Dead right, it is,' Geraldine Tode replied. 'I wouldn't still be hanging around if it weren't, I dare say . . . Or maybe I would . . .' She glanced at Alice, her bright little eyes revealing, in one moment, the infinite pit of her confusion. But it only lasted a moment. 'In any case,' she said, 'that's for another time . . . *Les mystères de l'univers* . . . [An abominable French accent.] I've been dead nearly fifty years, Alice dear, and these things are still no clearer to me.'

'That's incredibly disappointing,' agreed Alice.

'I think it may be Hell,' Geraldine said, briskly. 'On a brighter note, I get a feeling your new employer, Mrs Tode of Wandsworth, also has a touch of the narcissist about her. Do you think so? It's probably why she and Emma set each other's teeth on edge . . . More importantly, what do you make of Car Fizzy? I wouldn't trust him an inch.'

Alice remembered his hostile behaviour in the mausoleum; also how he'd lied to Violet about Dominic Rathbone. He probably did have something to hide. Plenty to hide, even . . . But then again, after a certain point in life, didn't everyone? Alice shook her head. 'He seems like a nice enough chap,' she said.

'Nonsense!' scoffed Lady Tode. 'You don't believe that!'

Maybe she didn't. But it wasn't the point. 'Well, that's your opinion,' Alice said. 'But all this finger pointing – it's not getting us anywhere, is it? Anyway, I'm sure if there had been any

131

funny business, the police would've been onto it by now. And I really don't think—'

'You're not listening. There are so many suspects in this case, it makes one's head ache simply trying to list them. And it's not that one *minds*, exactly. That is – one certainly has no intention of *reporting* anything to the police. God forbid.'

'I don't see how you could, anyway,' Alice said. 'All things considered. I don't think the police would take you very seriously ... Anyway ... It's been very interesting meeting you, Lady Tode. But if you wouldn't mind, I'd like to go back to bed. Unlike you, I have to get up in the morning.'

Geraldine continued just as if Alice hadn't spoken. 'Nevertheless it simply isn't healthy, *to hover in this sort of ignorance.* If there's been a murder, one ought to be told. You must agree, Alice. Otherwise it leaves one suspecting *tout le monde* ...'

'Not really.'

'Which is why I need you, Alice, dear, to help me find out what actually happened. Emma didn't "fall over" in that terrible place! She was *lured* in there by devious means, we know not which ... And then knocked on the head and left for dead. Either by Car Fizzy, who adored her, or by poor Mad Ecgbert, who adored her. Or by—'

'Ecgbert didn't kill his mother,' snapped Alice. Geraldine Tode noted this, filed it away with a private smirk.

'Of course it could have been Dominic. It might well have been Dominic ... Or it could easily have been India, who *loathed* Emma, by the way. Those two women were at loggerheads from the moment she set foot in the house. As one might expect ...'

'Oh nonsense! Why would Dominic want to kill her? Why

132

would anyone want to kill her? And as for India – it's ridiculous. This whole conversation is ridiculous.' Alice glanced at the broken laptop, and beside it, the discarded gentleman's shoe. Even if those two items were still sitting there on the kitchen table tomorrow, she told herself, it didn't mean this conversation had ever taken place.

She'd smoked too much cannabis before bedtime. Plus – she was in a new house, and a long way from home: all these factors were bound to give her unusually vivid dreams. 'You'd better be a dream,' she muttered. 'Either way, I'm very tired and I want to go back to bed.'

Geraldine Tode considered Alice for a moment. She said: 'Emma was murdered. There's no doubt about it. The question is, *by whom*?' She slapped her hand on the table, but on this occasion it made no sound because her hand didn't stop at the wood. '*That is what we have to find out!*'

There followed a moment of stillness and then, softly, Geraldine's teacup began to shake. The sugar pot shook, and continued to shake. It shook so much the lid flew open. Alice looked at it with terror – this, more than anything tonight, was what frightened her. She heard Geraldine chuckling, glanced up and was confronted by her face, gently contorting, its lower half – the jaw and smiling mouth – twisting like rubber; and then the nose and eyes and forehead following, and continuing the twist, transforming into a small, tunnel-like whirl; the neck and shoulders and the silky pantsuit merged and joined the dance, the whole of her whirling and twirling into a slim tunnel that swivelled and curled and twisted around the kitchen. It twisted faster, until a vapour began to rise from the mass; green and smelling of methane; and all the while, Geraldine, Lady Tode, continued to chuckle.

Alice could do nothing but stare. She said: 'Stop laughing!'

Which made what was left of Lady Tode – the wisping, whirling, stinking tunnel of green vapour – laugh even more, even harder. And then, without warning, the twirling stopped and the tunnel of vapour fired toward the open sugar bowl and dived inside. The lid snapped shut. The smell was gone. The room was quiet. All that was left of Geraldine Tode was her teacup, filled, as it ever was, with her ice cold tea.

CHAPTER 26

Alice woke to the sound of India banging loudly on the front door, shouting at her to get out of bed. She opened her eyes and glanced at the time. It was ten o'clock. Her alarm must have been blaring for the past two hours.

She stumbled downstairs in her kaftan/dressing gown, full of apologies. India, understandably, looked quite put out.

'Get it together, Alice!' she said, standing on the doorstep in mud-spattered Lycra biking gear and wellington boots. 'We've got a big meeting to introduce you to everyone starting in exactly one hour! ... What happened? It's your first day on the job! You can't just – *not turn up*!'

Alice apologised. 'Bit of a weird night,' she said.

India sniffed. 'Is that *ganja* I smell?'

Alice sniffed. 'I don't think so . . .'

'It is, you know.' India grinned. 'You naughty old thing. Don't worry. Promise I won't tell Egg.' She winked at Alice, pushed back the front door and, without invitation, stepped into Alice's hall. The smell of cannabis was faint, but distinct – if not to Alice, who carried it in her clothes, and in her nostrils, then to India, fresh from a twenty-mile bike-athon around the Yorkshire countryside. India suggested making them both some coffee while Alice dressed, and Alice – clearly on the back foot – had little option but to agree.

The door to the kitchen was closed. As Alice opened it, she remembered how she'd left the room last night: the abandoned teacups, the tarnished sugar dispenser. After Geraldine Tode's disappearing act she'd scarpered, fast as she could. Now, suddenly, it was vital to Alice, though she wasn't sure why, that India didn't spot the sugar dispenser. If she saw it, she might want to take it away. And if India took the sugar dispenser, she would take Geraldine Tode with her too. Alice did not want that. She very much wanted to see Geraldine again. This realisation hit her with some force, and took her by surprise.

She said to India, 'Take off your boots will you?' and moved quickly ahead of her to the kitchen table.

Behind her, India laughed. 'You've been living in London too long. Nobody takes their boots off around here. There's no point.'

'Why's that then?' Alice snatched up the sugar dispenser and stuffed it under the remains of Kveta's clean laundry pile.

'. . . About as pointless as taking a towel into the bathtub with you . . . It's not going to keep you dry.'

Alice searched for the teacups. They were gone.

'Come on in then. I'm fussing.'

India already had. She stood at the open kitchen door, smiling her dazzling smile. 'I didn't think you'd be the type to bother about that kind of thing! Where do you keep the coffee – Holy ker-rumpers, Alice!' She had spotted the broken computer, still on the table. 'What the hell happened there?'

'Oh yes . . .' Alice mumbled. The computer . . . the shoe . . . she'd forgotten them both. Her head was still fuzzy with sleep. She wasn't sure how much she wanted to reveal to India about her previous night's adventures. 'Yes – I'm afraid I dropped it. I'm so sorry . . .'

India said: 'Is it yours?'

'No . . . actually it's not. It sort of fell off the shelf when I was looking for the . . . I can't even remember . . . I'm so sorry. I was going to take it into Todeister– try and get it fixed.'

But India had already scooped it up. She was holding it close to her chest. 'I'll do it,' she said.

'But I dropped it,' Alice said. 'I can do it . . .' She stepped forward to take it back again, but India clung tight.

'Don't worry,' she said. 'I've got it. I'll do it. In fact – I'm going to take it back to the house right now. How about you get dressed and come on over as soon as you can? We've got a big meeting this afternoon. *Mega*.' India grinned, her good cheer already restored. 'I'm going to show you off to everyone and we're going brainstorm and you and I are going to dream up with some fab, fun ideas to put this house on the map? OK? . . . OK Alice? Are you ready for that?'

'Absolutely!' said Alice politely. 'One hundred per cent.'

CHAPTER 27

The contrast between the silk and gilt extravagance of the family and public rooms at Tode Hall, and the meanness of the wing which housed its Estate Offices was embarrassing: a sharp reminder of what a mean old bastard the late Sir Ecgbert 11th must have been as an employer.

The offices comprised five separate rooms: one for India, one for Egbert, one for Alice, and two larger ones that were shared by the finance man, who was mostly based in Darlington, and various secretaries and managers.

At the end of a long and dingy corridor there was also a staff room where instant coffee and a kettle were provided, along with a desultory collection of mustard yellow 1970s sofas. In the middle of the room eight Formica-top tables with plastic seats had been arranged in a U-shape. This was the room where India's 'mega meeting' was due to take place.

Aside from young Egbert, only four other people turned up. India, sitting at the head of the Formica island, a pretty Paperchase notebook before her, expressed a little annoyance at the low turnout. She had wanted to make a splash. However, everyone who failed to turn up appeared to have a reasonably good excuse, so there was no point in her making a scene. Also, which wasn't mentioned, but which hung in the air, after two months on the job, India's 'mega meetings' had developed a bad reputation: India, it was agreed, tended to waste everyone's time with an unending stream of silly suggestions, only to take enormous offence when nobody (except Egbert) supported them.

She could as easily have offered useful suggestions. The staff wouldn't have supported them either. They were old, long ensconced and stuck in their ways; implacably hostile to young people, to Londoners, and above all, to anyone who might attempt to replace Lady Tode. Since the day she arrived India had been met by a wall of unhelpfulness – she'd never experienced anything quite like it.

She had been born, whether she knew it or not, with more charm than most of England altogether, and she was accustomed to people falling at her feet. Her staff's relentless surliness came as a real shock to her and, as her husband knew only too well, she was finding it difficult to cope.

But now, here they were beneath the strip lighting, side by side in this most dismal of rooms; Egbert on one seat, looking kind and serious, and wanting to help; Alice on another, thinking about ghosts and smelling of ganja; and only four others, all female, all over fifty-five years old; all looking quite disagreeable.

'Right then!' said India, with her brave and dazzling smile. 'Shall we get started?'

'Good idea!' Egbert replied. 'Brilliant idea, India! Let's get started!'

'Right then!' she said again. 'Well there's *lots* to discuss, as always. Loads of ideas, and I'd love to hear any new ones. Any suggestions at all. I'm literally all ears! So please, I've said it before, but I really, *really* do mean it: don't be shy! I want us to work *together* to make this a fun place to be! A place where everyone wakes up in the morning and says to themselves, "Hooray! It's a work day today!"' This was meant to be a joke.

Egbert threw back his head: 'HA HA HA HA!'

Alice smiled.

India rolled her eyes, smiled at her husband. '*Thanks, Eggie!*' she said. 'Obviously that was a joke! I don't really expect anyone to think "hooray it's a work day". That would be silly. But I would like people to enjoy their work. If possible. So – first things first! Everyone say hello to Alice! As you know, Alice has joined the team here at Tode Hall to help me, help you, help us . . . And she's going to come up with loads of brill, fab, fantastic ideas to get this fantastic, amazing, beautiful house Back on the Map!'

A long pause. One of the disagreeable women said, in a flat Yorkshire tone: 'I wasn't aware it'd ever gone off the map.'

The other ones smirked.

'You're quite right!' replied India, delighted anyone was saying anything at all. 'That's a great point, Mrs Danvers. Thank you for making it. Of course Tode Hall hasn't "gone off the map"! That would be mad. Or magic. Or something. What I meant – well, I think you know what I meant *really*, don't you? Just – what we want is to add some SPARKLE to the place! Get people talking about it again. Get some film people up here filming a mega blockbuster. That would be fun, wouldn't it? *Spider-Man* at Tode Hall! Think about it! How many of you were here when they did *Prance*? I bet that was fun wasn't it? Or maybe a pop video – anything fun like that! I'm just trying to highlight the idea that, you know, historic houses don't have to be historic! And actually – Alice, Eggie – I think that's a really good point I've just made there. What do you think? Maybe that could be our slogan. Like: "Tax doesn't have to be taxing!" Remember that? Of course you do. So – you know, we could have a sort of "slogo", as I call it: "Historic houses don't have to be historic!" ...' She looked around the room.

'Brilliant!' said Egbert. 'Absolutely brilliant, India! What do you think, Alice? Would you get the T-shirt? "Historic houses don't have to be historic" ... I LOVE IT! Any thoughts, ladies?'

A long, long pause. Above their heads, the strip lighting ticked.

Alice said: 'Well, I'd get the T-shirt. Why not? Sounds fun.' She didn't mean it, obviously. But there was nothing else to say, and somebody had to say it.

Mrs Danvers, arms crossed over skinny bosom, sitting back on her plastic seat, said that she didn't agree: 'Doesn't make any sense though, does it? I mean – if you're saying a house is historic, then it's historic, isn't it? It's not a broad bean. It's a historic house.'

'A broad bean?' repeated India, still smiling. 'I'm not sure I understand.'

'No well you wouldn't would you? That's because it doesn't make sense.'

At which, all the disagreeable women stopped smirking and started laughing.

India, still confused, understanding only that she was being mocked, looked from one laughing face to the next, and then to her husband, who was smiling, but in a panicky way, and then to Alice. Alice could see that India was about to cry, or lose her temper: one or other, and as Fun Manager, she felt it was clearly within her remit to try to do something to help. Also she felt sorry for India, who was obviously trying; and faintly revolted by the older women, for ganging up on her. So she smiled at India, but in a non-panicky way; she rolled her eyes at the giggling women, and said:

'It's not very helpful, really, to be banging on about broad beans. India's talking about getting a slogan to advertise the house. It's a good idea. Why don't we talk about it?'

The women ignored Alice and continued to snigger. 'Come on, ladies,' pleaded Egbert. 'Let's be sensible!' But it seemed they couldn't. After so many years of turning up to work in those dowdy offices and failing to see the humour in anything, ever, this one joke had set them off. They were hysterical.

India's eyes were smarting. The skin on her beautiful face and neck had flushed into unpretty patches. She watched the women, whom she'd tried so hard to charm – and tears spilled down her mottled cheeks, and her mouth became a cold hard line. She picked up her Paperchase notebook and stood up.

'All right then,' she said, in her soft, sweet voice, '*be* like that!' And, to the sound of the women's snorts, she swept out of the room.

Egbert looked on in dismay. He stood up.

'That wasn't very kind,' he said. 'India was going to tell you all about her exciting plans to revamp this horrid staff room.

She really wants to make it lovely for you all. She just wants you to be happy. But the way you ladies are going, I'm not sure you deserve it.'

Somehow this only made the women laugh more.

Egbert looked at Alice. He didn't know what to do. He would have liked to stalk out of the meeting himself at this point. He would have liked to fire the lot of them, chuck them out their homes, all of which were owned by the estate, and leave them to rot, frankly, after the way they'd treated his darling India. But of course he couldn't do that. *With great power comes great responsibility*, as Spider-Man's Uncle Ben said. Egbert bit back his temper.

'Now *look here*,' he said. He knew he needed to regain control of the room – but his heart was dragging him towards India. He couldn't stand to think of her, crying, all on her own, hiding away in some dark corner of this horrible, hostile house.

Alice said: 'Why don't you carry on here, Egbert? You carry on with the meeting. When these people have stopped laughing. I'll go and find India. Check she's all right.'

'Good idea,' said Egbert, gratefully. 'Very good idea. Thank you Alice. *Ladies!* Mrs Danvers, if you wouldn't mind? We do have quite a lot to get through. So if you wouldn't mind, please, Miss Sharp? . . . Nurse Ratched? When you've quite finished, shall we continue?'

CHAPTER 28

There were too many corridors at Tode Hall. Though Alice knew the house well from childhood, it was many years since she'd last been in this section. When she followed India out of the staff room she was briefly disorientated. She didn't know which way to turn, couldn't hear India's footsteps in either direction, so chose a route at random: took a left and a right, and right and a left, and found herself outside the Long Gallery.

The Hall was packed with burglar alarms and she was afraid that by stepping into the Long Gallery she might set one of them off. She paused, uncertain where to turn, was about to call out India's name when she heard whispered, angry voices in the corridor behind her: Carfizzi and someone else – Dominic. She recognised his actorish vowels.

'I'm offended, Mr Carfizzi. I don't want it. What are you implying?'

She tiptoed closer, the better to hear.

144

But her figure must have cast a shadow, or maybe she made a sound. In any case, the two men sensed her presence and stopped talking. Mr Carfizzi, having rearranged his face into a polite smile, said he looked forward to welcoming her properly later, and stalked away.

Dominic was much more friendly. He held out his arms. There was a Molton Brown shopping bag hanging from one of them. Made him look a bit like a scarecrow. 'Alice! *Welcome* to Tode Hall!' he cried.

Alice didn't want Dominic to put his arms around her, but it was too late. She endured the hug, and the sharp bag banging against her. Thanked him for his welcome.

'Forgive my horrible manners!' he said, releasing her at last. 'I had every intention of dropping by yesterday, to welcome you to our happy clan. There's a marvellous tree in my garden, weighed down with the most gorgeous apples, and I was going to deliver a little basket of them to your door . . .' He gave her a charming, wolfish grin. 'It would have been a cross between Red Riding Hood and one of those US suburban horror movies.'

Alice laughed.

'You're in the Gardener's House aren't you? Lucky thing! How are you finding it? A bit quiet after London probably. It took me years to get to grips with the peace and quiet. Now I couldn't survive without it.'

Her first night had been neither quiet nor peaceful. But she certainly wasn't going to tell him that. 'It makes a nice change,' she said blandly. 'And it's such a pretty house. You're in the village, aren't you? I think I was originally meant to have the cottage next to yours.'

'That's right! We would have been neighbours.'

'Yes,' said Alice, and smiled awkwardly. She didn't know what else to add. She was still slightly dazzled by his famous face. ' . . . Actually I was looking for India. She didn't happen to come this way, did she?'

Dominic stopped acting. 'Has something happened?'

'Not really . . . Bit of a nasty scene in our first staff meeting.'

'Oh, they're *foul* to her! I wish I could help but they don't listen to me! Ha! No, I've been "the enemy" for years . . .' It didn't sound like it bothered him much. 'That's what *you're* here for Alice! You have to help the poor girl to assimilate. They're very hostile.'

'I noticed.'

'She's trying so hard. It's so unfair.'

'It does seem to be a bit,' Alice agreed.

'Trouble is, she flies off the handle. And you know how people are . . . brings out the sadist in them. When they know how easy it is to get a rise.'

'They weren't being at all kind,' Alice said.

'Bastards. I bet they weren't . . .' He thought a moment. 'I adore India. I think she's wonderful. She's a burst of sunlight here at Tode Hall. *The fact is* . . .' He dropped his voice. ' . . . and I know we shouldn't speak ill of the dead – and I adored Emma, too. But she didn't help India at all. It was almost as if she deliberately set out to make life difficult for the poor girl. That's what *I* thought. And I did mention it to her once, before she died . . . She didn't like it . . . And by the way, I say that as someone who loved Emma. We all loved Emma. But she could be quite unkind. When she set her mind to it. She made things very difficult for India. Right from the start.'

'Yes, I was beginning to get that impression.'

'I'm gossiping and I shouldn't be. No doubt you'll discover

all this for yourself in the sweetness of time. I'm just *saying* . . . wear a helmet and carry a stick! At all times! There's a lot of bad feeling flying around this place.' He laughed heartily. 'Only joking!'

Alice smiled: 'What were you and Carfizzi whispering about just then? It looked intense.'

A flicker of annoyance. He waved the question aside. It was nothing, he said. Nothing at all. 'Mr Carfizzi can be awkward sometimes. He was being a bit awkward.'

Alice said: 'What about? You both looked quite angry.'

'None of your business, I'm afraid!' Dominic grinned, and looked at his watch. He said they should definitely get together for a drink when she was more settled in. He would take her to the pub and introduce her to the village. And before she had time to thank him he was hurrying away in long, neurotic strides, in the direction of Mr Carfizzi.

CHAPTER 29

Geraldine, Lady Tode (1907–1971) was thumping impatiently from the inside of her sugar dispenser when Alice returned to the Gardener's House that night. The noise was mostly muffled by the laundry pile on top of her. It was the greenish vapour, seeping from between the clean towels, that caught Alice's attention.

Alice pulled out the little pot and placed it, seeping and warmish, onto the kitchen table. A moment passed. The sugar pot wobbled and jumped.

'Hello, hello?' said Alice. 'Anyone there?'

It wobbled again. It lost its balance and fell onto its side, landing in a blob of jam, left from Alice's breakfast.

That she might, without her unruly triplets, at last be able to live in a clean and tidy house, had been one of the job's attractions; and yet here she was at the end of Day One, and she'd not even managed to clear her own breakfast. Alice took a cloth and wiped the table. She wiped a smear of jam off the jumping sugar pot and at once the pot became scorching. She dropped it back on the table and watched, mesmerised, as it trembled and shook. A flurry of stinking green vapour, followed by another, forceful enough to pop open the lid. And then, slowly, from the depths, rubbery and elongated, scowling with discomfort, and accompanied by a loud farting sound, emerged Geraldine, Lady Tode.

It took a moment or two. And then there was her ghost, back at the table, her slim wrists, her straight back, her magnificent chignon, her sapphire jewellery catching the light. She was wearing a different outfit today – this one, a psychedelic, flared silk Balmain trouser suit, inestimably daring and chic. Before her, the cup and saucer, steaming with ice cold tea. A hint of the green vapour lingered around her, but in other respects her dignity was restored.

'Good God, I thought you'd never work it out, Alice. Have you never read *Arabian Nights*?'

'What's that?'

Geraldine Tode took a dainty sip of her ice cold tea, or pretended to. She didn't swallow. 'Of course nobody teaches anyone anything these days. It's a wonder young people even learn how to read. Have you never heard of Aladdin?'

'Of course I've heard of Aladdin.'

'Well then.'

Alice still looked confused but Geraldine Tode wouldn't say more. With her handsome chin, she indicated the sugar dispenser.

'Ah!' said Alice. 'I have to rub … if I want to summon you …?'

'Don't be impertinent. Nobody said anything about "summon".'

Alice chuckled. 'Well I'm glad you're back,' she said. 'I've got a lot of questions.'

'Never mind your questions,' replied Geraldine Tode. 'How was your first day of work? Are they treating you properly? India is quite mad. You will have realised that by now. She's a Daventy and all the Daventys are mad. And then she's got the Smetterson-Sythes on her father's side. Rather, her paternal grandmama was a Smetterson-Sythe, and – aheh – we know about *them* . . . The women [she clarified] are nymphomaniacs . . . And the men are all queer. As indeed are Daventy males. And of course *Lord* Daventy – I'm referring to Eric not poor, dear Derek – Eric was a well-known sadist. So what can one expect? My idiotic grandson might have checked this sort of thing before he married her. But people don't do that anymore. They think they know better. We shall see. Is she treating you well?'

Alice said she was.

'Good. Now then . . . ' Geraldine paused. 'Are you going to take off your coat, Alice? We have things to discuss and I need you to concentrate. Get yourself a drink, or whatever you want. Settle down. I shall wait for you here. And when you're ready, we can begin.' Alice didn't move. Actually she was wondering whether she could roll herself a joint. It didn't feel quite right. On the other hand, it was her house, her off-time. And Geraldine was only a ghost.

'Buck up,' snapped Geraldine Tode. 'Do hurry. I have some interesting news vis-à-vis our murder investigation.'

Alice didn't take issue with Geraldine's annoying reference to the non-existent 'murder investigation'. She had a lot of questions of her own, and she didn't want to send Geraldine scurrying back into her sugar pot without first answering at least some of them.

At some point, obviously, she would need to clarify to Geraldine that she had no interest in investigating 'murders'. She had come to Tode Hall because . . . well, because it was the only job she'd ever been offered, and she had nothing much else to do. Those were the main reasons. Also because her grandmother had been set on it. Also because – it didn't really matter. The point was, she had *not* come to Tode Hall to be a murder detective.

Geraldine Tode waited, watching with haughty impatience as Alice rolled and lit her joint. She said: 'Have you ever smoked opium, dear? One used to do that a little, as a young thing. It was tremendous fun.'

'I never have,' said Alice. 'I would love to though. I've heard it's wonderful stuff.'

But Lady Tode wasn't actually that interested. She said: 'Well I'll tell you what happened to *me* this afternoon. Guess who walked through that front door. And by the way he has a key. You must change the locks.'

'Not Ecgbert, again? cried Alice, indignantly. 'What do you think he wanted?'

'Not Mad Ecgbert, no,' Geraldine Tode replied impatiently. 'Of course not. And under what circumstances, I ask you, would his mother *ever* have given him a key? She couldn't abide him, Alice. Do you not understand? He was her nemesis. Emma was a classic narcissist. Do you know what that is?'

'Of course I do.'

'There was nothing she loathed more than people who spoke the truth to her. And poor mad Ecgbert has always been incapable of speaking anything else. He terrified her. She packed him off to that funny house at the bottom of the drive – not for drugs or drink or any sort of criminal

151

activity – not for anything, really, but simply for speaking his mind ... Well, maybe that *is* a form of madness ...' she added. ' ... And then she persuaded her ghastly husband – and I speak as his mother – to have the poor boy disinherited. As I said to you the other evening, dear, if anyone *ought* to have killed that dreadful woman, it was poor mad darling Ecgbert. Whether or not he actually did, well, we simply don't know ...'

'I do,' Alice snapped, yet again: 'It wasn't Ecgbert—' She seemed to be saying this a lot, lately. And the more she said it, the sillier it sounded. After all, how would she know? She'd not seen or spoken to him for nearly forty years.

'You mustn't be sentimental, Alice. Ecgbert *might* have killed her. He certainly had motive ... and opportunity. And he is quite mad.'

'But you just said he wasn't.'

'Well of course he isn't. Not really,' Geraldine continued. 'And by the way I tend to agree with you. I adore that boy. His mother treated him terribly, and if he did kill her, I would be the last person in the world to blame him.'

' ... You were telling me who it was who broke into the house,' Alice said.

'I'm aware of that.'

'Well, come on then, who was it?'

Geraldine Tode leaned toward her. She smelled of baked beans and milk, Alice noticed. Weird. 'Firstly,' she said, 'as I explained previously, our guest this afternoon did *not* break in. As I said barely a second ago, the gentleman in question *has a set of keys*. Which makes perfect sense, of course. However, if you don't want him climbing into your bed in the middle of the night, I strongly advise you, once again, to get your locks changed. He and my daughter-in-law have been using the place as a knocking shop for years.'

'*WHO? I still don't know who you're talking about,*' Alice said.

'Dominic Rathbone of course.'

'*Dominic Rathbone and Emma Tode?* That's – but he must be at least ten years younger than she is. Was.'

Geraldine Tode said stonily: 'And?'

'Well – that's amazing. I'm amazed.'

'Don't be idiotic.'

'She seems to have had sex with every man she met since the day she was married!'

Geraldine raised an eyebrow. 'Maybe so.'

'Crikey,' said Alice.

'But Dominic Rathbone was rather more than a fling, I dare say. It went on for years. Why else do you think she lent him a house on the estate? I don't recall what was the "job" she drummed up for him . . .'

'Archives,' Alice said. 'He's in charge of archives.'

'Archives indeed!' Geraldine laughed. 'Darling girl, he's nothing more than a gigolo! Anyway the point is – Dominic let himself into the house this afternoon while you were gone. He rummaged around downstairs looking for some-thing – I don't know what. But he was muttering a lot of filthy language to himself, getting quite tetchy. He went upstairs and came down with . . . Do you remember there was a tin cigar box in the cupboard where you found me? Do you remember it?'

'I do. It was locked.'

'Well he took that.'

'Do you know why? Do you know what was inside it?'

Geraldine Tode looked uncomfortable. 'Never you mind . . .

But it's probably a good thing he's taken it. We wouldn't want the staff getting hold of it.'

'I'm staff,' Alice reminded her.

Geraldine ignored her. 'Imagine if those half-witted sisters happened upon it! Or Car Fizzy! Dear God, just imagining it makes the blood run cold. You realise he's Mafia, don't you?'

Alice laughed. 'He's been living in Yorkshire the last forty years.'

'And you think the Mafia's tentacles, in this day and age, don't reach as far as Yorkshire?'

Alice had no idea. 'I'm just saying, it seems unlikely.'

Lady Tode raised another fine eyebrow, and left it at that.

'I bumped into them earlier,' Alice said. 'Dominic and Mr Carfizzi. Having quite a row.'

'*Did you indeed?*' said Geraldine. 'Well that *is* interesting. What about, I wonder? I wouldn't be in the least surprised if Emma, Dominic and Car Fizzy had been engaged in a *ménage à trois*. Don't you think? In fact, the more I think about it, the more likely it seems.'

Alice said: 'But you said Mr Carfizzi preferred men?'

'Oh for heaven's sake!' said Geraldine Tode. She inhaled: an appalling idea having struck her. 'You don't suppose Dominic was giving the cigar box to Car Fizzy, do you? No. Of course not. Why would he?'

'I don't know.'

'Car Fizzy would hock it, without a doubt. Though I'm not sure how much he'd get in today's market. Nobody much cares about aristocrats these days. And thankfully Dominic's acting career is dead ... ' She chortled. 'Nobody would have the faintest idea whom he even was.'

'Actually,' said Alice, 'he's doing a coffee ad at the moment on TV. My grandmother was very excited when she spotted him at the Tintin teddy—'

'Yes well. With the greatest respect. I don't think we can really use your dear, late grandmother as a particularly useful barometer, either for the state of Dominic Rathbone's career – nor for the price Car Fizzy could fetch for a pile of pornographic photographs of him with my late daughter-in-law *in flagrante*. So . . .' Geraldine took another pretend sip from her cold tea, shuddered at its absence of taste, and looked at Alice. 'That's my news. What's yours?'

CHAPTER 30

Life at Tode Hall settled down a little after that. Alice and India formed a bond over the failure of the mega meeting. Alice, with her eternally unruffled approach to everything in life, and by making a lot of quite funny references to broad beans, somehow managed to turn the incident into a joke.

'They'll come round in the end,' Alice comforted her, calmly. 'They'd be stupid not to.'

On Geraldine's advice Alice changed the locks to the Gardener's House. On her own advice, she brought in a locksmith all the way from York, paid him in cash, and organised everything without consulting anyone at the Hall. Since it wasn't really clear who at the Hall she could trust; who had keys, or who knew what about whom, or who ought to know what, or even whether she knew what she thought she knew about anyone (et cetera), Alice decided to say nothing about anything to anyone – except of course, to Geraldine, her new, most-irritating friend and replacement grandmother.

Her duties as Tode Hall Manager for Fun remained obscure. In truth, though nobody wanted to admit to it, Alice had been hired as nothing much more than a companion for India. She didn't mind. As long as she was paid, and she wasn't expected to work too hard, or investigate any murders, or to stand for too long in the cold, she didn't really care what the job entailed. She liked India, she liked Egbert, she liked her little house. She liked looking out of her window onto the Rose Garden, and above all, she liked gossiping with Geraldine Tode at night. In fact, most unexpectedly, and possibly for the first time in her life, she was almost – very nearly – happy.

At some point, maybe towards the end of her second week at Tode, India said to Alice: 'I'm still not sure what your job really *is*, Alice, are you?'

Alice lied. She said she had 'a pretty good idea'.

'Good,' India said: 'I just have faith that it'll become clear. I think the universe had a reason for sending you to me and I am humble enough to wait for that reason to be revealed.'

Alice chuckled. 'Good for you.'

'Anyway who cares? It doesn't matter, does it, as long as we're having fun! And I know *I'm* having fun. Are you, Alice? Are you OK? I'm just so happy you've come here. Because Egbert's a brick and all that. I adore him. You know I do. And the kids, obviously. I *adore* the kids! But I swear, I'd be so damn bored without you being around. I don't think I'd be able to hack it.'

CHAPTER 31

On her third Saturday at Tode Hall Alice, in an uncharacteristic burst of willpower, overcame her distaste for mud and freezing winds, and took herself into the blustery great outdoors, thinking, after all, that it might be more enjoyable than she realised. It was what other people did during weekends in the country, and many of them genuinely liked it.

She trudged slowly along the front of the house, where a few tourists still lingered in the wind and cold, and then further, towards Africa Folly and the mausoleum. It would be an hour's brisk walk there and back – slightly too far for perfection, Alice thought. She had only decided on doing it because she missed her triplets and there was nothing on the telly.

But it wasn't so bad once she got out there, of course. Perhaps, she thought, as she huffed up the hill, she should get a dog? It might encourage her to venture outside more often. It might stop her spending so much of her free time talking to a ghost.

At Africa Folly she paused to catch her breath and admire

the view. She remembered that sunny evening, forty years ago, with Ecgbert, before they put him in the funny house; and with herself, before her mother died. They'd been happy – well, of course. They were different people then. In any case, the memory didn't make her feel comfortable. She brushed it away. Looked back at the Hall, splayed out in the fading light below: vast and beautiful and outrageous; utterly unaware of the great burden it represented, the unending demands it made on its caretakers. Sometimes she glimpsed Egbert, on whose shoulders this vast responsibility now lay: such a loving husband, such a decent father, such a worried man. She wondered if there wasn't a part of him which longed to be back in Wandsworth, selling terraced houses to bankers.

But she didn't waste much time on sympathy. It was his fault for having accepted Lady Tode's offer.

Ahead of her, at the bottom of the hill, was the mausoleum. She'd not been back since the day she went with Egbert to see the body, but she felt she probably couldn't avoid it forever. She continued walking – after all, the sooner she got there, the sooner she could turn back, the sooner she could return to her sofa, her hot bath – and perhaps some spaghetti Bolognese if she could be bothered to make it.

She was preoccupied with thoughts of the Bolognese (and the tiresomeness of not having a mini Waitrose in the village), so it wasn't until she was directly in front of it that she noticed the door to the mausoleum was wide open.

Odd, she thought. It was beginning to get dark already, it being a quarter-to-four in late November. She hesitated: was it part of her job, as Monitor for Fun, to pull the door closed again? The image of Emma Tode's body lying in a black pool of blood flashed before her, and she decided that no – it was not her job.

On the other hand – she couldn't just leave it hanging open. Not when there were still tourists milling about. They might wander in, trip on a loose piece of stone, break a leg, sue the estate. Die. All this went through her head as she stood before the open door, hesitating.

She had to close the bloody door. She called out first – just in case. Nobody answered. She called a second time, just to be sure. Still no reply. Finally, feeling sick, and trying hard not to think of Lady Tode and the pool of blood, she took the last few steps toward the building, and grabbed the handle.

It wouldn't shut. It was a big door, old and heavy, and it had warped slightly over all the years it had stood there. The bolt and the latch weren't flush, and each time she tugged at it, the door swung gently ajar again. She gave up. When she let go of the handle for the last time she discovered that the door, left to its own devices, didn't just swing ajar: something about the tilt of the frame, or the weight of the door, compelled it to keep on swinging until it hung wide open, just as Alice had found it.

Mr Carfizzi's words rang, word for word, in her head. '*Of course she wasn't locked in,*' he had said. He kept saying it. '*The door was closed but it wasn't locked. That is why nobody never suspected something. Of course she wasn't locked in ...*' Hadn't he said that? Hadn't he positively snarled it at her, as they were gazing down at Emma Tode's body? There had been something odd and shrill and hostile about his insistence. It was why, now, she remembered it so clearly.

So he'd been lying. When Egbert and she and Violet had stood outside the mausoleum that day, complaining about the smell of sheep, the door had been shut tight. Egbert had said it wasn't possible to go into the mausoleum because he didn't have a key.

160

Carfizzi had lied. The door wouldn't shut unless it was locked and now it was hanging open. She decided against hanging around to find out why. She imagined dying in there. She imagined someone coming up behind her, *now*, and pushing her inside, locking the door and leaving her, surrounded by old coffins. And no electric light. And no one within earshot. That was enough. She backed up, turned away, broke into a panicky jog. She would send a text to Egbert when she got home. But right now, she only wanted to put some space between herself and that open door.

She didn't get far: ten yards at best. She heard footsteps behind her, and then a hand on her shoulder.

Fat hairy fingers. A gold signet ring. A waft of sickly aftershave. A flash of shiny white-capped teeth.

'Mr Carfizzi,' said Alice, trying to sound normal: 'Hello there! Goodness! Hahaha. You scared the life out of me!'

His mouth was grinning, but the smile didn't reach his eyes. He kept his hairy hand on her shoulder.

'How lovely to see you!' Alice said.

He was wearing a leather tanner's apron over his two-tone tailored winter coat, and in his other hand he was clutching a hammer.

'And to see you, Alice!' he said, his white teeth clanging, 'We must stop meeting like this!'

'What?' said Alice. 'But we haven't! What do you mean?' She looked at his hand, still resting on her shoulder, but he didn't move it. After a moment, she couldn't stand it any longer, and brushed it off. 'We've never met like this. I was trying to close the door, but it—' She stopped. Thought better than to finish the sentence. She said instead, 'I had no idea you were inside . . .'

'You look terrified,' he said blandly.

161

'Well I . . .' Again, she stopped. 'Well, I suppose the last time I was up here was when Lady Tode was – you know – lying on the floor there. I just . . . The memory of it . . . That's all.' She glanced behind him. The door to the mausoleum gaped open, just a few steps away; and beyond it, pure darkness. There was no one around; only her and Carfizzi. If he wanted to kill her, right now: if he wanted to push her into that black hole and close the door and lock it – there was nothing to stop him.

But why would he want to do that? There was no reason. None whatsoever. She tried to smile. 'Doesn't it give you the creeps, just a tiny bit?'

He shook his head. 'I am very comfortable around death,' he said. 'In Calabria my father was a mortician. I have no problem with it.'

'Oh,' said Alice. 'Gosh.'

'Gosh,' he repeated, and smiled. To Alice, it sounded menacing. 'I am here arranging the shelf in preparation for Lady Tode's coffin. I want to be certain everything is perfect when she is ready to rejoin us. Of course we can't trust Mr Groper. He's only been with us five years. Why would he care?'

'Mr Groper?'

'Our carpenter,' Carfizzi explained. 'Mr Groper didn't know Lady Tode. Not really. Not like I did. He can't be trusted to do it properly.'

'All right then,' Alice said. 'All right. Well then, that's nice. I'll let you get on. Good luck with that. And have a good evening. I'm probably going to head home. If that's all right with you.'

'You do that,' he said. 'That's a good idea. It's getting dark.'

She backed away from him and he stood there, watching her, as if daring her to return.

162

CHAPTER 32

'Don't laugh,' India said. 'I've actually been thinking quite a lot about it.'

He tweaked her nipple.

She pushed him away. 'I'm serious. I actually don't think I've had sex with anyone over the age of, like, thirty-four – and by the way that's only Egbert, so it doesn't count. You are literally very nearly *double* the age of anyone I've had sex with, *ever before*! Apart from Hamish Tomlinson, I suppose,' she added. 'He was pretty old. But that was yonks ago.'

'Hamish Tomlinson?' he muttered. He wasn't really listening. 'Is he a threat? Should I send a hitman?' He ran his hand along the inside of her thigh, burrowed his grey head beneath the duvet . . . She batted him off, irritated. 'It's not funny Dominic, I think what we're doing is probably a bit gross and perverted.'

'It's neither, darling. It's fun,' he said. 'It's what people do in the country . . .' He rolled back onto the pillow, lit himself a cigarette.

India made a show of waving the smell away and coughing but as they were in his bedroom she couldn't much complain. He ignored her anyway.

'What was that pop song?' he asked. 'You're probably too young . . . "*We dance and drink and screw because there's nothing else to do . . .*" Welcome to rural life, sweetheart. There's nothing perverted about it. What's *perverted*,' he added, 'is the puritanical work ethic of our miserable town folk . . .' But he was talking to himself. In any case, India could never have been accused of puritanical anything.

She said: 'I do feel a *bit* guilty, Dominic. Poor Eggie, working his socks off . . .'

Dominic laughed. 'You don't feel remotely guilty, India my love, and nor should you. He's dragged you away from your beloved London. You've literally sacrificed your entire life to look after this place. What more does he want? What more can he ask for? . . . Besides, sweet girl, Egbert can't expect to have you all to himself. That would be unfair.'

A silence fell. India said: 'Do you think I should cut my hair? I think it's a bit long.'

'Darling, your hair is liquid gold. Why would you want to cut it? Don't cut it, I beg you.'

'You're so lovely to me, Dominic!' She smiled at him. 'I'm so happy I found you.'

'And me you, darling. And me you.'

It had been a nice afternoon for both of them. Egbert had gone to a meeting of Yorkshire landowners to discuss – India didn't actually know. Something to do with grouse, maybe. Or subsidies. Who cared? The children had woken up insisting on spending yet another session at the Boathouse. India couldn't face it. So she'd offered the au pair, whose day off it was, an extra fifty quid in overtime to do it for her. Everyone was happy.

'I ought to leave,' India said. 'Duty-Dinz tonight with the awful vicar and his disgusting, creepy wife.'

'She *is* creepy, isn't she?' agreed Dominic. 'Always sucking up.'

'She sucks up to Egbert like crazy. He's so sweet though, I'm not sure he even notices it.'

'Men generally don't,' Dominic said.

But she'd moved on. 'How *on earth* do you think Emma put up with Mrs Carfizzi's cooking all those years?' she said. 'Why did she never say anything? It's a mystery – more than a mystery, actually. It's *torture*. We can smell the food she cooks for herself and Carfizzi. I can smell it, seeping up the stairs – the most delicious Italian cooking smells come wafting through the back of the house. And then she comes into our kitchen and serves us boiled cabbage. And she won't change. She refuses. It's a nightmare, Dominic. Everyone's still so in love with that woman, they won't change *anything*. It's driving me mad.'

'In love with Mrs Carfizzi?'

'Obviously not. I mean fucking Emma. She's *dead* and I still can't get her off my back. What's it going to take?'

Dominic didn't reply. He dragged on his cigarette and considered his response. It wasn't nice of India to refer to Emma as 'fucking Emma'. But India knew that. So he left a silence.

'I don't mean *fucking Emma*,' she muttered. 'Of course not. But you know what I mean. Everybody adored her so much. And she was a bitch to me. You saw it. You did, didn't you?'

'I did, sweetheart. But she's gone now. You can move on.'

'I wish I *could* . . .' She stopped. It seemed she wanted to say more.

Dominic glanced at her. 'What's up?' he said.

She shook her head. 'Nothing.'

He turned. 'What's up, India?' he asked again.

'Nothing. Nothing . . .' And then, in a rush. 'She told me that morning she'd cancelled the trip. She told me she wasn't going to Capri. That she was talking to her lawyers about maybe booting us out of Tode Hall. I didn't believe her but . . .'

There was a long pause then. Very long.

Dominic said, 'Did she? . . . Why didn't you say something?'

India shrugged. She looked shifty. 'Well . . . She didn't. She didn't say it exactly . . . Maybe she didn't say it. I don't think she really did . . . Honestly Dominic, I was just so relieved to see the back of her at that point. When she disappeared, I didn't think: "Oh, she must be lying dead in the mausoleum." Obviously. I assumed she hadn't cancelled the trip after all . . .'

'You knew she was missing?' Dominic said. His voice was cold.

'No! No – of course I didn't *know* . . . I didn't *know* know. If you know what I mean.' It sounded unbelievable, even to her own ears. 'I mean – no, of course not.'

'Well then.' He leaned back on the pillow again. 'What are you worrying about?'

'I just feel so awful . . . I couldn't stand her. But all that time we thought she was in Capri . . .'

'. . . She was dead in the mausoleum.'

India shivered. 'Horrible, isn't it?'

Dominic took some time to reply. 'Yes. It's horrible,' he said slowly. 'But you mustn't blame yourself, darling. You weren't to know.'

India said: 'Don't tell anyone, will you? I mean, there's nothing to tell. But—'

166

'Of course not.' He tried to smile, but it didn't quite work. The old acting skills weren't up to it. His handsome face had lost its colour.

'Do you miss her?' India asked at last.

He said: 'Who? Emma?'

'Obviously, Emma. You two were friendly, weren't you? I used to see you, chatting together like old chums. You must miss her.'

'We got along well, on the whole,' he said carefully. 'Yes, of course we did. But – as you know – she was a difficult woman. Absolutely delightful ... as long as she got her way. But she could be cruel, sometimes. Quietly unkind ... You weren't the only one who felt it.' He smiled. ' ... Do I miss her? I suppose I do, a little, yes.' He had finished his cigarette. He stubbed it out, and turned again towards India, naked on the pillow beside him. 'But having you here makes all the difference. If Emma hadn't died, and the shock of all that ... Really it was the shock of it all that threw us together. Wasn't it?'

'I suppose it was.'

'We might never have found each other. We might have carried on, like ships that pass in the night ...'

India smirked. 'I don't think so,' she said.

She climbed out of the bed. It was a pretty room – old fashioned, with thick chintz curtains at the cottage windows – and it belonged to the Todes. The cottage, the ebony bed with angel carvings, the mahogany bookshelf, the light fittings – everything, except for the old clock radio, the books and Dominic's clothes. It was all India's. But she didn't think of it like that, and neither did he.

He stayed in bed and watched her dress. 'Why don't you come to dinner too?' she said. 'Might make it a bit more fun if

167

you did. Will you? Perhaps I could get Alice to come as well. That would be nice. You could get to know her better. Do you like her?'

'We haven't really talked too much yet. But I like the look of her *very* much,' he said.

'Well that decides it then. I'll see you later. I'll ask Alice to be with us by eight. Assuming she's free. Which she probably will be.' India giggled. 'At least I hope so. Not sure I can face the evening if she isn't.'

CHAPTER 33

Mr Carfizzi served them dinner in the Red Dining Room. India drank much more she usually did, mostly out of boredom, and by the main course was already quite drunk. Everybody drank, mostly out of boredom – except for the vicar's wife, who didn't drink at all, and Egbert, who was in training for a high altitude triathlon, scheduled to take place in Chile in the spring: '*Our* spring, *their* autumn, of course,' as Egbert was always quick to clarify to anyone who showed the slightest interest, and sometimes to people who didn't.

The vicar's wife, aged fifty-eight, with a neat white bob of shiny hair and clean white fingernails, was exceedingly polite, and dull, and inexplicably bitter. It was obvious to Alice that she was jealous of India, disapproved of Dominic, didn't think much of Alice or of her own husband, but was keen as mustard on young Egbert. She listened with twittery solicitude as he bored on about his fitness targets and the dangers of protein deficiency in stamina-dependent, oxygen-deficient situations.

After a while, India groaned, and said to the vicar, 'We have entered the Egbert Tode High Altitude Triathlon Portal. Somebody change the record. I swear he'll never shut up!'

She pulled a face at Dominic, who chortled encouragingly. 'Egbert, darling, have pity,' she shouted. 'People are falling off their chairs around you: they're literally *dying of boredom*.'

Egbert was mortified. 'Oh God, am I doing it again?' he said. 'You're quite right, Munch. I'm an intolerable bore.' He turned to the vicar's wife. 'I'm *so* sorry . . .'

'Not *at all*!' cried the vicar's wife, sending India a small, hygienic hate vibe. 'I'm finding our conversation most absorbing. I've never been a great one for fitness regimes, speaking personally. I'm just happy walking my dog, enjoying all this gorgeous countryside. But I'm fascinated by triathlons . . .'

India rolled her eyes in her head, her head on her shoulders, and then, feeling that even this wasn't quite enough, pretended to fall off her chair.

'Are you all right?' cried the vicar.

'Oh she's fine!' Egbert laughed. 'Come on Munch. Give me a break!'

The vicar's wife glared at the empty chair. 'I'm sorry you don't find your husband's interests worth learning about, India . . .'

India returned to her seat. 'Just mucking around, Penelope!' she beamed. 'Anyway, never mind triathlons. Are we ready for pudding?' She rang the bell, and in came Mr Carfizzi to clear the plates. It being a dinner party, he had banished his wife to the kitchen. He'd changed out of the tanner's apron, washed the mausoleum grime from beneath his fingernails and put on his butler's gear. He always wore his butler gear when Dominic came to dinner.

170

'What's for pudding tonight then?' Dominic asked him playfully. 'Has Mrs Carfizzi done us her marvellous chocolate profiteroles?'

'Unfortunately not,' Carfizzi replied. He shot a killer stare towards India, who was busy refilling her glass and didn't notice. 'Mrs Carfizzi and I were only made aware that you and Mrs Liddell would be dining with us shortly before dinner. So it was rather difficult—'

'Ya-ya. I apologised to your wife already, Carfizzi,' India said irritably. 'She was perfectly OK with it. And by the way, since she's actually the cook . . .'

'As you know,' Carfizzi interrupted her midstream. He was looking at Dominic. 'Mrs Carfizzi always prepares her profiteroles when she knows you are coming.' He fussed about with the plates, taking them one at a time to the sideboard. 'But unfortunately nobody informed us you were coming,' he said again, '*until it was much too late*.'

India shrugged. '*Whatevs*, Carfizzi. I'm sure Dominic will survive without his profiteroles just this once. Anyway, he needs to watch his weight a bit, at his age. Don't you Dom?'

The comment landed. Alice, who watched and learned, and said very little, noticed Dominic Rathbone tightening his grip on his water glass. She noticed contempt – repugnance, even – flitting across Carfizzi's clean-shaven, sweet-smelling face; and around Egbert, at the head of the table, a gentle dipping in spirits.

Alice said: 'I suppose we all have to watch our weight, really, don't we? I used to run a cookery course before I came here. It was all anyone wanted me to teach them: how to make food that wouldn't make them fat.'

'Ah! The Holy Grail!' replied Dominic, gratefully.

'Too right!' said Egbert. 'If anyone could come up with food that tasted good and didn't pile on the pounds, well they'd probably turn out to be richer than God! By which I mean—' He glanced apologetically at the vicar: 'Obviously I don't mean *God*, God – I mean: what's the name of that chap who owns Microsoft?'

'Bill Gates,' said the vicar.

'That's the one,' Egbert said. 'As rich as Bill Gates.'

After that, after pudding (which turned out to be baked apples with sultanas and vanilla-flavour easy-scoop ice cream on the side) the party removed themselves from Red Dining Room to Chinese Drawing Room, where Mr Carfizzi had put out the coffee.

India, having had more than enough polite conversation with the vicar and his wife for one night, took care to place herself as far away from them as possible. She parked herself onto a sofa closest to the fire, slipped off her shoes and patted the seat beside her.

'Alice!' she said. 'We've hardly spoken all night. Come and sit next to me. I want to hear all the gossip.'

'I'm not sure I have any,' said Alice, settling beside her.

Dominic and Egbert were left to entertain the vicar and wife. Both men rose valiantly and affably to the challenge. Conversation flowed so smoothly that when, at length, the couple returned to their vicarage, they would agree with each other that it had been a very nice evening, despite the odd hiccup, and that Egbert Tode was proving to be 'a wonderful thing' for the estate. They wouldn't mention India. It wasn't nice to be nasty and in any case there was no need. On this, they knew they were united. *India was a dreadful woman.*

And so, while Dominic and Egbert listened to the vicar's

wife's observations regarding the nesting habits of pintail ducks on the Upper Lawn Lake last spring, India confided in Alice some of her ambitions regarding Dominic, whom she felt was being 'under-exploited as Tode Hall's resident celebrity'.

Alice asked India how she thought he might be better exploited. India glanced across at him, chatting so nicely with her husband and the vicarage duo. She said: 'He's *gorgeous* isn't he, though? As well as being quite famous. We should organise a coffee theme-day, you know? A grand coffee tasting; a coffee expo . . . What do you think? People LOVE coffee – and people LOVE seeing famous people. And we do happen to have the most famous face-associated-with-coffee-drinking, probably in the whole world, right now, *living and working on the estate*. We should be exploiting that. Don't you think?'

'Sounds like a good idea,' said Alice, even though it didn't. 'Maybe we could—'

'*I know*. We definitely need to think more about it,' India said. 'We can do it later. Seriously Alice, what do you think about Carfizzi?'

'Sorry. What do I think about—'

'I just – he is driving me *insane*. Egbert thinks we couldn't survive without him but I think he's wrong. I know he's wrong. We've got to get rid of him . . . Both of them, actually. But specially him. I actually can't stand being in the same room as him anymore.'

'Yes. You make that pretty clear,' Alice said.

'Do I?' India looked surprised. 'Well I don't think he likes being in the same room with me, either, frankly. We can't stand each other.'

Since their encounter at the mausoleum this afternoon, it happened Alice didn't much like being around him either.

'He's a strange man, isn't he?' Alice said. 'Lots of silent fury, I get the feeling.'

'Because he's still in love with bloody Emma, just like everyone else around here ...'

'Yes I'd heard that ...'

'Sometimes I catch him looking at me like he ... I don't know ...' She let out a burst of unhappy laughter. '... I swear, it's almost like he thinks *I* was the one who killed her!'

'But no one "killed" her,' Alice said quickly. 'Surely – you don't think that?'

'Hm? No! No, of course I don't. I'm talking crap. I just think *Carfizzi* thinks – never mind. Who cares what he thinks? It doesn't matter, does it? I've drunk too much. I probably shouldn't be saying all this anyway ...' India fell silent for a moment. She looked at the fire, and then across the room at the men. '... He really is gorgeous, though, isn't he?'

'Egbert?'

'*Dominic!* He must be thirty years older than me at least. Seriously, how pervy is that?'

'It's not "pervy" being older than people.'

'No!' she whispered. 'It's pervy how much I fancy him.' She giggled. She put a finger to her lips. '*Shhhhh!* ... By the way I've decided to take your advice and have a media-people house party. It's going to be a "murder mystery" theme. Otherwise they won't have anything to do except sit around talking crap. It's going to be MEGA, Alice.'

'A house party?' Alice was tired. Much as she generally enjoyed India's company, she'd had enough of it for the night. She wanted to go to bed. But she smiled anyway. 'Did I advise that?'

'Egbert thinks we ought to wait until after the inquest. But

174

it's a bit late for that. He should have said it before I sent the invitations out.'

'You've sent invitations out already?'

She giggled. 'Egg's a bit peed off tbh. Turns out it's literally the weekend before. The inquest's on the Monday ... So. Anyway,' she looked gloomy for a microsecond, and in the next microsecond, remembered what a blast it was going to be, and brightened up again. 'I don't even know them, Alice!' she said. 'I just made a list of all the most famous, glamorous media-type knob-heads I've ever met, got hold of their emails and thought, *why not*? Let's get this house back on the map! Half of them won't have the faintest idea who I am. But they'll recognise the house, won't they? If they Google it. How many of them do you think will accept?'

'Well it depends ...'

'No it doesn't! Remember? Don't you remember what you said? It's going to be hilarious, Alice. They're all going to suck up *massively*, because I live in this crazy house.' She laughed her precarious laugh and Alice wondered if India was more unwell than anyone realised.

'Anyway,' India added, suddenly serious. 'Enough chitchat. You look exhausted. And I've definitely had enough of today. I'm going to bed. We'll talk about the Big Media Murder Weekend in the morning, OK ... We're going to need the biggest Xmas tree in the world, Alice. But Ollie Mellors can probs organise that ... And Dominic doesn't know it yet but he's going to be the star – He's going to show off his acting skills to all those big media fuckers, and they'll be stuck here for the weekend and they won't be able to get away!' India touched her nose, and winked. 'I'm going to make Dominic a star again! See? *Big Plans!* ... Contrary to popular opinion, I'm not just a pretty face!'

175

CHAPTER 34

I t transpired that Geraldine Tode had only needed the one ferocious polishing, followed by a couple of desultory rubs, to liberate her into the big wide world again. She was now able to escape her sugar dispenser at will. This was good and bad. Good for Geraldine, who could wander the estate at her leisure. Not so good for Alice, because it meant Geraldine was almost always around. There were times when Alice found her quite irritating.

'Call it whatever you like,' she said to Alice, one night, a couple of evenings after the vicar's dinner, and apropos of nothing much, 'but you're only employed here, really, as a "companion", to keep that silly girl out of trouble. Nothing more than that. It's very old fashioned.'

'Well I'm not sure I'm doing a particularly good job at it,' Alice replied.

'She seems to keep you amused.'

'She's funny. I like her.'

'Well then, don't complain.'

'I wasn't.'

'Sounded to me as if you were.'

Not for the first time it occurred to Alice how much Geraldine, Lady Tode reminded her of her grandmother. She'd commented on it once, but it had made Geraldine livid, because of the class divide. Sometimes it was difficult for Geraldine, knowing that her chief companion – her only companion in the world – was the granddaughter of her former lady's maid. Sometimes she would feel the need to assert to Alice the differences between them, and she would spiral off into boastful stories from her past, about all the smart people she used to know, and how much they used to admire her. On these occasions Alice thought her companion was a sad, unlikeable figure. She would gaze out of the window and let the old dame run with it, just as she used to when her grandmother got the wind behind her.

She told Geraldine she thought India might be having a fling with Dominic Rathbone.

Geraldine said: 'I'm not remotely surprised.'

Alice fell silent.

'Well don't be coy,' Geraldine snapped. 'How do you know? And how long have you known? Have you actually seen them at it?'

Alice said, 'Of course not.'

'More importantly, do you suppose India knows she's retreading old ground? Do you think she has the slightest inkling that he and Emma were involved for all those years? She'd be furious, wouldn't she?'

'Probably,' agreed Alice.

'*Well? Do you think she knows?* Seriously, Alice. We'll likely have another murder on our hands if she ever finds out. Daventy women are narcissists and nymphomaniacs. A dangerous mix, believe me. She'll kill him if she works out she's only a rebound.' Geraldine gave a chilly laugh. 'Especially when she discovers from whom . . .'

'Well,' Alice said, blandly, 'with any luck she won't find out. There's no reason she should.'

'Excuse me, there are a million reasons why she should,' said Geraldine. 'I'm astonished she hasn't already.'

Geraldine's voice grated. Her snobbery grated. Her gleeful, ungenerous spirit was giving Alice a headache. Outside, it was a cloudless night, and through the window she could see the moon shining bright. Suddenly she didn't want to sit there listening to her anymore. She didn't want to spend the rest of the evening discussing Daventy narcissism.

She'd been at Tode Hall for less than a month and already her feelings towards the land outside her window were changing. She was warming to it – literally. She didn't feel the cold the way she once had. And when she looked out at the garden – it didn't all merge into a smudge of green and brown. There was, for example, a beautiful winter-flowering clematis she had noticed and admired in the Rose Garden; and a robin redbreast she thought she recognised, which often appeared on a branch by her kitchen window. Small things perhaps, but big for Alice. She told Geraldine she needed to go outside.

She put on coat and boots, and left Geraldine at the kitchen table with her stone cold tea, tutting, and telling Alice she was a fool.

The Rose Garden was peaceful without the tourists, and spectacular in the moonlight. Alice thought of her grandmother and how much she would have loved to be living here, and missed her; she thought of her triplets, and the mess they made, and missed them, too; and it occurred to her that she felt more contented, here at Tode Hall, living alone with an irritating ghost, than she'd ever been before. It was an unusual moment in Alice's life, brought on by fresh air and moonlight (and a very small spliff); a moment when her battered heart seemed perhaps to be considering the possibility of kicking back to life, just a little bit. She realised how much she had always loved this place.

The moment was rudely interrupted by a noise on the other side of the hedge: slightly unnerving, as noises when alone in a dark place must always be. At first Alice assumed it was a fox. But then it grew louder, drew closer . . .

'Hello?' she called out. 'Is someone there?'

She wrapped her coat a little tighter around her and stepped towards the noise. There was an archway cut into the hedge. Beyond it was a pathway to the village. She poked her head around the archway and found Dominic Rathbone standing there, grinning like an idiot. He was wearing a cowboy hat and carrying a vaguely familiar string-handled shopping bag from Molton Brown.

'*Dominic? Is that you?*'

'Certainly is!' he said. 'Hello there! I'm so sorry. Did I frighten you? I didn't mean to. Actually, if it's any comfort,' he laughed, 'you frightened the bejaysus out of me!' For some reason he said it in an Irish accent.

'What are you doing out here?'

He said: 'Well, I was coming to see you, Alice. Actually I thought I might fulfil my promise to you, and drag you to the pub. What do you think? Are you busy?'

She clearly wasn't busy. Alice cast around for another excuse.

179

Didn't find one and settled for the second least exhausting option that presented itself. She invited him in for a drink.

'What a marvellous idea!' said Dominic. 'Thank you Alice, I would love that.'

As they approached the house, Alice prayed Geraldine would hear them coming and disappear into her pot. Not that Dominic would have been able to see her. But it would be awkward if she insisted on sitting there, tutting and sneering and pretending to sip tea. So Alice spoke loudly as she opened the door.

'I don't know if I've got much in the house in the way of spirits,' she shouted. 'That is, unless you count my resident ghost, ha ha ha. I know I don't have whisky. BUT I MIGHT HAVE SOME GIN.'

'Why are you shouting?' asked Dominic.

Alice said: 'I just wanted to make sure you heard.'

The house was messy, but not in an unpleasant way. In the kitchen was a faint smell of methane, and – if you happened to look – a wisp of green smog, floating into the far corners of the room. But Geraldine was gone.

The light and warmth inside, combined with the weed she'd smoked, made Alice feel light headed. She giggled as she offered Dominic a drink. Dominic assumed it was because she fancied him, which helped him to feel more at ease. He thanked her for the glass of red wine. Put his hat and the bag onto the kitchen table and plonked himself into the seat just vacated by Geraldine.

'*Well*,' he said. 'This is awfully nice! You've made it terribly cosy.' He frowned, trying to work out how, exactly. 'What have you changed? It feels so much more welcoming.'

'Oh, nothing much,' Alice said. 'Bits and bobs. Pictures

180

and things – nothing much.' But Alice, accustomed to think-ing very little of her small efforts in life, undersold herself on this occasion. It turned out, now she didn't have the triplets wreaking havoc, that she had quite a knack for making a living space agreeable.

'Well whatever it is you've done, it's marvellous. You've trans-formed the place,' he was exaggerating. Alice was aware of that.

She said: 'You knew the place from when Lady Tode was living here, I suppose?'

'Lady Tode, yes ... Dear Emma.' He sighed. 'You knew her as a child, I think? Didn't your grandmother work for her, donkeys' years ago?'

'She did. My grandmother was very fond of her.'

'Ah yes, well. A lot of people were.'

'Including you, I imagine?'

'Indeed. Very much so. I was very fond of her,' he said. He sighed again, looking quite miserable. He fiddled with the shopping bag, and after a moment, glanced up at Alice with a forced smile. 'Well, that's life isn't it! Emma had her difficult sides, but she was a very special lady.'

'I'm sure she was.'

He looked nervous, Alice thought. He kept fiddling with the bag, as if he wanted to hand it over, and yet something was holding him back. She said: 'Are you all right, Dominic? What's in the bag?'

'Nothing.' He snatched it off the table.

'Nothing?'

'Nothing at all,' he said.

She laughed. 'Come on! What have you got in that posh shopping bag? I'm curious now.'

But he didn't want to tell her. In fact, for a moment he

seemed to have lost the power of speech. He simply clutched the bag tight and shook his head. And then – he could only have been in the house for five minutes – he picked up his glass and swallowed its contents in one. 'I really ought to be going,' he said.

'What, already? You've only just got here.'

She glanced at the shopping bag, clasped tight between both hands, and tried to make out a shape. He clasped it tighter. Alice couldn't help laughing again. 'What have you got in there? Body parts?'

'Body parts? *Body parts!* What a ridiculous idea! Of course I don't have body parts. If you must know,' he said, 'it's a cream. A face cream. Not mine.'

'Oh.' Alice waited to hear more, but Dominic, it seemed, felt he had already said more than enough. He placed his Stetson back on his head, adjusted it to the right angle, without the aid of a mirror, and stood up. It suited him, she noted (as she assumed he was aware). He was certainly a handsome man. If you liked actors. Alice had endured a couple of relationships with actors over the years, and overall she wasn't sure that she did. They tended, she thought, never to know when to stop acting. Dominic looked silly standing in her kitchen, in the middle of a Yorkshire rose garden, talking about face cream and worrying about the angle of his hat. 'Well it was good to see you,' she said. 'Thanks for dropping in.'

'The pleasure was all mine,' he said. 'Thank you for inviting me in.'

'All right then.'

They stood opposite each other, looking at each other: Alice wondering what had put the wind up him so; Dominic not really knowing what to think. The room smelled strongly of cannabis, he noted. And he wasn't certain he liked her. She was weird and unforthcoming, and harder-than-most women to charm. Nevertheless for his own sake, for everyone's sake, he realised, it would be easier if they were friends.

So he hugged her tightly. (She didn't like that.) He thanked her much too effusively for inviting him in, and apologised much too effusively for having to leave so soon. He gushed about the wine, the kitchen décor, the smell of her perfume, the colour of her mud-brown hippy dress, and shimmied out into the darkness whence he came, clutching tight to the mysterious bag of beauty cream.

CHAPTER 35

| ndia had not overestimated the extraordinary pull of her big house. Not a single guest turned down her invitation – even after India, who was fond of her own children but found other people's tiresome, told the guests that they had to leave their children at home. 'Aren't people *snobs*!' India said to Alice. She thought it was hilarious.

She had invited twenty guests, most of them couples. They were the flashiest she could muster at the exact time she was mustering, and she'd not done badly. Several were quite famous: a TV presenter, an actor, an heiress 'style icon', a clothes designer, a celebrity chef, a publisher, a celebrity ecologist, a film producer, a radio show host, two TV producers, a film director, four bankers, including one featured on the *Sunday Times* Rich List, two former *Vogue* cover girls (both now banker spouses), an American-born gossip magazine editor . . . and finally, India's afterthought: the house party's least glamorous, least impressive and (which was quite something) most toxic guest, Hamish

Tomlinson, society painter of pets. India had emailed him as an afterthought, post the dinner with the vicar and his wife and when she was still quite drunk – only because his name had come up when she was in bed with Dominic that afternoon.

Their relationship had ended after he 'ghosted' her – decades before the verb was invented. She called and wrote, and wrote and called, but after the one measly shag (albeit an adept one, and indeed her first) he had never contacted her again. What a bastard. Hamish Tomlinson. Society painter of pets. Society shagger. Society vulture and creep.

He was a friend of her parents, briefly, and the only man who ever came close to breaking her heart, for which she had never quite forgiven him. India invited him to join the glamorous house party in a flash of carefree malice, because she imagined it might, at last, make him feel a fool for having treated her so badly.

'Plus,' she said to Alice, as she was talking her through the guest list, 'he thinks he's cleverer than everyone. And he's got massive status anxiety, due to only being a *quite* successful painter and not having any money. So it's going to make him feel really rotten, seeing me here queening over everything!' She cracked up, laughing merrily at the prospect of his unhappiness, and Alice laughed with her. India's laugh was infectious.

On India's insistence – she told Egbert she was 'sick to death of looking out the window and seeing nothing but grockles and weirdies peering in' – it had been agreed that the gardens be closed to the public for the Saturday.

This was unpopular with the Estate Offices. Mrs Danvers and Nurse Ratched both took Egbert aside to warn him of the dire consequences of an unscheduled garden closure – and Egbert, with his sensible hat on, found it hard to disagree with them. Tode Hall Gardens were always open. It was one of Yorkshire's great certainties. That and the rain. If people started not knowing whether the gardens were open or not, there was a grave danger they would decamp to Chatsworth, where there was also an excellent gift shop, and a café selling top-of-the-range cakes. Egbert knew this. He also knew that the estate staff hated his wife, whom he loved. So he thanked them for their concern, tried his best to make them feel appreciated – and went ahead with the closure anyway. India had wanted to close for the entire weekend. As a compromise, they had settled for just Saturday.

He might never have worded it quite the way his wife did, but Egbert, too, would enjoy a day at the Hall without the tourists. Aside from that, though, as he confided in Alice, he 'probably wasn't massively looking forward to the weekend'. He didn't know any of the people India had invited – any more than India did of course. But India was an extrovert. She thrived in these sort of social situations; Egbert, on the other hand, tended to feel lost and unnecessary, and generally longed to be allowed to slip off to bed.

Some of the guests had wanted to arrive on Friday night but India was quick to put a stop to that. She sent out a round robin email to clarify, and laughed as she showed it to Alice: 'Why do they want to come for two nights anyway? They don't even know us.'

'Because they're already paying for the train fare?' suggested Alice.

'Nonsense! They're all very rich. Apart from Hamish, obviously. They're only coming so they can put it up on their stupid Instagram ... Seriously, Alice,' she added earnestly, 'do you think a single one of them would have spared Egbert or me five minutes if we were living in Wandsworth, and poor Eggie was still just an estate agent?'

'I doubt it,' agreed Alice.

'You see?' said India. 'So it's my way or the highway. I've got it seriously planned out. They have to arrive on Saturday in time for dindins, and definitely not before tea. And I've told them they have to bring black tie or fancy dress ... and then at the dinner I'm going to make a big announcement about the house being a film location et cetera et cetera, which they're going to have to listen to. Don't tell Eggie, though. He'll think it's a bit much. But otherwise, seriously, what's the point of having them there?'

'Good question,' said Alice.

'Right. So during dinner, I'm going to get Dominic to do his thing. Haven't told him yet, though. So don't. Don't tell him, OK?'

'What "thing" are you going to get him to do?'

India looked at Alice as if she was stupid. 'He's going to kick off the whole murder mystery thing, *obviously* ... With his acting. Come on Alice! Wakey-wakey! And Mellors has agreed to be the dead body, which we'll "discover" during the after-dinner runabout. *Please don't tell Eggie, Alice. He'll think it's super inappropriate, what with the inquest and everything ...*'

'Maybe it is, a little bit?'

India rolled her eyes. 'And then Dominic, once he's done his acting bit, is going to sort of "recover", and lead the guests, whilst sort of pretending he's still dying, but being very brave

187

about it, so it's a good opportunity for his acting, into whatever room we decide Mellors will be found dead in, and then—' India waved the details aside, 'we – rather, the stupid guests – have to work out who killed him! What do you think?'

Alice frowned, quite confused. 'Well – but who did kill him?'

'What? I don't know – there's stuff on the internet. Just got to look it up. All the instructions for, "How to organise a murder mystery weekend". It's very easy, apparently. You just have to get a few clues, like in Cluedo. And basically, dot them around the house, and then accuse one of the guests of having done the deed. Laughs-all-round. Everybody's pissed, so nobody much cares either way. The end. Keeps the guests busy . . . Plus – and I know you think I'm an idiot, Alice, but I'm actually not. Not *really* – it emphasises the house as a setting for *drama*, do you see? So the idea gets implanted into the brains of all our stupid coked-out guests – *hey, this would be a good place to set a TV drama-stroke-blockbuster movie-stroke-whatever*. Get it? Film set comes to Tode Hall. We hang out with movie stars. Tode Estates gets rich. No more tourists in the garden every day of the bloody week. We all live happily ever after.'

' . . . OK . . .' said Alice.

'Don't *worry* Alice! I've got it all worked out!'

CHAPTER 36

Only Hamish was permitted to arrive before tea. He arrived on the midmorning train and India herself drove to the station to pick him up. Egbert was working (he was always working) and the children had been taken by Weronika to a funfair in York. So India and Hamish had the day to themselves. They spent it roaming the estate, India showing off her newly acquired empire and completely forgetting to remember not to flirt, because it turned out she still quite fancied him, after all these years – despite his looking even more like a rat than she remembered.

Hamish had lately discovered a passion for poisonous plants, which he claimed, with his artist's eye, tended toward a specific kind of beauty. He showed her some pictures of deadly nightshade on his iPhone and India said, 'Oh, we've got some of those!'

'Of course you have,' said Hamish. 'You've got some of everything.'

She smirked. 'You should have been nicer to me when you had the chance, Hamish Tomlinson. I am probably the richest and most important person you know!'

He didn't respond. She was wrong, in any case. Hamish only knew rich and important people. He didn't know anyone else. Didn't even know the name of his cleaner. So.

The thing about Hamish: he just wasn't very nice. At some point (quite early) in the maturation, Hamish Tomlinson had simply curdled. Most people have a saving grace: and it's true, Hamish was a decent painter. He had a good figure. He was well read. He could be witty, sometimes. And he was, in his chilly way, mysteriously adept in the sack. Other than that? *Niente.* Hamish wasn't even kind to dogs. He didn't tip waiters. He never gave up his seat to pregnant women on buses. He never spent his own money if somebody else had a wallet nearby. In fact he never did anything for anyone else, ever. And yet, here he was, once again, with one of the prettiest and richest women in the country, eating out of his hand.

He and India found a bed of winter foxgloves during their flirtatious ramble, and they chortled and flirted a great deal, discussing which of the guests they might decide to poison during this weekend of murder and mystery, should they feel inclined. They would take a few leaves with them back to the house, crush them up and drop them into somebody's food ...

'It might add some genuine drama to the weekend,' as Hamish put it. 'At the moment it all sounds more like a mid-management team-building away-day than a civilised house party.'

India was stung by that. But she didn't show it. She told Hamish she would very much like to poison Carfizzi. Which wouldn't be at all hard, she said, because he was very greedy.

She could just sprinkle the leaves on a box of chocolates and leave the box open in the kitchen.

Hamish said that if she felt that strongly about Carfizzi, she should go ahead and do it.

'You make it sound like a dare,' said India, flirtatiously.

'It is,' he flirted back.

They picked a few leaves, giggling as they did so, and wrapped them in Hamish's clean handkerchief.

He said, 'While you're at it, could you be a sweetheart and poison that bastard, Dominic Rathbone? I can't believe he's still hanging around at Tode Hall.'

This took India by surprise. She hadn't been aware that they knew each other. Hadn't, in fact, been aware – until he let it drop on the way back from the station – that Hamish had been to Tode Hall before – which he had, in the eighties, many times, when employed by Emma to paint her cocker spaniel, Dante, now dead.

Dominic would probably know where the Dante paintings were stored. He would have known all about Hamish, and yet when she'd mentioned his name, in bed that afternoon, Dominic had never said a thing (because he hadn't been listening, but this didn't occur to her).

'I didn't know you two knew each other,' she said, making it sound lighter than she felt.

'Rivals in love,' Hamish replied, which piqued India's interest no end. But, typically, he refused to go into details.

Aside from that, which India found irritating, also a little disturbing, it was a wonderful afternoon. They were both sorry when it grew dark and India had to return to the house to catch up with the children and check in with arrangements for dinner.

The Red Dining Room – the dining room the family usually used and which was closest to the kitchen – was too small for such a large number of guests. And the problem with Tode Hall, as India once explained to Alice, straight-faced, was that it didn't really have a 'medium-sized' dining room. There was either the Long Gallery which could seat 150 or more; or the Red Dining Room, or the East Dining Room, both of which could comfortably seat up to twenty, but which, when the numbers rose any higher, became what India called 'a disgusting squish'.

Tonight they would be twenty-four, including India, Egbert, Dominic and Alice. Nobody wanted a disgusting squish, so India asked Mr and Mrs Carfizzi to lay up in the Long Gallery. 'And spread everyone out, will you?' she said. 'It'll be hilarious. Like in those *New Yorker* cartoons when they have to telephone each other, to pass the salt . . .'

Mr Carfizzi tipped his head as if to imply receipt, but inwardly he seethed: India seemed to think these grand occasions were an opportunity for humour. She completely missed the point.

When Lady Tode had run the show, she'd developed a typically elegant way to get around the lack of an appropriate-sized dining room. Diners would be arranged around the long table's centre, with a roaring fire behind them, and candles in silver candlesticks winking and glittering the full length – not just of the table but of the entire, enormous room. This is what he intended to do, and it would be beautiful. Whether India liked it or not.

CHAPTER 37

The guests arrived *en masse*, in a convoy of shiny four-wheel drive Mercedes and Range Rovers, and in good time to change for dinner. Carfizzi welcomed them in, served them drinks and gave them instructions to reconvene for further drinks, in black tie or fancy dress if they had brought it, in the Chinese Drawing Room at seven. He showed them to their rooms.

India didn't go down to greet them. She had spied on them from her bathroom window, which overlooked the Great North Door, and decided they looked even worse than expected.

'They look awful, Eggie.'

It wasn't the only reason she didn't go down to greet them. But it was the one she gave to Egbert, when he asked.

They were upstairs changing into their finery. He'd only just joined her but he could tell at once she was in a strange mood. He said:

'Munch, what's up?'

'Nothing,' she replied.

It wasn't true. To distract her husband from examining her mood more closely, she changed the conversation: 'By the way, did Mellors find you? He was looking for you earlier.'

'Munch,' Egbert said, undiverted. 'Darling, you look miserable! Are you getting cold feet about this bloody weekend? I don't blame you if you are. I know I am.'

'Of course I'm not, Eggie. Did you meet up with Mellors? He seemed a bit frantic.'

'I didn't, no. But I tell you, I met that little actor chap in the hall just now. With the skinny girlfriend. *God* they were rude! I don't think they realised who I was, but even so . . .'

'Oh?' said India, distracted from her troubles, briefly. 'You mean . . . What's his name again? I can never remember his name . . . I thought he might be the best of them. He was actually at prep school with my cousin Archie. What did he say?'

'Nothing! That's the point. They were sort of dry-humping against the sofa in the Great Hall—'

'No! That's disgusting!'

'Well, I agree with you. So I sort of went up to them to introduce myself . . . I thought Mrs Carfizzi might see them . . . Or, you know, Kveta . . . I sort of said, "Hello, I'm Egbert." And they looked at me, India. Literally – they looked directly at me, *and carried on*! They just *carried on humping*!'

'No!'

'Also,' he added, 'I don't mean to be rude, but there's something wrong with the girl. She's so thin . . . and she had this ludicrous *hat* on . . . the most massive hat . . .'

'Oh. She's a style icon,' India explained. 'She's a Guggenheim or Rockefeller . . . or a – one or the other. Super rich.'

'Well I don't know about that,' he said. 'She looked like she

194

was about to die . . . ' Egbert paused. An idea had occurred to him. The most wonderful idea. He looked hopefully at his wife. ' . . . I don't suppose,' he said, 'we could just pull a sickie . . . just sort of send our apologies and stay up here and leave them to get on with it?'

'Just skive the whole thing? . . . Oh, *Eggie*,' India cried; and gasped and breathed and whimpered and murmured. 'That's an amazing idea!' She was reminded, briefly, of how sexy he could be – sometimes, very occasionally. '*Shall we?* We could just sidle out the East door, and Egg – *we could spend the week-end in Venice!*' she said. 'We could! We absolutely could! Kveta can take care of the children. Shall we?'

But in the end, of course, the ever-dutiful Egbert's nerve abandoned him. He straightened his black tie, combed his hair, told his wife she looked lovely, which she did. And together, they headed down the stairs to greet their horrible guests.

CHAPTER 38

Nobody had bothered with fancy dress. Except, possibly, the style icon, Poppy Rockefeller, who was wearing a gauze sack with holes cut out at crotch and nipples, and no underwear. Compared to India – her usual slinky, understated self in an expensive grey wool dress – the guests looked uncomfortable in their finery: gussied up and over dressed. Everyone drank a lot.

Dinner rolled along. Mrs Carfizzi, having already dined with her husband on some delicious *melanzane parmigiana*, served up the usual Tode Hall banquet fare: individual prawn cocktails with Thousand Island dressing, leathery beef stew with long-boiled brussels sprouts and boiled potatoes, cheddar cheese and dried biscuits, and stewed apple with custard. The guests, used to the finest London restaurants, hardly knew what had hit them. Even so, they finished their plates and gushed to Mr Carfizzi as he cleared them, lauding – as James O'Shea, the bearded talkshow host put it – 'the amazing retro scrumminess of everything'.

Meanwhile, in the West Wing's Lady Laverty bedroom, Oliver Mellors, holding a letter he'd been trying to deliver to his employer all day, settled onto the bed in a corpse-like pose and fell asleep.

... And at the dining table an oblivious Dominic, not real-ising the plans had been changed, tapped his foot and awaited India's nod. Once the coffee was served, he was supposed to get the murder mystery game started by making a short comic speech (much rehearsed) and then suddenly collapsing into a terrible coughing fit and pretending to be dead.

The brassy crowd grew brassier. They yelled at one another across the glittering 250-year-old dining table, gossip about people their hosts did not know, and commentaries on spa hotels they'd visited in the Maldives.

Mr Carfizzi cleared the pudding, and listened in, and despised every one of them. He despised India for inviting them into the house. He despised Egbert Tode for marrying her, and Emma Tode for inviting her to become mistress of the house. He despised Hamish for the attention he was giving to Dominic Rathbone, and he despised Dominic Rathbone for tolerating it. Inside his butler suit, he was burning with misery and rage. But there was one thing that kept him smiling.

Earlier that evening, before India had gone upstairs to change, Carfizzi had let it drop: the piece of gossip that almost everyone at Tode Hall knew, except her; that her new fuck-buddy Dominic Rathbone, and her nemesis, Emma Tode had been involved in a love affair for almost thirty years. He had watched with sly relish as the news sank in. *Almost thirty years*, he said again ... Until that moment he had only suspected there was something going on between India and Dominic. But India's reaction to his news confirmed everything.

She said nothing to him (of course) and he had continued to potter this way and that, fussing with the overnight safe, rearranging bits of silver for the table. But he could feel her anger. She was livid.

Carfizzi hated India; he hated her golden hair and her happy-go-lucky laugh, her lack of formality, her openness, her selfishness. He hated that she was mistress of Tode Hall, and mistress of Dominic. He hated her more than he had ever hated anyone.

Later that night, he noticed an open box of chocolates lying on a side table beneath where his butler's coat hung. *How typically careless of her*, he thought. *But how delicious!*

CHAPTER 39

ndia's and Mr Carfizzi's were not the only undercurrents festering in the Long Gallery that night. Far from it. Egbert was also out of sorts. Nobody was talking to him. This was a good thing, on the whole, because even if his guests had been polite enough to try, he wouldn't have known what to say back. On occasions like these he became acutely aware of his own dullness. He longed to be anywhere else.

Which minor social discomfort troubled him a good deal less than the fact that his beautiful wife was flirting madly with Hamish Tomlinson. It was, of course, part of the price of being married to someone so beautiful and charming. Egbert understood this well and had learned, on the whole, to tolerate it. But this evening, she was flirting more brazenly than normal. He would go so far as to say that his darling Munchkin was teetering on the edge of making a grand old fool of herself. And the more she seemed to throw herself at Hamish, the more Hamish seemed to direct himself to Dominic, and the more miserable Dominic seemed to look. Dominic, like Egbert, had barely opened his mouth all night.

Alice, sitting beside Egbert and noticing his sadness, said something bland about how nice it was to see the room by candlelight.

'Yes, doesn't it look fabulous?' he replied, glumly. 'Mr and Mrs Carfizzi have done an absolutely terrific job.' But then he sighed. 'It's all a bit much for me to be honest with you, Alice.'

'Me too!' Alice said, laughing. 'Don't worry, it'll soon be over!' She looked around the table. Egbert was right. More than 'a bit much', it was appalling. India's celebrity guests, sealed inside their members-only bubble, were throwing bits of bread at one another across the table. The Long Gallery echoed to their *double entendres*, brazen namedrops, their louche laughter. India, meanwhile, was obviously very drunk. What Egbert couldn't see from his seat but Alice could from hers, was India's hand beneath the table, groping blindly at Hamish's crotch. Alice wondered whether Dominic was aware of it – and decided, from the look on his face, that he probably was.

All this, for Alice, was far less distracting than the presence, at the furthest end of the Long Gallery dining table, of Geraldine, Lady Tode. She was sitting bolt upright, in an Yves Saint Laurent scarlet flowerprint pantsuit, the ubiquitous cup of cold tea in front of her and a look of majestic disdain on her face. She'd been sitting like that, occasionally barking unintelligible comments down the table, ever since the prawn cocktails had been cleared. It was the first time Alice had seen her outside of the Gardener's House, in public, and she found it very disconcerting.

'Is this gorgeous, amazing mansion actually haunted?' Pinkie Simpleton asked Egbert suddenly. Pinkie was probably the most well-known person at the table. She was the presenter of a popular Saturday night talent show, and her face was smooth and orange. She shouted the question across the table, over the stewed apple and custard, just as Geraldine Tode was reminding Alice of the nymphomania tendencies of the Leybert-Sorringtons of Derby, also related to India (albeit by marriage).

'Oh my goodness, I wouldn't think so!' Egbert said, blushing, because he hadn't expected to be spoken to. He recognised her from the newspapers, vaguely. He'd never actually seen the show. He thought she looked much smaller and thinner and older and more orange than she did in the pictures. A bit like she was made of plastic. 'No, no,' he reassured her. 'No ghosts at Tode Hall! Or not that I've come across!'

'Yes there *are* Eggie!' India corrected him. 'Famously. And by the way – Hamish, I bet you know this. Hamish, tell everyone what Tode means in German!'

'Tode ... *tor-der*, as it's pronounced, means death,' he said.

'Bing Bing Bing! Correct! *Dix points* to Hamish. Tode-pronounced-*tor-der* means death in German. How spooky is that? So welcome to Death Hall, everyone! And yes, of course Death Hall has a ghost! Crikey. We've got loads of them. There's the ghost of the fourth Baronet. Remember Egg? He went crazy and murdered his wife with a cutlass. Or something. And now he roams the East Wing, banging on doors and calling her name. It's very romantic. He's usually in the Pineapple Room. Who's sleeping in the Pineapple Room?'

'Ooooohhhh!' went the cry. 'That'll be you then, Pinkie. Watch out, he'll probably be wanting to hump you in your sleep!'

'HA HA HA HA'

'He should be so lucky!' Pinkie said. She winked at her husband. 'Right Andy?'

'HA HA HA HA'

'Oh, dear God!' exclaimed Geraldine. And with that, she disappeared in the usual explosion of noxious green smoke, which nobody seemed to notice but Alice.

India, meanwhile, was on her feet, pinging her glass with a fork. Her eyes gleamed with a wild kind of mischief that her parents might have recognised, also her old housemistress, also her oldest, closest friends; and which Egbert noted, with a sickly dread. She was very drunk.

'Ladies and gents!' she said. 'Now that I have your attention ... I just want to welcome you all to Tode Hall ... or Death Hall, as we like to call it!'

'Yay!'

'Whoopeee!'

'Spooky!'

'Thank you guys,' said India. 'Thank you all so much for coming. And now ...' She cleared her throat. Swayed a little. Gave a dazzling smile to the room. '... I want to introduce you to Tode Hall's resident celeb, *drum roll please*! Everybody say hello to ... the world famous DOMINIC RATHBONE!'

Dominic hadn't been listening. He'd been muttering to the rat-like Hamish Tomlinson. On hearing his name, he looked up, a little bewildered. This wasn't what they'd rehearsed.

But the guests didn't know that. They were, obligingly enough, whooping and cheering and banging the table. India was smirking at him. She'd been ignoring him all evening and the smirk looked far from friendly. He had no idea what was going on.

But he dug deep, felt his breathing. There was no hint

from his manner of anything but good nature, amusement and diffident delight as he chuckled and bowed to acknowledge the drunken cheering. Eventually, India raised a hand for hush.

'Well, that was unexpected!' Dominic said. 'Not at all sure what I did to deserve it. But – as you know – applause is every actor's life-blood! I am greatly obliged to you all!'

'Wait a bit!' Pinkie said. 'I've seen you before. Aren't you the guy from—'

'That's exactly right, Pinkie!' India interrupted her. 'He is the one and only Dominic Rathbone, star of the 1990s TV adaptation of *Prance to the Music in Time*, which was of course filmed here in this house and which, don't laugh, I *still haven't got round to watching*! But we *must* Egg. We *must*. It's too ridiculous!'

'No, that's not it,' said Pinkie. 'I've never seen that show either. I'm too young!'

'Ah, but you can get it on DVD,' Egbert interjected. 'So that's no excuse!'

'OMG I don't even know what a DVD player *is* Eggie!' Pinkie replied. 'Do they even exist in this day and age?' She turned back to Dominic. 'Seriously though, where have I seen you before?'

'He's also in the coffee ad,' India said, slightly irritably. 'But that's not why I'm standing here making a speech, right?'

'Of course!' cried Pinkie. 'You're the guy in the coffee ad! Hello Mr "shake-the-coffee, makes-the-coffee" Guy in the coffee ad! Nice to meet you!'

India sent Pinkie a frosty look. 'Dominic, aside from being the guy-in-the-coffee-ad is our resident superstar, here at Death Hall. As everyone knows, he played the character of Tintin and, as such, is probably *the* face of Death Hall, in most people's minds. Don't you think, Dominic?'

'No, not really . . .'

'Of course you are, Dominic! Don't be modest!'

'Well, I would've thought . . .'

'Anyway,' India continued, 'it's such a treat to have the house full of all you lovely, super-successful media-types, and it was so *sweet* of you to have schlepped all the way North to visit us, here on the outer edges of civilisation . . .'

'Yay! Woo! Outer Hebrides, darling! Not on yours! HA HA HA' (They weren't making sense but, as the professional communicators among them knew well, it was the ambient sound that counted.)

India grinned and waited. 'I invited you here – *we* invited you here,' she corrected herself, 'Egbert and I invited you here because we miss all you clever London folk, don't we, Egg?'

Yay, Clever?! London, Woah.

' . . . And ALSO . . . because you lovely people all – in case you hadn't noticed – almost all of you work in MEDIA! And for that reason I believe you can *help* us! I want you all to get a real sense of this fantastic house, which is so full of history and romance and so TIED UP in people's minds with the fab TV series/book/film/whatever . . .

HAHAHAHAHAHAHAHAHA.

'I want you all to look at Tode Hall and let its romance and beauty really sink into your hearts, and *then* with a bit of luck, you'll take such fabulous memories home with you that when you go back to all your amazingly important jobs and all your fabulous, showbiz friends—'

Woo Wozzat? Oop, Important?!

'You will realise that no film, no pop video, no porn movie,

204

no cooking show – will be worth anything unless you set it here at Tode Hall! *And* – let me just stress this: there is nothing – no project – we won't consider! Literally nothing!'

'Porn show might be a bit much,' muttered Egbert. Everyone ignored him.

India said: 'We want to make TODE HALL the backdrop to every "Screen Experience" literally on … people's screens, whatsoever screens they may be … OK?'

YAY! Super screens! Tode Hall! Wowza!

'We want to share this beautiful house with the world! We don't want to keep it to ourselves, do we Egg?'

'Sort of,' muttered Egg.

'We want *everyone in the world* to benefit from the amazing beauty of this amazing house!' cried India.

'And of course double your take at the ticket office in the process,' said Hamish, with a ratty smile.

India turned to him, sitting beside her. She bent down so that their eyes were level, laid a soft, sparkling finger onto the centre of his ratty lips, and muttered, with a little smile: '*Cheeky!*'

For a moment it looked very much as if she might replace her soft sparkling finger with her soft, smiling lips which, even in this boisterous atmosphere, didn't feel quite right.

Alice said, loudly: 'The gardens already sell a quarter of a million tickets every year. I think what Egbert and India would like is to offer the house as a location so they can reduce the number of tourists and get a little privacy.'

'Thank you, Alice,' Egbert said. 'Hamish, I think you're being a teeny bit unfair …'

India straightened up. 'Where was I?' she asked. 'Before I was so rudely interrupted?' Another secret smile for Hamish.

'So . . . what I've planned – and this is a surprise for Dominic too, so bear with him. However, seeing as he is employed by us here at Death Hall I don't think he's likely to complain, are you Dominic?'

Dominic made his face look light and cheerful, though he was seething inside. With a chuckle, he said: 'Well it rather depends, young India! What are you going to ask me to do?'

CHAPTER 40

ndia had slipped out during the prawn cocktails to fetch the props. She had an iPhone under her seat, and a small attachable speaker. She'd snatched a Dogmatix teddy bear from the basement gift shop, and from the back of Egbert's cupboard, a straw boater with old, dried flowers pinned to its brim. The boater had sentimental value. But not to India, and not tonight.

She plonked it on Dominic's head, shoved the Dogmatix teddy into his arms.

'Stand up!' she ordered. 'Come on Dominic! This is your moment!'

He stood, and his bones creaked. 'We had a little thing prepared, India,' he grumbled. 'What happened to that?'

'Forget that,' India snapped. She fiddled with her iPhone.

Egbert said: 'My goodness, India, you are full of surprises! What *are* you up to, I wonder? And what on earth are you doing with my old Fourth of June boater? I'm actually rather fond of it . . .'

'He's got to look the part, hasn't he? Wait a bit. Hang on – *oops*!' In a burst, from her tiny speaker, that famous theme tune filled the room.

'AHHH! THE WONDERS OF MODERN TECHNOLOGY!' India yelled. But nobody could hear her over the music, so she switched it off.

'Dominic Rathbone, coffee ad superstar, is now going to take us all on a guided tour of the house – by candlelight! How about that?!'

Yay!

The cheers were noticeably less heartfelt than before. The last thing anyone wanted to do, after a night of merry drinking, was to trail around this big, cold house, in uncomfortable shoes, listening to a washed up old actor wheeze on about boring architecture. What they wanted to do at this point (and would, as soon as they got the chance) was to slip off to the nearest lavatory and chop themselves out some lines.

India ignored their subdued grumbles. She rang the bell for Carfizzi.

'And because Dominic's an actor,' she continued, 'and because he is still best known for the role he played twenty-five or thirty years ago, or whenever it was, in this very house, and because I want to remind you all of what a fantastic performer he is, and what a fantastic house this is, and what a fantastic novel *Prance to the Music* is (even if I haven't read it hahaha) and because basically I want to remind you it's about time one of you guys organised a remake, and paid us loads of money to film it here . . . ' She paused for breath, gave a wobbly, wild laugh. 'Because of *all* of that, Dominic is going to do the house tour *in character*! All right Dominic? All right everyone? So come on, cheer up! It's going to be fun!

This is a murder mystery weekend, after all! So if Dominic gets too boring we can just kill him! *Only joking!* Oh. And here is the amazing Mr Carfizzi! Carfizzi, Dominic's going to lead us on a grand tour of the house, by candlelight! Isn't that fab?'

Mr Carfizzi was feeling very ill. He'd spent the last fifteen minutes emptying his guts into the pantry sink. But nobody would have known it, not even if they had been looking at him really hard (which of course they weren't). Carfizzi's guts may well have been dissolving inside him, but he stood upright in his butler's coat, proper and professional to the end.

'As you can see,' India said, 'our lazy guests are going to need a bit of encouragement – can you please bring in some champagne? Don't give any to Dominic though, will you?' She grinned at him evilly. 'Dominic's got to keep his wits about him, haven't you Dominic? Actually Dominic, I'm going to call you Tintin from now on. Everyone, you have to call Dominic "Tintin" until the end of the tour, just to keep him in character. All right?'

Woop ... Yay ...

'It's called "method acting",' she explained. 'So come on, everyone. On your feet! Let's GO!'

'Are you sure this is a good idea?' muttered Egbert, standing up and tucking his chair in. 'It seems a bit much ...'

'Nonsense! It's great fun. Carfizzi – catch us up with the champagne will you? And keep an eye on Hamish. He's been cross-questioning me about Tode Hall security all evening, haven't you Hamish? I'm pretty sure he wants to rob us.'

Hamish gave a nonchalant shrug. 'I'm a starving artist, India, darling.' He looked directly at Dominic. 'In any case, I never leave Tode Hall without taking a little treasure away with me. It's tradition. Isn't it, Dominic? You can't expect me to make an exception this time.'

'What's that?' India said, but she wasn't really listening. 'All right Tintin, are you ready to roll? We're going to begin in the Great Hall, and I'm starting the music now. EVERYONE! STAND UP . . .'

Reluctantly, the guests clambered to their feet.

CHAPTER 41

Dominic stood beside the twenty-five-foot Christmas tree, in the middle of the huge marble floor, the dead-flowered boater on his head, Dogmatix the teddy in his hand, trying his best to look dignified. There was a fire roaring in the grate, and logs crackling, and the *Prance* theme tune, bouncing off the seventy-foot ceiling. He took a breath to begin.

'The Great Hall, designed in 1699 by Vanbrugh, is, as you will be aware, one of the great architectural masterpieces of eighteenth-century Britain. This remarkable dome which you see above you was, for its time, a miracle of engineering. It . . .' India was holding the iPhone that controlled the music, and the small speaker that amplified it.

For no clear reason, she suddenly whacked up the volume, deafening everyone and making the decorations on the twenty-five-foot Christmas tree shake. Dominic's mouth kept moving but nobody could hear anything he said.

It made India laugh, helplessly. Nobody else thought it was

211

funny; nobody wanted to be standing in this echoey hall at this stage in the evening, watching somebody mouth the words to a lecture about eighteenth-century engineering: that India seemed now intent on prolonging their discomfort, was beyond irritating. Everybody groaned. She apologised, shoulders still shaking with the funniness, and turned the music down again.

Dominic continued as if he hadn't noticed. 'Of course Vanbrugh was first and foremost a playwright, as I'm sure you know. He was not an engineer and he could never have realised his extraordinary vision without the help of—'

She did it again.

'Come on Munch,' shouted Egbert. 'This really isn't fair on anyone . . .'

She stopped laughing, turned the music down, apologised, told Dominic to continue . . . But after that, each time he took a breath, she'd do it again. It wasn't malicious, any longer. She just couldn't resist it. She'd whack up the volume, drown him out, and at once fold into helpless laughter . . . apologise . . . turn it down . . . and then do it all over again. Until everybody's irritation became comical in itself, and Alice began to laugh, and Hamish began to snigger, and even Egbert started laughing.

'For goodness sake,' said Dominic, eventually.

India said: 'OK, OK, sorry, sorry, *sorry* . . . I won't do it again. I swear . . . I absolutely swear . . . Also Tintin, remember you're meant to stay in character! Tintin's LBGTQRS-BMW or whatever . . . apparently. He really is. So do it super-gay as well. Come on. It'll be funny!'

Again, Dominic ignored her. 'The Great Hall was initially the dream child of Sir Ecgbert the First,' he continued, 'who had distinguished himself at the court of William III . . .' It was a speech Dominic had delivered many times before, if never to music, or to such a bawdy, drunken and uninterested audience. Nevertheless, he was professional, and he knew what he was doing. 'This extraordinarily beautiful ceiling which we are standing under now is the highest of its age in the county of Yorkshire, and at the time the First Baronet imagined . . .'

Before she had a chance to do it again, Egbert snatched the phone off her. Which was a mistake because it meant Dominic was able to carry on.

. . . And on . . . He was (at least according to the original plan) supposed to be leading the guests to the Lady Laverty Suite. But instead, perhaps in revenge, he led them through the back of the hall, along 'what we now call the Corridor of the Ancients, so named as a consequence of the multitude of remarkable busts from the ancient world, as you can see, each one wonderfully framed by its own baroque archway . . . Here we have a bust of the great Cicero, rescued by the fourth Baronet during what I call his Grand Shopping tour of seventeen forty-five . . . And beside Cicero . . .'

The guests began to talk among themselves. Rather, they never stopped talking among themselves, but as Dominic and the theme tune drilled on, and on, they began to talk louder, the better to hear themselves above his racket.

'And on the left here . . .'

The guests tripped along behind him, from the Corridor of the Ancients, to the Imperial Singsong Room, with its harpsichord, once strummed upon by Mozart, and its remarkable rococo painting, *Lady and Violin*, thought to be the work of . . . India turned to Alice and said: 'Do you think this was a mistake?'

Alice said: 'It depends what you were hoping to achieve.

I don't think anyone's having any fun.' She looked at India's shining face, her glazed eyes: 'But I'm not sure that was really the aim, was it?'

India said, slightly indignantly but without looking directly at Alice: 'What else was supposed to be the aim? You're right though, it's bloody boring. Maybe we should cut it short? Mellors is playing dead in Lady Laverty – *I'm pretty sure* ... Maybe we should just head over there?'

Too late. She glanced back at Dominic just as Hamish was tapping him on the shoulder. Dominic paused, an expression of fierce irritation on his face. Hamish was a half-head smaller and altogether less well built. He tipped his face upward and whispered something into Dominic's ear.

Dominic turned to him, stunned. Before anyone knew quite how it happened, Dominic had dropped his Dogmatix teddy bear, knocked Hamish Tomlinson to the ground, straddled him, and was punching him in the face.

Egbert was the first to react. He said: 'For Christ's sake, you two, watch out for the harpsichord!'

But Dominic kept pounding.

Annoyingly, no one had heard what Hamish said, and even after the TV producer and the film director had prised Dominic off him, and an element of calm had been restored, nobody ever did get to the bottom of it.

India, looking gleeful, said: 'Shall we carry on, or shall we call it a day? Dominic you are *awful*! You should be ashamed of yourself! Whatever got *into* you?'

'I think we should carry on,' Hamish said, holding a tea towel and ice to his weaselly cheekbone. 'I'm absolutely fine. Dominic – or should I call you Tintin? – India wants you to give the guests a murder mystery tour. I'm prepared to overlook

214

the pounding you just gave me, as long as you grant the wish of the lady of the house, and carry on!' But he was smirking beneath the tea towel, and there was a moment when Alice thought Dominic might relaunch his attack.

'*Ignore him*,' she muttered.

Dominic glanced at her, ignored her. He said to Hamish: 'You're bloody lucky they pulled me off when they did.'

'Shall we have a post mortem?' Hamish said. 'I'd want to move on as fast as I could if I were in your boots, Tintin … Except I'm not, am I? Not in your boots *exactly* …'

The words meant more to Hamish and Dominic than to anyone else standing around in the Singsong Room. Dominic glared at Hamish, and Hamish smirked at Dominic. And finally Dominic said: 'Frankly, you can all *fuck off*!' And he stormed away, out of the Singsong Room, along the Ancient corridor, past the baroque archways, beneath the feat of engineering … to his own bed. Rather, to the bed he'd been sleeping in these past thirty years, which belonged, like everything else in his life, to Egbert and India.

CHAPTER 42

It was generally agreed that Dominic and Hamish's fight had pepped up the midsection of what was already an excellent evening. After Dominic stormed off, the party returned to the Chinese Drawing Room for coffee, champagne, brandy and further merriment. The Londoners, all fired up on their marching powder, didn't retire to bed until four in the morning; Egbert left at about half past twelve, and Hamish and India, neither of whom was offered any of the Londoners' cocaine, sidled off to bed at about two. For a short period, they sidled off to the same bed. India had put Hamish in the Russian Room, one of the less good bedrooms: partly to punish him for not returning her calls when she was seventeen, and partly because she had half known all along how this was likely to play out, and the Russian Room was discreet, far away on the third floor.

She might have saved herself the trouble because the encounter didn't go well. Not as she had planned. India, confronted by his ratty nakedness and weirdly vast – elephantine – erection, sobered up. She thought of Dominic, his comparative neatness, and of how cruelly she had treated him earlier: also, more powerfully, how cruelly he had treated her. She thought of Egbert, one floor below, sleeping the sleep of the innocent, and realised she missed him.

'Oops,' she said, staring at Hamish and feeling a bit sick. 'Serious second thoughts. [Hic] Sorry!'

He didn't try to change her mind – beyond a desultory 'Are you sure?' It wasn't his style. So she slipped back into her grey dress, hiccupping but otherwise silent.

'See you at breakfast,' she said, as she closed his bedroom door. 'Thanks for not making a fuss.'

But he didn't look up. He was lying naked on the bed, erection slowly deflating, apparently already engrossed in an article in yesterday's *Times*.

CHAPTER 43

Breakfast was served from 9 a.m., but India advised Mrs Carfizzi not to expect the London guests to appear before noon.

At 10 a.m., having dropped the children at their weekly riding lesson, she herself could be found in her seat at the head of the dining table, glossy haired and smelling of roses, eating toast and marmalade. Her husband sat in his seat, at the other end of the table. He was wearing mud-spattered biking gear, eating kedgeree and reading the *Mail on Sunday*. Between them, also eating kedgeree, and reading the latest edition of the *New Yorker*, sat the bruised and rat-like Hamish. No one else had yet surfaced, of course: and the silence, and the munching, and the men, with their complacent reading faces, and the smell of the kedgeree – not to mention her own hangover – were putting a terrific strain on India's patience.

She wondered what had become of Dominic. Even though he wasn't staying in the house for the weekend, she had made it clear that he was expected for breakfast. His celebrity presence was part of the entertainment, after all. She rang the bell.

A moment longer than India had wanted to be kept waiting, Mrs Carfizzi poked her head through the connecting kitchen door. This was doubly annoying. India had been expecting to see Mr Carfizzi, and was not in the mood to deal with Mrs Carfizzi's useless English. She scowled.

'Where's Mr Carfizzi?'

'He sick.'

'Really? Why?' India remembered something, and laughed. 'Oh! He is, is he? Poor fellow. Tell him to get better soon.'

Mrs Carfizzi shrugged. 'He try.'

'No. I mean – send him my best. Never mind. I'll come and visit him later. Will you tell him?'

Mrs Carfizzi shook her head. This, she seemed to understand. 'No, he no want it.'

'Of course he does! He'll be delighted!' India chortled. 'Tell him I'll bring him some more of his favourite chocs!'

Mrs Carfizzi looked terrified. 'NO!' she said vehemently. 'Chocolates. He kill.'

'What? Who kills?'

'Chocolate he kills.'

India shook her head. 'Never mind. Where's Mr Rathbone?'

Mrs Carfizzi said: 'Mr Rathbone very angry today. Train for London.'

'What? This morning? He's supposed to be working! He's supposed to be entertaining the guests!'

Mrs Carfizzi shrugged. She glanced nervously at Egbert, but he was engrossed in his newspaper and didn't appear to be listening.

'Well, never mind,' India said again. 'Please will you ask Alice to join us for breakfast?'

Mrs Carfizzi didn't move.

'Ask *Alice*. Please *ask Alice Liddell* at *the Gardener's House* to come and join us for breakfast. As soon as possible. Please. Do you understand? Also can you please get rid of the kedgeree. The smell is making me feel sick.'

'Bit much, Munch,' muttered Egbert, watching Mrs Carfizzi clear the dish away. 'Don't chuck it out, will you Mrs Car Fizzy? I'm sure when the other guests appear they'll want to eat it . . . Terrific stuff. Thank you so much . . .'

Just then, behind India, the large mahogany door slammed open and in barged Mad Ecgbert, 12th Baronet Tode: looking, India thought, when she turned to see the source of the noise, even madder than usual.

'For goodness sake, Ecgbert,' said Egbert, mildly. 'There's no need to smash the door like that. One day you'll knock the Reynolds right off that wall and Christ only knows if the insurance would cough up . . .'

India rolled her eyes.

'You may well roll your eyes, India,' her husband snapped, sounding unusually sharp. 'But actually we have a responsibility . . .'

She turned towards her husband's cousin. His long, lean frame was clothed, this morning, in a slinky, wide-collar orange shirt and slim-cut purple velvet suit, and his thick hair was like a Brillo pad on top of his head, woolly and grey. There was nothing too unusual about the hair – it often looked wild – but the clothes were something else. Normally he wore jeans and an ancient tweed jacket. This morning he looked like a beatnik version of Beethoven. Mad, perhaps; but not unattractive.

220

'Ecgbeeeeeeerrrrrrrrt!' she cried, mostly to shut up her husband. 'Nice suit! We haven't seen you for a bit! Where have you *been*? Come on in! Mrs Car Fizzy has made kedgeree. It smells gross, to be honest. But my husband says it's delicious.'

'I haven't come here to talk about kedgeree,' Mad Ecgbert replied. He looked around him impatiently; from the scowling, mud-spattered Egbert, to the smiling, rosy India – and then to Hamish Tomlinson, peering at him over his *New Yorker*. 'What the hell are *you* doing here?' Mad Ecgbert asked.

'I'm eating breakfast,' Hamish smirked. 'How very nice to see you again, Ecgbert. An unexpected pleasure.'

'Definitely not reciprocated,' Mad Ecgbert replied, and slammed the big mahogany door shut behind him, making the Reynolds shake on its wire again.

'For God's sake,' muttered Egbert. He turned back to his *Mail on Sunday*.

Mad Ecgbert, still standing by the door, pointed an angry finger at Hamish, turned to India and demanded: 'Seriously. What is that creep doing here again? I thought we'd all seen the back of him. My mother's dead, you silly bastard. We all hate you. Why don't you fuck off?'

Hamish snickered and stretched across the table for another triangle of brown toast. He didn't offer a reply, and it seemed that Mad Ecgbert wasn't expecting one. He pulled out a chair – beside India, opposite Hamish, and slumped into the seat.

'By the way, somebody needs to pay the cab driver,' he added. 'He's in the Great Hall. With that insane Christmas tree. Where's this famous kedgeree then?'

'I asked Mrs Carfizzi to take it away with her. I'll ask her to bring it back again,' India said. 'Unless,' she added hopefully, 'you want something else? Wish I hadn't mentioned it now. Are you sure you don't want eggs?'

Behind him, the door opened again, and in came Alice.

'Morning all!' she said. 'Sorry I'm a bit late—' A pause. Quite a long one. She had stopped still. When she next spoke she didn't sound herself. Ecgbert hadn't turned, so she addressed the back of his woolly head. She said:

'Hello Ecgbert. Long time no see.'

He spun round, wide eyed. There was a triangle of toast hanging out of his mouth. But even so – and greatly to her surprise – Alice's heart missed a beat. She gave him a flat, sad smile. It had been almost forty years, and life had taken its toll on them both. She felt the weight of the years, but also – mostly – the triumph of the fact that here they were, still standing. To Alice, who usually felt so little, the emotion of the moment shot through her like a horrible electric pulse: a physical pain from her fingertips to the top of her head, centring – or stopping – with a massive punch in her heart, as if, for a moment, her heart had stopped. She had no idea, not the slightest inkling, that the sight of him would have had such an effect.

' . . . *YOU!*' he said. It was not friendly. The toast fell to the table. He leapt to his feet. (She had forgotten how tall he was.) 'What are *you* doing here? What's going on? . . . ' He turned from Alice to Egbert, and then to India. And then back to Alice again: 'Sorry about your Ma,' he said.

Alice shrugged. 'Long time ago now.'

'Still . . . ' He gazed at her.

' . . . Yep . . . ' Alice said.

' . . . I'm an orphan as well, by the way. Now. Just like you.'

'Yes, I know.'

'Mind you, at least your mother got the chance to do *herself* in,' he added.

'That's true,' Alice said. 'That's a very positive way of looking at it.'

'My mother was done in, as you probably know.'

'Oh, I don't think she was "done in",' Alice said, automatically, lazily.

'What's that?' he snapped.

'I said—'

'Oh you don't think so? Maybe that's because *you* did it! It could have been you.'

Alice gave him a thin smile. She sounded quite calm again. She said: 'Why would I have "done her in", Ecgbert? I don't have any reason—'

'You think *I* did?'

'No. I didn't say that—'

'How?' he shouted.

'Well, I didn't actually—' Alice began.

'You haven't got an answer! Because there *isn't* an answer! Of course I didn't. What a stupid idea!'

His rudeness annoyed her. She said: 'It's not that stupid, actually. Now you mention it.'

They eyeballed one another, and then Mad Ecgbert lunged towards Alice. At the far end of the room, Egbert, in his biking gear, leapt to his feet to protect her. But there was no need. Alice didn't flinch. She looked into Ecgbert's eyes as he flew towards her: and then, as abruptly as he began, he stopped, and they both giggled.

'Mad as ever, I see,' Alice observed.

He ignored that. 'I knew you'd come back here eventually.

You had to. But you should have come and seen me ... I was waiting. Why didn't you?'

'Like you came and saw me in London?'

'But I didn't,' he replied, confused. ' ... Car Fizzy tells me you're living in the Gardener's House.'

'That's right.'

'You realise it's haunted? Ma didn't realise, either. She used to be furious when I mentioned it.'

'Guys,' interrupted India, feeling excluded, 'I'm getting neck ache following all this madness. Come and sit down.'

But the sound of her voice brought Ecgbert back into the room. It seemed to awaken his fury again. He pointed at the smirking, kedgeree-munching Hamish Tomlinson. 'I will die,' Ecgbert declared, his long, lean finger quivering, 'before I sit at the same table as *that shit*! Did *you* kill Ma, Hamish Tomlinson? You probably did. After you had sex with her. You probably fucked her and then killed her, like one of those spiders—'

'Easy does it, Coz,' mumbled Egbert. 'Bit much. It's only breakfast.'

'Well it was probably "only breakfast" when he fucked Mummy and then killed her!' Mad Ecgbert cried.

Hamish frowned in mock confusion. 'I don't know what breakfast has to do with all this. But then again ... '

'Oh shut up,' snapped India. 'Both of you. Ecgbert, for Christ's sake, please don't dump your Oedipal weirdness on us this morning. We've all got hangovers and we're trying to have a nice, peaceful breakfast. So either join in, or bugger off.'

'Bugger off?' repeated Ecgbert, outraged. 'I'll have you know, Miss *India* whatever-the-fuck you call yourself, from Wandsworth. This is *my* dining room. And nobody – *nobody* tells me when to bugger off in my own dining room. *Comprendi?* And where is my fucking kedgeree?'

Mrs Carfizzi saved what might easily have turned into a nasty moment by just then popping her smiling face through the interconnecting kitchen door.

'Ah! Sir Ecgbert!' she cried. 'I think I hear you! You home again! Very good, very good.'

Mad Ecgbert, mollified by her warmth, forgot about the fight. He crossed the large room and hugged her.

She bustled off to pay the waiting cab driver and fetch the kedgeree, and the crisis passed. Or it would have passed. But Hamish hadn't quite finished. He waited until Ecgbert sat down, and then he said:

'So – did you?'

Mad Ecgbert said: 'Did I, what?'

'Did you kill your Mama? I wouldn't blame you if you had. *Nobody* would blame you. She was vile to you. I often used to tell her so . . .'

India was only half listening. Her mind was spinning. Had Emma Tode and Hamish Tomlinson been lovers too? Was there any man in Yorkshire Emma Tode hadn't got to before her?

And then Ecgbert started shouting again.

'You think *I* killed her, Hamish? Well that's funny because I think *you* killed her. That is, I think you would have killed her, if you'd had the imagination to think of it. How dare you come *slinking into my house*, with that disgusting smirk on your face, telling me who killed my mother, when I *know perfectly well* who killed her, and it wasn't me?'

Hamish said: 'Sorry to break it to you, old man, but it's not actually your house. It belongs to your cousin Egbert. The fellow over there, who's sitting at the head of the table, paying your taxi fares. See? It's not your house.'

'Come on, Hamish,' said Egbert. 'It's really not necessary . . .'

'Eggie's right,' India said: 'Shut *up*, Hamish. Apologise to Ecgbert. Apologise to him, or leave. Go back to – wherever it is you live.' She couldn't remember. Not London. He'd had to move out for financial reasons.

Hamish held up his hands: still smirking, but beginning to sound peevish. He said: 'Sorry, India. But I seem to be getting abuse left and right this weekend. First Dominic, then Ecgbert. You have to admit—'

'Forget about Hamish,' Mad Ecgbert shouted over him. 'He's an idiot. Don't give him another thought. I actually need to talk to Car Fizzy. I only came here to talk to Car Fizzy. And Mellors, obviously. I *must* talk to Mellors. I'm pretty sure he knows what's what. On the murder front. Because Ma used to tell him everything. I'm actually quite surprised she didn't leave him all her dosh . . . Has anyone apart from me actually bothered to read Mummy's will yet? Maybe they should. More importantly, where's Mellors?'

Young Egbert had had enough. Whether his mad cousin did or didn't kill his mother, frankly: whether anyone did – it was a matter for the police and certainly not a matter for Sunday breakfast. Nor, come to that, was the very delicate matter of Lady Tode's will which, it so happened, had only yesterday landed on his – and presumably Ecgbert's – desk. The time had come to take control.

'Ecgbert, my cousin and friend,' he began.

'Fuck off. I'm not your friend.'

'But you are my cousin.'

'In name only.'

226

'Well – no. You actually are my cousin. Look the point is – I am sorry, but you really do have to leave, now. We have a houseful of very important guests, and much as I love your visits, and I *really* do ...'

'Pah!'

'I do, Egbert. Believe me. I am always pleased to see you. But on this one occasion, I really do think—'

Mad Egbert cut him off. He turned to Alice. 'Trudy, I'm sorry I accused you of killing Ma. I obviously didn't mean it. You know that, don't you? You look well, by the way. Did I say that? You look scrumptious, Trudy ... Truly scrumptious.' He smiled at her. *Trudy*. (Her heart skipped. It's what he called her when they were children.) 'Perhaps you and I can have a drink when all this is over ...'

She didn't know what he meant by 'all this'. She didn't even know if he'd murdered his mother. But at that instant, she didn't care.

'That would be lovely, Egbert,' she smiled at him. 'You know where to find me.'

CHAPTER 44

ndia had decided to serve Sunday lunch up at Africa Folly. There were tables and chairs kept there for the purpose, and she'd asked for a fire to be laid in the grate. The Folly wasn't normally used in winter, as Mrs Carfizzi tried to explain. But India was set on the idea. *It'll be fun*, she said.

Not much fun for Mrs Carfizzi, with a husband sick in bed and twenty-four people to cater for, but India had managed to persuade Kveta to work extra time, and now Alice had been roped in to help, too. Egbert said he would give her a lift up there on his way to fetching the children at the riding stables.

First, Alice stopped by the Gardener's House to fetch her phone. She'd meant to rush in and out, but then there was Geraldine at the kitchen table, waiting for her, determined to waylay her.

Geraldine was wearing an emerald green turban, satin pantaloons and a Chinese embroidered jacket, and looking, Alice noted, even more magnificent than usual. One day, when there was more time, she might ask Geraldine where, in that tiny sugar pot, she stored her magnificent wardrobe. But for now she had more pressing concerns – the whereabouts, for example, of her mobile phone.

'Where did you go?' Geraldine asked her irritably. 'You sidled off. I've been waiting for you all morning.'

'Oh. Hi, Geraldine. Good morning. I'm in a bit of a hurry, actually. I've only come back to fetch the phone. But guess who turned up to breakfast? Your grandson, my old friend Egbert! At last! He burst into the dining room this morning, mad as a—'

'*Eccentric*,' Geraldine corrected her.

'Eccentric. You're quite right.'

'And half-witted, obviously. Not mad.'

'Either way – I haven't even laid eyes on him since I was fourteen. If you don't count the first night when he broke in and – I don't count it because I didn't even see his face. It was . . .' Alice paused to consider how she felt – which, in itself, was unusual.

But then she spotted her phone. 'I should go,' she said, picking it up. 'India's insisting on everyone having lunch at the Folly. Carfizzi's ill in bed, Lottie and Lisa have both got colds, apparently. Kveta's agreed to help but she's sulking about it . . . Et cetera, et cetera . . . And Egbert's waiting for me.'

Geraldine said: 'Dominic dropped something on the doorstep this morning. Did you see it?'

Alice hadn't. She wanted to know when he'd dropped it. He was meant to be half way to London. But Geraldine had no real concept of time. She couldn't tell Alice when the object had been dropped; it might have been in the middle of the night. In any case, she'd seen him, stumbling through the darkness. He'd put a shopping bag on the doorstep, and then stopped and returned to it, and moved it. He'd left it propped behind a garden pot on the terrace.

'*Do* go and get it,' said Geraldine. 'One finds oneself beyond curious.'

'I can't . . . I'm meeting Egbert in three minutes,' Alice said, peering through the window onto the terrace.

'Just quickly, Alice. Be sweet. Please.'

'I really can't . . .' Alice said. 'I can't see it, Geraldine. I'll fetch it later.'

This was a bitter pill for Geraldine. She was not accustomed to being told 'No'. Not before she died, and not since she'd befriended Alice, either. Thin curls of vapour began to seep gently from the base of her neck and a most noxious smell filled the room. Alice bit her cheeks to stop herself from laughing, but then – something about Geraldine's helplessness made her hesitate. It was a Sunday, after all. Fun Managers weren't supposed to work seven days a week. And in any case – she was quite close to *beyond curious* herself. What could he have left for her?

Egbert would have to wait.

CHAPTER 45

Outside, a blustery wind had picked up. There were pots and plants and garden equipment strewn across the terrace and Geraldine couldn't be very specific about where, exactly, Dominic had hidden the bag, so Alice took a while to find it. As she bent to look beneath a wheelbarrow, she thought she heard something or someone approaching from behind. She yelped. It was unlike her: uncharacteristically jumpy.

Inside, Geraldine's booming voice demanded to know what was happening.

'Nothing!' said Alice. '... Just the wind, I think. Here it is! I've found it!'

'Hurry up!'

The bag had been tucked behind a laurel bush that grew right up against the wall of the house. It was the same bag – the Molton Brown shopping bag that Dominic had been carrying first, when she bumped into him outside the Long Gallery, looking like a scarecrow, and again, when she found him roaming in the garden, what now felt like a lifetime ago. She took the bag back into the kitchen and opened it, with Geraldine looking on.

There was a sealed envelope inside, addressed in flowery pen to 'Alice Lydell' (spelt wrong), and with it a pot of face cream, just as he had claimed the last time: not just any face cream, either. It was a massive, 250ml pot of Crème de la Mer.

'What the hell . . . ?' Alice muttered.

'What is it?'

Alice held it up. ' . . . only *Crème de la Mer*!' she said. Apparently this stuff was magic: worked like no other moisturiser in the world. She opened the pot, dipped in a finger . . . *marvellous, rich texture*, she thought.

'What *is it*?' snapped Geraldine. Impatience was causing her to distort again, very slightly. Her head was stretching, and there were wisps of smoke appearing from her left ear. 'What have you got there? For goodness sake, Alice. *What is it?*'

'Amazing!' muttered Alice. 'Geraldine, this is probably the largest pot of what is probably one of the most expensive face creams in the world . . .'

'How peculiar,' said Geraldine. 'Why's he left it here?'

Alice sniffed the open jar. 'Smells good. Smell it.'

Geraldine Tode put her nose to the jar and pretended to sniff. She said nothing.

'You can't smell?'

Geraldine looked straight ahead and Alice, sensing her *faux pas*, quickly moved the jar away again. 'There's a letter. Shall I read it aloud?'

Geraldine nodded. 'Please.'

Alice put the jar aside and opened the letter. Sat down. Cleared her throat.

'*My dearest Alice,*' she began. '*By the time you read this I shall be gone . . .*'

'Oh, my dear,' cried Geraldine. 'It's a suicide note!'

'*I have a flight to catch, and I need to pack . . .*'

'A flight? Where the devil is he going?'

'*. . . I have left Tode Hall for ever. Something I should have done a long time ago, and I would have done, if only I had been able. But I had fallen in love with Emma. For the past twenty odd years, until she died, I was caught up in the most wonderful love affair. Why am I telling you this? I am telling you about my love for Emma Tode because it is important for you to understand this before I tell you what I am about to tell you next . . .*'

'He's very repetitive,' Geraldine complained. 'I thought he had an airplane to catch?'

'*. . . When Emma died, my world stopped.*'

'Yes, yes, I dare say.'

'*. . . You were there when the news arrived. Do you remember? Of course you do. When Carfizzi told us, my heart broke in two. Of course it did. But do you remember how India took the news? Try to picture it, if you can.*

'*We were standing together, she and I. I was judging the Tintin & Dogmatix costume award, and beside me India was haranguing me to hurry and announce the winner . . . Can you picture it, Alice? On some level I think I have known this all along – only I couldn't allow myself to acknowledge it. But when Carfizzi arrived to tell us that my darling Emma was lying dead in the mausoleum, it is quite clear to me now, that India already knew. She knew what had happened to Emma before Mr Carfizzi had uttered a word. She grasped hold of my arm and she said – at the time I thought I had misheard her. She took my arm and she said: "They've found her . . ."*'

'Tommy rot!' exclaimed Geraldine. 'Balls and bunkum! Well, Alice? Did *you* hear India say that?'

Alice tried to picture it. Where had India been standing? Beside Dominic? Had she grasped hold of his arm? She might have done. But had she *said* anything? Alice tried to imagine India's face when the news came in. Dominic had looked thunderstruck. Shattered. And India? India never looked shattered. Had she spoken? Maybe, yes. *Maybe.*

'Maybe you remember, maybe you don't. There was something out of whack about all of us – about everything – that terrible afternoon. Nothing seemed quite real.

'You, of course, and your remarkable grandmother, went with Mr Carfizzi and Egbert to investigate the scene, leaving India and me to hold the fort, as it were. Egbert was determined not to upset the tourists. (His alpha and omega! No matter who is dead or how they may have died, we Must Not Upset the Tourists!) In any case, India and I did, somehow, manage to keep the show on track, got the prize giving wrapped up, and as my car was so close, we decided to return to my cottage for a drink. We needed one.

'There's no pretty way to put this. The fact is, we had several drinks and within a fairly short time, India and I found ourselves in bed together. I should have stopped it. Then or now or at any time since. I did try – but not hard enough and there is no excuse … except my own grief, and I suppose, that I am only human – but I'm not justifying our actions. We did what we did.

'India hated Emma. I never dared tell her the extent of our deep friendship, and I tremble for the day she discovers it. But I won't be here, thank God. You could say I am running away. I don't know what else to do. After what happened last night, I can't stand by and say nothing any longer.

'The tub of Crème de la Mer is something not I, but Mr

Carfizzi, found in India's bathroom cupboard. He gave it to me some weeks ago, because he didn't know what to do with it himself. Neither did I. Except for that night when you found me roaming in your garden. (I had come with the intention of giving it to you then, only to get cold feet and scurry away again!) I, like Mr Carfizzi, have kept the wretched thing hidden. I most likely would have continued to do so, but, Alice, last night I am almost certain that India struck again.

'*Mr Carfizzi called me from his sickbed at about 2 a.m., convinced that she was trying to poison him. There is only circumstantial evidence for this. However, I know that Hamish is currently interested in plant poisons because he and India talked about little else at dinner. Mrs Carfizzi says she found a handful of dead foxgloves in India's bedroom wastebasket ... Mr Carfizzi says he found a box of his favourite chocolates lying open beneath the hook where he hangs his jacket ... Five hours later he is blinded by headaches, vomiting so violently that he ruptured his own stomach. Perhaps it's just coincidence. (How I wish I could believe that.) Mrs Carfizzi has been feeding her poor husband hot water and mustard powder, which she swears is the only antidote to foxglove poisoning, and we must keep our fingers crossed.*'

'He's lying!' cried Geraldine. 'He must be!'

'*IN THE MEANTIME – I realise my loyalty is no longer to the Todes, nor to the Carfizzis, nor even to my darling Emma, but to Society.*'

'Oh for heaven's sake! The man's a gigolo!'

'Shh!' said Alice. 'Listen. Listen to this.' She read on: '*India Tode is a killer.*'

'Nonsense! How dare he?'

'*... And I believe that India has it in her to kill again and again, unless she is stopped. Shortly before she disappeared, Emma*

235

told me she was having second thoughts about leaving India in charge at Tode Hall. She told me she was already in secret discussions with her lawyers about reversing the situation, and I suspect that on the day she was due to leave for Capri, she may have said as much to India, and that India, as is her wont, simply lost her temper. An opportunity arose for India to abandon Emma in the mausoleum, and she leapt at the chance, knocked Emma to the ground, locked the door and left her to die ...'

'This is preposterous,' muttered Geraldine. '... Really ... It is ...' But she didn't sound her certain self. Not quite.

'... You will have opened the jar of Crème de la Mer by now. (A tub of that size costs £800, Alice, and yet, after Mr Carfizzi took it off her all those weeks ago India never said a word. Not a squeak! Never mentioned that an £800 tub of face cream had gone missing from her bathroom cupboard. Don't you think it strange?) What you find buried inside that jar may not count as evidence in law – I have no idea. But it's evidence enough for me. India must be stopped before she kills again. After all, who knows who might be her next victim? Who might offend her next? I don't think I am being too melodramatic when I say to you – she frightens me. Be careful. Watch your back.'

'He's a coward and a liar!' interjected Geraldine. 'How dare he. How *dare* he? The man's nothing but a washed up old ham, Alice. I hope you're not swallowing any of this tripe?'

Alice held up a finger – *wait* – and continued reading.

'I have left India's face cream exactly as I found it. I would suggest, if it's not too late, that you do too ...'

'Well, open the jar again, for God's sake!' cried Geraldine. 'What's in there? What's she put in there?'

Alice opened it, and this time delved deep into the pot. Her fingers touched on something hard.

'What? What is it?'

'... Feels like a ...' Alice pulled it out, wiped away the cream and held up to Geraldine a large and ancient-looking key. Especially distinctive thanks to the family crest at the tip of the key's handle.

'Well, what the devil ...' Geraldine stared at it. They both did. There was only one key that looked like that – or two, to be precise. The one that was hanging in the key cupboard, and the other one, the missing key to the mausoleum: missing since before Alice started at the Hall. Missing since Lady Tode was meant to have left for Capri.

Alice said: 'We should hand it over to the police.'

'What?'

'This – everything. The letter, the key ... There's the inquest tomorrow. If India did this, we should ...'

Green vapour filled the room. It spouted, dragon-like, from her ears and nostrils.

'**NOOOOOO!**' The word emerged as a roar, not from Geraldine's slim chest, but from somewhere way beneath her, from the depths of her purest darkness, and it made the windows shake.

Alice stared, terrified. The key slipped from her fingers and clanged to the floor.

And the moment passed. The vapour thinned. Geraldine cleared her throat and apologised.

'—Don't be silly, Alice,' she said. 'There's absolutely no need for the police to be poking their noses into this. This is Tode business. We can deal with it ourselves.'

Alice looked at the key. 'Geraldine, this may be evidence of ... a very serious crime indeed ... I mean ...'

'Of course it's not evidence.'

'But it is.'

Geraldine tried another tack. 'Not really. Anyway how do we know Dominic didn't put the key in that pot himself? He probably did. Or Car Fizzy, come to that. Or anyone, frankly. How do we even know this Crème de what not even belongs to India? We don't. And even if it did, even if she did do . . . whatever Dominic is trying to imply. . . which I don't believe for a second, by the way, what's to be gained from telling the police?'

'Well—'

'It's *absolutely* none of their business, Alice,' Geraldine continued without waiting for a reply. 'Do you really want to drag India's name through the mud over a bit of worthless tittle-tattle? A lovers' tiff? I thought you liked her? I thought you said she was a friend? And think of India's darling little children! Think of her sweet, brave husband! Do you really want to put them through all that . . . over a silly pot of over-priced face cream?'

'It's not about the face cream . . .'

'It most certainly is about face cream. If it's not about face cream I don't know what it is about.'

'Well it's about murder . . .'

'Nonsense.'

'You're the one who has always insisted that Emma Tode was murdered.'

'And even if Dominic's story added up, which it clearly doesn't, I ask you again, what is to be gained from bringing PC Plod into the *mélange*? For heaven's sake, Alice, wake up! Emma is already dead. Do you really want to ruin any more lives?'

'But what if she kills someone else?'

238

'Whom? Whom might she kill?' Geraldine asked.

'I don't know! Me? Egbert? The children? How do I know? She may already have killed Mr Carfizzi, according to Dominic ... I mean ... I haven't seen him this morning. Mrs Carfizzi says he's too sick to work. I don't think he's ever been too sick to work before ...'

'You're talking twaddle, darling. Because you're tired. And no wonder, when they're making you work seven days a week. I suggest you dispose of that ridiculous pot of cream and its contents as soon as possible. Also that odious and very silly letter ... in fact I think you should go for a drive into Todeister this afternoon, as soon as the guests have left us, and throw them both into the bottom of the River Tode—'

'Throw away the Crème de la Mer?'

'With a bit of luck, we can brush this whole unfortunate episode under the carpet and move on ... And as for Dominic Rathbone: good riddance. I hope he catches his airplane, and I hope it crashes. I hope I never set eyes on him again.'

CHAPTER 46

Alice didn't want to believe the letter. She wished she'd never read it. She didn't want to have to think about the questions it raised – certainly not now, and preferably ever again. So she filed it away, buried it in a dark and distant corner of her mind, and hoped it would quietly die there. (An unfashionable system, but it worked better than people often realised.) So she tucked both the letter and the incriminating beauty cream into a kitchen drawer, and headed out to find Egbert.

He was already waiting for her, sitting in the Land Rover with the engine running and a glum, slightly self-pitying expression on his face. She swallowed any irritation, and climbed up into the seat beside him.

'Sorry I'm late,' she said.

'Nonsense!' he cried. 'If anyone should be apologising it's me. And possibly India . . .' There was 'literally no reason on earth,' he said, that Alice should be working through her weekend, let alone be expected to help with the laying up of lunch.

'I don't know why we have to bother with the Folly, to be honest with you Alice. It seems a lot of trouble, with Car Fizzy ill. But when India gets an idea into her head ...'

He felt disloyal and didn't finish the sentence. A long silence. And then, sounding slightly whiney: 'She just so wants the weekend to be a success, after everything's been so difficult, you know?'

'I do,' said Alice, only half listening.

'She's not used to people disliking her, Alice ... It really is really horrid for her ... And the fact is ... Sorry, Alice, do you mind? Am I clear your side? The fact *is* ... most people, by the time they reach India's age, have had a certain amount of experience in that area. But I honestly don't think India has ... Bless her. I don't think she's ever encountered an individual she's not been able to win over. Never in her life.'

'Amazing,' said Alice.

' ... Not until Emma Tode came along ...'

Alice didn't know what to say. An image of Emma Tode lying dead in the mausoleum obstructed everything else. And Dominic's words, which she'd been trying to forget ... *India, as is her wont, simply lost her temper.*

'Emma invited us to take over the Hall,' Egbert was saying, 'and then, as far as I can see, did just about everything within her power to make it impossible for us to fit in ...'

An opportunity arose for India to abandon Emma in the mausoleum, and she leapt at the chance ...

'And look, I just get on with the job,' Egbert droned on. 'But *I worry for* India ... She's actually *terribly* sensitive.'

... knocked Emma to the ground, locked the door and left her to die ...

It was unlike Egbert to be so communicative. Alice

would have preferred it vastly if he'd stayed in character, on this morning of mornings. But it seemed there was no stopping him.

'Well I wasn't here when Lady Tode was alive of course,' Alice mumbled. 'So I don't really know what went on.'

'Of course you don't. And I don't even know for sure that you would have noticed even if you *had* been, Alice. That's the strangest thing. I'm not sure *I* noticed, really ... not consciously. Just – there were these subtle remarks; these ever-so-subtle ways of mocking us in front of the staff. Both of us, actually ... ' He sighed. 'You probably think I sound completely mad.'

'No, no ... ' said Alice.

'But you know, when I see the way Car Fizzy looks at my wife ... It's *really* upsetting.'

... Mrs Carfizzi has been feeding her poor husband hot water and mustard powder, which she swears is the only antidote to foxglove poisoning ...

Egbert glanced across at Alice. He found himself miraculously comforted by her quiet presence; wanting to confide more to her than he usually confided to anyone, not even – or least of all – his beloved wife.

'This is probably a terrible thing to admit,' he said, steering politely round the tourists. 'But I'm actually *jolly glad Emma's gone* ... When I saw her lying there – and you were with me, Alice: you'll remember what a shock it was – but when I saw her, lying there on the floor, and all that dried blood everywhere, and goodness knows ... the pants ... ' He shuddered. 'Do you know, I didn't feel a single thing? Rather,' he added, 'that's not strictly true ... I'll tell you what I really felt. And you must never breathe a word. Never tell a soul. Certainly not,' he laughed, 'to our friends at the local constabulary! But I tell you what I thought. I thought: well that's you sorted, you silly old bag. Bloody well serves you right!'

'Goodness,' Alice said. 'I had no idea how much you disliked her.'

'I should hope not!' he laughed again. 'Or we'd have a couple of our local bobbies dropping in at the Hall, brandishing handcuffs and arresting me for first degree!'

Alice felt a little sick.

'. . . How are you finding it here?' he asked, changing tack. 'Actually what I really mean is, how are you finding *India*? I worry about her. Do you think she's happy?'

There was a toddler posing for photographs in the middle of the drive.

'Watch out,' she said. 'There's a toddler . . .'

Egbert swerved neatly round. 'What I'm trying to say is . . . *I love her so much.*'

'Good. . . I mean, I'm sure you do . . .'

'And I'd do anything to make her happy.'

'Please – Egbert,' Alice said desperately. She hated heart-to-hearts at the best of times. This was beyond any call of duty. This was hell.

'The thing is, I know she confides in you, Alice, and I just . . . Well I just want to say that I'm so happy . . . *so happy* . . . that she has someone to confide in. It could be awfully lonely for her otherwise. I think that was actually part of the problem for Emma . . .' He laughed. '*Emma* was an absolute man eater, it turns out! Turns out there was barely a male on the estate she didn't sort of . . . you know . . .'

Alice fiddled with the door handle and longed for the journey to end. Or for another toddler – a family of toddlers – to fall in front of the car. Anything. 'My goodness,' she said. 'Nearly there!'

'... From what I can gather she was having it off with pretty much every male within a twenty-mile radius of the place! Lady Chatterley move over!' He laughed, and then apologised. 'Sorry. Not appropriate. Anyway ... I was just ... Christ ... I don't know ... I suppose I was just – I wanted to thank you. For being such a good friend to my wife. She'd be so desperately lonely here if it weren't for you ...'

'No need to thank me,' Alice said. Was he fishing? What did he know? Alice couldn't be sure. She wanted to say something else, to help him to feel a bit better – but at that point all she could think of was Dominic's letter. And India, ogling him across the Chinese Drawing Room, declaring herself a 'perv' for finding him attractive; and India, with her hand on Hamish's thigh last night; and India, discovering Lady Tode didn't want to make her mistress of Tode Hall after all ... And India, grasping Dominic's arm when the news came through... And Lady Tode, lying in that pool of blood, and India, turning the key to the mausoleum door and leaving her there to die. India, never commenting on her absence, even though she knew ...

'Did India ever mention losing a massive jar of very expensive face cream?' she interrupted Egbert suddenly. 'Silly question, I know.'

But he absolutely wasn't listening. He was on his own jag, jabbering on ... Alice wished she'd been paying attention '... she'll probably *hit the roof*,' he was saying. '... India's not *really* vindictive,' he added. 'I mean, she has a dreadful temper. But she's incapable of bearing grudges ...' He left a pause. 'Plus – of course, these things are all tied up so tight by the lawyers. So, I mean, the estate will obviously have to cough up, no matter what, *whatever* India says ... And listen, I'm just an executor. It's nothing to me, not really. But I mean – it's a bit much, isn't it? I worked out this morning we could buy two hundred plus freshly calved heifers with that. Or a terraced house in Broadstairs ... albeit in need of updating. But it's a lot of money.'

Alice wasn't quite sure who or what he was talking about. She said: 'Sorry, Egbert. I'm confused. India bearing grudges about what? What have the lawyers got tied up?'

'Hm?' He glanced across at her. 'Oh I'm *sorry*! I've been blathering on! Ignore me, Alice. I do apologise. I've been unloading all my sorrows on you, as if you don't have plenty of your own ...'

'No but – I don't understand ...'

'Never mind!' he said. 'Consider it a lucky escape!'

Alice could have kicked herself. What lawyers? Pay *whom*, what money, why? 'It's not a burden at all, Egbert—'

Too late. They had arrived at Africa Folly at last. He was quite relieved, now, that she hadn't been listening. It had been most inappropriate of him to be discussing it at all ...

'Right then!' he said, pulling up. 'Heart to heart over, you'll be relieved to hear. Let's get this stuff unloaded shall we? And I'll pop back to fetch Mrs Car Fizzy and the lunch. Alice I really *cannot* thank you enough for giving up your time ...'

CHAPTER 47

India visited the gift shop first, and helped herself to another box of chocolates, similar to the ones she had left for him the previous night, and while Mrs Carfizzi was busy in the kitchen, preparing the lunch that would be taken up to the Folly, she slipped into the pantry to pick up a set of keys, tiptoed down the back stairs and softly, softly let herself into the basement flat.

It was the first time she had been inside the Carfizzi residence, and she was astounded by its luxury: though humble in proportions, and with a view looking directly onto a wall, the little sitting room might have been the plushest in the entire house.

India was not an excessively educated woman. On leaving school, she'd attended an art foundation course in London and then a history of art course in Florence. She wasn't a reader, and didn't care for politics. Maths had never been her thing, and she'd been given a special dispensation from studying sciences because her mother told the school they made India's brain ache. But that didn't mean she was stupid. And it certainly didn't stop her from recognising top quality Italian design when she saw it. In all its smoked glass, leather and gilt, the place looked like a Versace Home show room.

As she stood there with her chocolates, wondering which of the three doors before her would lead to Carfizzi's sickroom, she calculated the value of what was laid out before her. There was no way they could have created a room like this from what the Tode Estates paid them. It must have cost her caretaker and his wife a minimum of £200,000 to decorate the place to this standard.

'Thieving bastards!' she muttered gleefully.

She found Carfizzi's bedroom behind the second door she opened. Even plusher than the sitting room, it was clad from floor to ceiling in dark brown leather and dominated by a bed shaped like a giant gilt-winged swan. She found Carfizzi sleeping peacefully, his bald head nestling between the swan's withers, amid an overpowering smell of high quality leather, mustard and vomit. Above him soared the arch of the swan's golden neck. On either side of him, on the matching tables, were two plastic bowls, brimming with bright yellow sick.

'Oh my God, Carfizzi!' India burst out laughing.

He woke up with a jolt. Glimpsed her, looming above him.

'You look a bit *peely-wally*, as they say in Scotland. What's up?' She indicated the two bowls, and sniffed. 'Is that what I think it is?'

He groaned, and turned away.

'Don't turn away!' she said. She sat on the edge of the bed. '*Look at me*, Carfizzi.' He didn't. 'Look at me,' she said again.

Slowly, he turned to face her. He looked sick and afraid.

247

After a while, India smiled. She waved the chocolate box under his nose. 'I brought you chocolates,' she said. 'I know how much you like them. But perhaps this isn't the moment?'

'Take them away!' he said.

'Certainly not!' she replied. 'Don't be silly! You'll love them when you're better. I'll put them here, by the sick bowl, all right? And then you can gobble them all up the moment you feel better!'

He groaned and again turned his head away.

'Please look at me, Mr Carfizzi,' she said politely. 'We need to talk ... Seriously ... I'm deadly serious, Carfizzi. We can't carry on like this. We need to sort out a better way of working together.'

'You *poisoned* me,' he whispered. 'You tried to k—' But it was too much for him. He began to gag on the word. India had to wait while he reached for the bowl beside the chocolates, and coughed and spluttered and emptied what stringy mucus remained in his stomach. He wiped his mouth. Put the bowl back. 'You tried to kill me,' he said.

India laughed. 'God, you're such a drama queen! Of course I didn't try to "kill" you! It was a *joke*. J-O-K-E, geddit? I just got a *teeny bit* fed up with you sending me hate vibes, day after day after day. Can you blame me? So finally I thought, *why not*? I might as well actually *do* something to deserve it!'

He stared at her. 'You think I'm stupid,' he said. 'But I know. I know all about it, India. *Dominic told me.*'

A long pause.

'What did Dominic tell you?' she asked at last.

Carfizzi started crying. 'You disgust me. Get out of my home. Get out or I will call the police.'

India stood up. She bent over the bed, so that their faces

248

were only centimetres apart. The smell of vomit on his breath would, normally, have been enough to make her recoil, but at that instant, her anger superseded everything.

She detested him, the sight of him, the smell of his breath. Above all, she hated how much he hated her. Egbert was right. She liked to think she could cope with almost anything in life. But she could not cope with dislike. It was Carfizzi's rejection of her; the look of disdain on his face that made her want to squeeze the life out of him. Her two hands hovered, just above his throat. He stared at them. He whimpered – and it broke the spell. The helplessness of the sound made her laugh. She took his nose between finger and thumb and pinched as hard as she could.

Mr Carfizzi yelped in pain.

She released it, and headed for the exit.

'You hurry and get well now, Mr Carfizzi,' she called back to him from the sitting room, in quite a different voice. 'Poor Mrs Carfizzi is worried sick about you!' She pulled back the door that opened into the main house, and stepped slap into Mad Ecgbert.

'India!'

'Oh. Hello Ecgbert.'

'We have to talk. I have something of the utmost urgency—'

'I thought you'd gone to Todeister with Egg?'

'I'm going in a sec. Just one sec. Mrs Car Fizzy has ordered me a cab but I needed to speak to you first. I wanted to discuss it with Car Fizzy but now I've found you obviously I should tell you, instead. I've already spoken to Mellors . . .'

'Mellors?' she said vaguely.

'It's spectacularly important—'

India grasped both his shoulders and gave them an

affectionate shake. Warmly, she smiled up into his wild (but handsome) face. 'Not now, Ecgbert,' she said.

'What? No, *wait*! India, I'm serious. I've got emails. Off Ma's computer. I've got evidence.' He waved something in her face – a piece of plastic. A memory stick. 'I just need to print them out. That's all.'

The smile died. In a flash she had snatched the memory stick and shoved it into her jeans pocket.

'Hey! Give that back!'

'No.'

'Give it back!'

'*Nobody cares*, you crazy fuck,' she said. 'Can't you get that into your stupid skull? *Nobody cares about your horrible mother*. Just – do us all a favour. Just this once. Shut the fuck up, and go home.'

He stepped back, shell shocked, and she swept past.

He didn't follow her. If she wouldn't speak to him, he would speak to Car Fizzy. Fine. After that, he would take the taxi that was waiting for him and head home. There was a back-up memory stick on his bedside table. Actually there were about ten of them. Not to mention a back-up portable hard drive. And a printer too of course. He would print out the salient messages – several times, to be sure that everyone got to see them. And then he'd come back to the Hall and explain to the assembled company – a bit like Hercule Poirot – who killed his mother. India couldn't silence him so easily. Certainly not. He chuckled.

'Crazy bitch,' he muttered. 'You're the crazy one.'

India shouted back at him: 'I heard that!'

'Yeah, you were meant to,' he replied (nervously). It wasn't true.

CHAPTER 48

Most of the guests skipped breakfast altogether. Just after noon, the small English actor whose name no one could remember, and his anorexic heiress girlfriend, Poppy Rockefeller, slopped into the dining room together. They sat side by side at the table, sipped coffee, and sent silent hate vibes to one another, to the world, and above all, to Hamish who, two hours and twenty minutes after he'd first sat down to breakfast, was still at his place at the table, munching his way through the controversial kedgeree.

Poppy Rockefeller lit a cigarette and asked if her small actor boyfriend couldn't organise for someone to remove the smell of kedgeree from around her nostrils.

He said he couldn't.

Hamish munched on.

India breezed in. She was annoyed by the sight of them all, sitting there relaxing, when the morning was going so badly for her, and immediately rang the bell for Mrs Carfizzi to come in and clear. She told them breakfast was over, and that the important challenge at this point was to get the rest of the guests out of bed in time for lunch.

'It's an early lunch,' India said, 'because I'm sure you'll all be wanting to head back to town before the afternoon rush. In my experience,' she added, 'you're best setting off not much later than three p.m. That way you'll avoid the Sunday night tailbacks. So . . .' India glanced at the skinny heiress, and realised she couldn't remember her name, either. It was awkward. 'I'll see you all up at the Folly. And I warn you – it's a good fifteen-minute walk.'

The small actor muttered something surly under his breath.

India beamed at him. Sunlight and roses. 'But I absolutely promise you it'll be worth it! It's a wonderful view. Plus this Yorkshire air is very good for hangovers.'

She breezed back out into the hall again, bored with the dining room and feeling very unhappy, really, about the way the weekend was unfolding. Not at all as she'd planned. She was bored with her guests and couldn't wait for them to leave. She couldn't stand the sight of Hamish, with his stupid bruised face, and she hated Dominic, who – so far as she could see – was indirectly responsible for everything. The whole debacle. She'd only dreamed up the stupid weekend in the first place as a way to help him relaunch his useless career . . . This was how he thought he could repay her. No.

She was saved from any more brooding by the vision of handsome Oliver Mellors, looking quite angry, and advancing on her with an envelope. His appearance confused her: he didn't normally come into the house, and he never normally looked angry. Then she remembered – in all the upheaval last night, they had abandoned the murder mystery walkabout.

She'd completely forgotten about him, playing dead, in the Lady Laverty Suite.

'Mellors!' she cried. 'We never found the corpse! Oh my God, I am *so sorry*! ... *What did you do?*'

He brushed aside that question. His corpse-like slumber had been interrupted at 4 a.m. by James O'Shea, the bearded talkshow host, and his girlfriend the American-born magazine editor, stumbling into their bed. What the three of them did next was none of his boss's business.

However the letter he was carrying, most definitely was.

'I've been trying to give this to your husband since yesterday,' he said. 'But I can't find him. I'm tired and I want to go home.' He shoved it into her hand. 'Lady Tode gave it me before she died. I forgot about it, 'til I saw it peeping out the secret pocket yesterday.'

'Peeping out the secret pocket, Mellors? Not sure I fully *comprendi* ...'

'Well it doesn't matter, does it?' he said shortly. 'You've got it now, haven't you? Safely received. Do what you like with it. It's not my problem.'

Emma Tode had always been giving him things: little treasures that he generally soon lost; boring little cards and newspaper cuttings that she thought he might find interesting. He often didn't bother to look at them. This one had fallen out of the lining of his hat yesterday morning (a place he often put annoying paperwork). He thought, having finally opened it and read it through, that he should pass it on before the inquest. Just in case anyone decided it was important. Now that he'd finally delivered it he could go home and watch *Game of Thrones* with his wife. He left India standing by the fireplace with the envelope in her hands. She could throw it in the fire, for all he cared. He had done his bit.

She didn't throw it in the fire. She opened and read it – of course – and then she read it a second time, to reconfirm her initial and every following impression. Emma Tode had been an unusually nasty woman. She deserved everything she got.

India laughed. An unusually nasty laugh. Now she only needed to find Dominic.

CHAPTER 49

One-twenty p.m. at the Africa Folly. Blustering wind, dark clouds, drizzling, miserable rain. A hell of a lot of low level disgruntlement in the air. And still only half the guests had turned up.

Alice and James O'Shea the talkshow host found themselves standing opposite one another while they were waiting for more people to arrive for lunch. Alice offered him a bland smile/grimace at the general state of affairs.

'Bit chaotic, isn't it?' she said.

He replied: 'I'm not actually clear. Are you guest or staff?'

'Staff,' Alice said.

'Oh, right.' Mr O'Shea believed passionately in equality, diversity, fairness, tolerance etc, and 'had a lot of time' for gender fluidity ... but he hadn't come to Tode Hall to talk to a middle-aged housekeeper/secretary or whatever the hell she was. Not with a hangover. He turned away.

At this point it struck Alice, quite forcefully, how little she would be missed if she sidled off home … It was a Sunday, after all. She'd already helped to lay up the table. And what with the face cream developments, she had a lot to think about. It seemed pointless to hang around.

She muttered something about a headache to Egbert, who was excessively sympathetic, and headed home.

'Ah. Excellent,' declared Geraldine when she saw Alice trudging through the door so much earlier than expected. 'Where were we? Sit down, Alice, dear. We have so much to discuss. But first things first. We really do *need* to deal with Dominic Rathbone's *soi-disant* "evidence" as it were. If you won't throw it in the river, the least you could do is put it in the bin.'

Alice said (she was in a foul mood): 'I'm not throwing anything in the bin if it's evidence of a murder.'

By 1.45 p.m., lunch was shrivelling in the gas-powered warming trolley and tempers in the Folly were fraying. Having been dragged from their beds and forbidden any breakfast, the guests were hanging around in clothes that didn't keep out the Yorkshire cold, feeling hard done by and hungover. The poshness novelty of staying in such a massive house had worn off, and they longed to be home in their luxurious, centrally heated metro-pads. They weren't even being allowed to start

lunch because neither India nor Hamish were yet present, and Egbert didn't want to start without them.

He wandered outside briefly, to escape everyone. His children didn't notice him leave, and didn't follow, so he stood for a while and allowed himself to breathe the lovely air. It was a rare moment of solitude in his busy, dutiful life, and he tried to enjoy it. The view to the house was spectacular from here. *What a fine house it is*, he thought. He thought of his wife: his beautiful, lovely wife, and he felt a short stab of confusing sadness.

The fishing leases in the North Lake needed updating. There should be a waiver added to the contracts, to protect the estate against people drowning ... His mind wandered back to his beautiful, lovely wife, and he felt a short stab of confusing sadness.

The loose paving outside the Old Stable Yard needed seeing to before some idiot tripped over and sued— *Where the fucking hell was India? Where was that rat, Hamish? And Dominic? Where were they? Where was Dominic?* Egbert felt a short stab of confusing rage, and quickly turned his mind to other matters. A meeting with the traffic chap at Todeister town council on Monday, after the inquest, to discuss the possibility of shuttle buses. *Could he get rid of Dominic? Could he fire him? He'd like to kill him, frankly.* But firing him might be easier. Or it might not, actually. In this day and age. Impossible to fire anyone these days.

There was a car from Todeister Minicabs making its way up the drive. Egbert saw it and thought: *Oh God, not Ecgbert again!* Was he back already?

Tourists weren't allowed to bring vehicles onto that part of the drive. They had to park by the Old Stable Yard, and could only enter the grounds via the courtyard with its loose paving and many retail opportunities ... Which meant that whoever it was in the minicab had some sort of dispensation or family pass. *Where the bloody hell was India? Why wasn't she answering her phone?*

The guests were fed up. So were the children. So was he, frankly. Perhaps they should just start lunch without her?

Except she might be furious.

Also – what if that really was Mad Ecgbert coming back up the drive? Egbert couldn't very well leave him to roam about the house without supervision, and Carfizzi, normally so good at dealing with him, had chosen this weekend – of all weekends! – to pull a sickie.

Egbert imagined the worst. These days that was all he ever tended to do. *What if* the burglar alarms weren't switched on properly? *What if* the insurance on the farm vehicles had accidentally been allowed to lapse? *What if* a tourist accidentally toppled onto a Gainsborough and ripped the canvas? *What if the Socialists got in?*

More to the point: *what if* Mad Ecgbert, seeing he had the run of the house, started taking pictures off the walls and loading them into his minicab? *What if* Mad Ecgbert, seeing he had the run of the house, literally decided to establish squatters rights, and move in? *What if*, even as Egbert stood there, admiring the view, his mad cousin was moving into his dressing room, his bathroom, his bedroom; literally, at that instant, and still with his shoes on, climbing into his marital bed? It was more than a bit much. It was much, much, much too much.

Egbert popped his head round the Folly door. The Londoners were standing in surly, homogenous clumps, looking miserable. He shouted out to them all ...

'Really sorry about the delay folks! Not sure quite where

India's got to. I'm going to nip back down to the house and check everything's OK – but do start without me. You must be starving!'

There was a rumble of protest. The guests had been dragged up here through the rain and the cold, when they would have much preferred to continue in the grand dining room – which, after all, was the whole point of the weekend. Now here they were, stuck up a hill, hungover, hungry, and fully abandoned by their hosts.

Nevertheless they plonked themselves at the table and began, dutifully, to throw bread rolls at one another and wait for their shrivelled lunch to be finally presented.

Mrs Carfizzi placed a large, flat dish of grey vegetables onto the middle of the table and gestured to the guests that they pass it around.

The meat she brought out next was even greyer. Not only that, as the little actor loudly pointed out when spooning the tiniest sliver onto his plate, 'This smells of farts'.

That was actually the moment when the mutiny took root. Nobody wanted to be there: not a single person present would not have preferred to be somewhere else. And when someone – again, the little actor – gave voice to this obvious fact, it begged the question: *so why the hell were they sticking around*? One by one, the guests sniffed their plates and agreed that the food smelled of farts. Enough was enough.

'I vote,' declared the little actor, 'that we go back to the house, fetch our cars and fuck off to the pub. What do you all think?'

As usual, Poppy Rockefeller didn't seem to think anything. She stared sullenly ahead. But the others thought it was a great idea. 'Brilliant!' they cried. 'Let's go!'

And so they did. The children quickly followed, leaving Mrs Carfizzi alone, holding the last of her trays. She glanced around the empty room, noticed the bread rolls lying on the floor, the meat dishes that smelled of farts, and she shrugged. She had left her husband sick in bed. Not only that, there was a passage in *Crime and Punishment* which troubled her, now she was reading in the original. She wanted to check against the translation. If nobody wanted to eat her food, there was no reason for her to stick around, either.

'Bollocks to this,' she muttered, and dumped the tray where she stood.

She was the last to leave the Folly. She didn't waste any time locking up – what did she care?

Being quite fat, and a little lame, and physically very lazy, she never quite caught up with the rest of the party, so – for better or worse – she missed out on all the drama that followed.

CHAPTER 50

For the second time in twenty-four hours the 12th Baronet Tode swept up the long drive in the same minicab. This time, however, he didn't stop at the Hall. He asked his driver to take him on to the Gardener's House instead.

'We owe Derek fifteen quid,' he informed Alice, when she opened the door. 'It's the second time he's driven me out here today, and I know for a fact my conversation has been getting on his nerves, so do you mind giving him a splendiferous tip? He's actually one of my best friends. Along with you, Trudy. You're my best friend.' He stepped around her and into the kitchen, where he found his grandmother.

'Oh you're here, are you, Granny?' he said. 'That's nice.' He sat down in the seat that had been Alice's, and took a slurp from her wine glass. Grimaced. 'Crikey, Trudy! Cat's piss!' he shouted. 'Have you got any whisky?' But she couldn't hear because she was outside collecting a receipt from Derek. 'Have you got any whisky?' He stood up again and started opening cupboards.

'New bottle above the fridge,' said his granny.

He thanked her. Sniffed. 'Somebody around here been smoking doobies? Granny I'm shocked.'

'Don't be impertinent, Ecgbert.'

He sat back down again. Looked at his grandmother, complimented her Chinese embroidered jacket, which was exquisite. She was pleased with that. He said: 'So you're up to date with the dramas, I take it?'

'I think so. Dominic's run off to London, leaving behind him a lot of vile and unbelievable accusations. It's most disagreeable.' She sipped the tea. 'You must help me to persuade Alice not to report all this nonsense to the police.'

Vigorously, he shook his head, spilling whisky on his chin as he did so. 'WRONG,' he said. 'You've got everything wrong, Granny. God – that's very disappointing ... Ah. Here you are, Trudy. You've made friends with Granny, I see. Not everyone does... I have so much to tell you. But first – was Derek OK? Did you give him a splendiferous tip?'

'Yes I did.'

'Thank you ... Sorry to barge in by the way. Are you busy?'

Alice told him not to be ridiculous. 'It's lovely to see you, Ecgbert. Are you all right though? That awful man, Hamish ...'

He said he was in better shape than Car Fizzy, but that he hadn't come here to waste time on small talk. (His grandmother nodded approvingly.) He had information, he said, about his mother's death. 'I know who did it!' he declared. 'And I have evidence. The game is up!'

Geraldine said: 'Dominic seems to think he knows who did it, too. Alice and I were just now discussing what we should do, or rather, *not* do, with the so-called evidence. Alice, tell him about the letter, and the key and the pot of cream and so on.'

'Forget about the cream. It's a red herring. I know all about the cream. I've spoken to Car Fizzy . . . And by the way he's going to be absolutely fine. In case you were worrying. Better still, he's very happy to blame the poisoning on Hamish, if need be. So.' Ecgbert shrugged. 'That works quite well, I would have said.'

'Ecgbert,' said his grandmother sternly, 'I like *very much* the way you're talking. Please pay close attention to me. This is very important. As I said to Alice, we need to . . . ' She was winking at her grandson, pointing at Dominic's letter, lying open on the table, and the key beside it, still covered in cream – and then, none too subtly, indicating the wood-burning Aga behind her. '*We need to make sure we put the evidence in a safe place.*'

Mad Ecgbert ignored his grandmother. From his pocket he brought out a small metal box, slightly larger than an iPhone, with a short electric coil attached to it. He slapped it on top of Dominic's letter.

'Is it a bomb?' Geraldine asked.

'By the way, Trudy – really sorry. It was you, was it, who chased after me when I broke in here the other night? I'd sort of assumed it was Granny. Did I frighten you?'

'You did. You scared the life out of me.'

'Point is,' he said, 'it was worth it.' He tapped the hard drive. 'I've got the whole thing backed up on here. Everything. Emails, iMessages, everything. Not only that . . . '

'Ecgbert,' Geraldine said. 'Would you kindly speak the Queen's English?'

Ecgbert ignored her. He rummaged beneath his shirt and pulled from his jeans waistband a wad of paper. 'I've printed everything out. All the important bits ... I knew it, Trudy. I knew something was up from the moment she went missing ...'

'But she never did go missing,' Alice said. 'Nobody *missed* her. Everyone thought she'd gone to Capri.'

Mad Ecgbert looked at Alice. 'The last time I saw Ma alive,' he said, 'I asked her to come with me to the mausoleum. Actually, I insisted on it.' Which admission begged various questions. He hesitated to go into the details, but he had no real choice. His shrink had put him up to it: a last ditch attempt, on the eve of her long departure, to trigger a spark of warmth, a flash of maternal feeling. (Emma Tode had been extremely busy at the time. She'd only agreed to come along because he had promised her, in return, that afterwards he would leave her in peace to get on with her packing.)

So they'd gone together to the mausoleum on the last day she was seen alive, in the place she was found dead ...

'I really wouldn't bother to mention this to anyone else, dear,' his grandmother said.

Mad Ecgbert had stood beside his mother. He had gazed at her as she rested her eyes on the shelf where her dead husband lay. As his shrink had instructed, he waited a moment or two and then asked her *what she felt*. She'd sniffed (surprised by the question) and replied: 'It's such a gorgeous place to be buried, isn't it? I should think Papa's very happy here.'

At that moment Ecgbert, who was not a violent fellow, experienced what he described to Geraldine and Alice as 'a *murderous flash*'.

'Darling. Honestly,' tutted his grandmother, 'these are the sort of personal details that *nobody* wants to hear. Especially in these circumstances. A little self editing, please ...'

He would have liked to bump her on the head and leave her for dead, he told them. He *longed* to bump her on the head, actually (he said). Instead, he stepped back. He stepped away from her. He realised, at last, that his rainbow's end could never be reached because 'Trudy, it never existed!' The thing he was seeking from his mother, she simply didn't have to give. She would never be able to say something she truly felt or believed, because she had never in her life truly felt or believed anything. 'I had clarity, Trudy! Clarity at last!' It was as if a great weight had lifted from his chest.

So he had left her there, in the mausoleum. And she had stood politely and let him leave. They didn't say goodbye.

'. . . *Anyway*,' Ecgbert said. 'The point is, I left her alone in the mausoleum on the day everybody thought she was leaving for Capri . . . on the day she obviously died. And I left the door wide open. *My mother had brought the key with her, and she had left the key in the lock.*'

Geraldine nodded. 'Hm. So. It was serendipity, was it? Whoever it was . . .' She glanced at Alice. '. . . Car Fizzy, for example – or some other non Tode: Mellors, perhaps? Dominic Rathbone? Those fatuous little twins who never turn up for work? They just happened to be passing by at that moment. They found Emma alone, bopped her on the head, slammed the door, locked it, and put the key in the err – into India's pot of cream . . . Sounds good,' Geraldine said. 'I'm happy to believe that. Are you Alice? It was probably Mellors, I should think. His father was a ghastly man.'

Ecgbert shook his head. 'Everyone around here thinks I'm a halfwit . . .'

'They most certainly do not!' declared his grandmother, quite angrily.

'... But I'm the one who's managed to stitch this thing together. I only came over, really, to make sure Trudy is with me when I tell everyone what happened—' He glanced bashfully at Alice. 'After my rotten start this morning. But Granny since you're around, come along too! I'm going to gather everyone in the Great Hall, celebrities included if they want. And explain more or less exactly what went down. Think Monsieur Poirot, or rather ...' He pulled himself up. 'Think Sir Egbert Tode, Twelfth Baronet, Not as Useless as Everyone Thinks ...'

'Egbert darling, you are ridiculous. *Nobody* thinks you're useless,' said his grandmother.

'Anyway the point is, I know who dunnit.' He couldn't resist adding, 'And it's all about THE MONEY! Always is though, isn't it? Money and power. Isn't that so, Granny? Mummy changed her mind about stuff just before she died ... Honestly, it's no wonder she got done in.'

At exactly that moment, a cacophony filled the room. This time it wasn't coming from the darkest depths of Geraldine, but from an intruder alarm that was linked to the Hall, the Estate Offices, and the police station.

'Holy Christ,' said Egbert. 'We'd better get over there. Here I am showing off to you girls. Meanwhile a killer is on the loose! What kind of an idiot does that?'

Egbert, Alice and Geraldine scampered (or glided) over the silent grass and let themselves into the house via the East Wing. On opening the door they were blasted by another wall of hellish sound, and in front them, careering through the baroque arches, they saw Hamish Tomlinson, with a bundle under his arm. Oliver Mellors followed close behind, shouting at the top of his lungs (or so they assumed: nobody could quite hear it):

'Stop thief!'

They followed the action as best they could, through the arches, down the Corridor of the Ancients, into the Great Hall, where a vast fire burned in the grate, and the Christmas tree decorations shimmered and shook to the throb of the alarm.

Hamish Tomlinson was wearing soft leather soles. As he tried to avoid the Christmas tree he lost his footing. Mellors seized the moment, launched himself through the air and landed on top of Hamish, crushing him to the marble floor, sending his stolen booty flying. The alarm stopped. And started again. It seemed to come in waves. In the sudden, short silence, Hamish flailed. But he didn't stand a chance. Beneath Mellors's manly bulk, he looked like a weedy grasshopper.

'You thieving bastard!' panted Ecgbert triumphantly. 'I always knew you were a shit. And it's no good trying to escape. We've got you now! Well done Mr Mellors! What a show! The police will be on their way any second. So you can just lie there – if you don't mind Mellors? – and think about what you've done ...'

Ecgbert stooped to pick up the fallen treasure. It was nothing much: nothing the Todes would have missed. A Bronze Age shield, possibly for a child: or a very small one, in any case. Dominic Rathbone could have told Ecgbert its value and provenance in a flash. So could Hamish, who had done a little research on the Tode treasures, over the years (though not,

267

apparently, despite his efforts at dinner last night, updated himself on their new motion-sensitive alarm systems).

The alarm stopped again. And started. Like a child having a tantrum, it seemed to need to pause intermittently to refill its lungs.

Unfortunately neither Mellors nor Ecgbert knew the code to turn it off. They would have to wait until someone came – the police, Egbert, Carfizzi.

So they waited. On-Off, it went. On-Off. A minute or two passed, the symphony of torture, drilling intermittently into their brains. It paused once again, and in the silence, fluttering down from high above them, there came a single sheet of paper.

And then, from the gallery, a bay of rage.

Seventy foot up, Dominic Rathbone was stretching over the empty space above, reaching in vain for the fluttering sheet. And beside him, India. They were grappling, tussling, yelling.

Ecgbert cried out. 'India! He's going to kill you. Get away from there!'

Too late. The alarm had struck up again. And Dominic had turned back from the railing, grabbed for India, tried to launch her over the edge, but in the process lost his balance, and launched them both.

The bodies plunged, flying through the air together, and the paper fluttered slowly behind. It caught on a branch of the Christmas tree, and never landed.

CHAPTER 51

The Great North Door was only unlocked on very special occasions. Today wasn't one of them. Egbert had trudged round the side of the house, to the family's private entrance. He tapped in the entry code, pulled back the door – and was, as Ecgbert, Geraldine and Alice had been, hit at once by the great wall of sound. Never had he heard so much of it. Tode Hall's alarm system seemed to be screaming from every room in the house.

Ahead of him were the stairs that led up to his and India's private apartment. To the left lay the Red Dining Room, the Chinese Drawing Room and the staff kitchen. To the right, via a long passageway, past artworks and arches, and out of sight, lay the Great Hall. He hesitated, uncertain which way to turn, what to protect first—

His children. Of course. They were out of harm's way, up at the Folly.

India ...

From the Great Hall, more shrill than even the burglar alarm, he heard a scream – two screams – then a third. Three separate voices. Three separate screams, followed moments later by the SILENCE – and the *thud* . . . The alarm struck up again, and then, over it, just the one voice, still screaming.

Egbert sprinted past the artworks and arches, and in the Great Hall skidded to a halt.

Before the hearth, with its warm roaring fire, not seeping, not flowing, but gushing over the black and white marble floor, was a river of blood. More blood than Egbert had ever seen. And kneeling in the blood, bent over a mangle of limbs, a splay of long golden hair, was his cousin Ecgbert.

'*India?* . . . India!' Egbert's feet wouldn't move fast enough. He splashed through the blood towards her.

Mad Ecgbert said: 'I could've stopped it . . .' he pointed upward, to the gallery above. 'They were fighting. They were falling through the air . . .'

They? Egbert repeated. He had seen the blood, the hair, the tangled limbs, but he hadn't looked properly. There were two bodies, one on top of the other: India, in a Barbour jacket and wellingtons; on her way to lunch, of course. And beneath her – the crushed remains of her assailant – of Dominic. He was dressed in the suit he always wore for London. All this, Egbert registered. The London suit, because Dominic was meant to be in London. The Barbour jacket because India was meant to be on her way to the Folly. Dominic – what was left of him – had cushioned her fall. Somewhere beneath the flow of blood, the halo of golden hair, Dominic's skull lay, flattened, its contents spilling onto the floor. Neither body moved.

The burglar alarm rang on. Ecgbert and Egbert, kneeling side by side in the blood, didn't register it. They didn't hear the running footsteps; or notice Mr Carfizzi joining them, his face waxy, his breath smelling of vomit, his Daniel Hanson dressing gown hanging open. They didn't notice the London guests gathering to gawk behind them, staring at the mess and taking surreptitious photographs; nor did they appreciate Alice covering the children's eyes, shepherding them and the Londoners back down the corridor again.

The paramedics arrived with the police. They lifted the two grieving men out of the blood. They separated the broken bodies; placed India's onto one stretcher and Dominic's onto the other. And at some point, young Egbert would recall much later, someone took Hamish Tomlinson away in an arm-lock and dumped him in the cells.

CHAPTER 52

There's not much that doesn't seem better after a good night's sleep. Unfortunately, on this night of nights, nobody enjoyed that luxury, except for India. India slept like a baby. Not only had she survived a seventy-foot fall onto a hard marble floor, she emerged from the incident the following morning as beautiful as ever, her wits and bones perfectly intact, and even – what was truly miraculous – revealing a glimmer of a sense of humour.

First to visit at the hospital (after Egbert of course, who was sent off in search of decent coffee) came Mr Carfizzi, quivering with soon-to-be-shed Italian teardrops, and filling the cubicle with the sweet smells of aftershave.

'I am so sorry,' he whimpered. 'I am ashamed.'

India listened to his meandering confession with a stern face. 'That was actually seriously wicked of you, Mr Carfizzi,' she said when he had finished. 'Fabricating evidence ... Stealing keys and putting them in cream pots ... You would have left my children without a mother! And what do you suppose would've become of Tode Hall? *National Trust*, Mr Carfizzi. Think about it!'

But she could never stay cross with people for long. Especially when they apologised. She said, 'You must have loved Dominic very much.'

The Italian teardrops flowed. Yes, he had. He had loved him very, very much.

'I'm sorry I poisoned you,' she said.

'And me, I'm sorry I tried to frame you for murder.'

They hugged it out.

India still had one more question:

'. . . There was a letter. From Lady Tode. I tossed it over the railing just before Dominic sent me over . . .'

'Hm?'

'Did you happen to see it? It was a legal thing . . .'

He shrugged. 'I don't know about any letter.'

Next to join them was Alice, with Geraldine in tow. India wanted to know if the story of her fall had reached the newspapers yet.

'There is a *little* interest . . .' Alice said, having battled her way through a hundred-strong pack of journalists, first at the top of the Hall drive, and then again at the doors to the hospital. 'A couple of your guests put pictures up on Instagram so – the image of you and Dominic on the hall floor is . . . well, it's pretty much everywhere . . .'

India shuddered. 'Can you see my pants?'

Alice smiled. 'You were wearing trousers.'

'*Lucky*,' said India, relaxing back on the pillows. Alice patted her leg.

'Are you all right?' Alice asked.

'Me? Oh, I'm fine …'

'Can you remember what happened?'

'Not really, no,' she said. 'Well … Actually there was a letter – do you remember? I threw it over the edge … You don't happen to know what happened to it?'

Alice frowned. 'I think it got stuck in the tree, didn't it? But there was so much going on …'

Next in: Sir Ecgbert. He'd somehow wheedled his way past the press and through the hospital's security. He arrived hotly pursued by Egbert, who was trying and failing to keep him away.

With great panache Sir Ecgbert pulled back the curtains surrounding India's bed and smiled warmly down onto the gathering.

It was quite a squash in there: Alice, Geraldine, Carfizzi, India – and now Egbert and Ecgbert, all jostling for space. Somebody in the next door bed grumbled about the disturbance, but everyone ignored him.

'Worry no more, India, my friend,' Sir Ecgbert cried. 'And by the way, it's good to see you're alive. I have the letter! Plus – thanks to my computer wizardry, not to mention my excellent, outstanding intuition, my nose for a crime, et cetera – I've got all the emails and all the messages Mummy and Dominic sent each other before she died. They had a massive row because she didn't want him with her in Capri.'

'Why, yes. Now you mention it, it was *ferocious*,' Geraldine nodded. 'I'd quite forgotten.' She waved this small detail aside. 'But darling, they were always rowing.'

Ecgbert rolled his eyes. 'You might have said something. We could have cleared this up long ago.'

'Who might have mentioned it?' Egbert asked. 'Mentioned what?'

'Granny. Never mind. The point is: Mummy was so completely fed up with him, she decided to change her will. Mellors and his wife were meant to be witnesses. They were about to sign the damn thing that day – the day Mummy was meant to go to Capri. But then – well actually it was me who put a spanner in the works by turning up and absolutely insisting she come with me to the mausoleum. So she never got round to it. Never got the chance.' He paused. 'By the way Granny and Alice already know most of this. Sorry to repeat. Dominic killed Mummy to stop her getting it signed off—'

'Getting *what* signed off?' Egbert interrupted.

'*This*. Obviously.' He waved the sheet of paper retrieved from the branches of the Christmas tree. 'The addendum, disinheriting him. The addendum which your wife so idiotically took up to the gallery and presented to him . . .'

'I didn't take it up to the gallery to *present* it to him,' India protested. 'He lured me up there . . . he was crying his eyes out. He seemed really upset. Little did I realise . . . '

'The point is, he needn't have troubled himself. The addendum was never was signed off. Which meant, as long as nobody accused him of her murder, he would get the two hundred and fifty thousand pounds promised in the original will.'

275

'. . . So?' said India.

Sir Ecgbert shrugged. 'Maybe he thought you were onto him?" he said. 'Or maybe he just wanted to feel safe. Get that letter off you and destroy any possible evidence . . .'

'What an absolute *heel*,' said Egbert. 'Very brainy of you, Coz. I must say. I wouldn't have worked that out in a billion years . . .'

'Super brainy,' agreed India.

'Exceptional,' said Geraldine.

'. . . By the way . . .' Egbert leaned in, dropped his voice: 'I don't think this needs to go any further, does it? I mean . . . really. Every family has its problems. We all have our "little secrets", as it were. There's absolutely no necessity to go bothering our excellent law enforcement friends . . . especially, you know, vis-à-vis this morning's court proceedings. Mr Carfizzi, sir, are you on board with that?'

'Of course,' he said. 'You can rely on me.'

A pause.

Everyone turned to look at Alice.

From: India Tode
To: Nicola Tode, Esmé Tode
Cc: Sir Ecgbert Tode, Egbert Tode, Alice Liddell
Subject: Hello!!!

Dear Cousin-in-Laws!

Eggie wanted to reach out but I thought it would be nicer (-: if I did, as probably the last time you saw me was on the front page of your newspaper, splattered all over the Great Hall, with the tragical Dominic R beneath me, who as I presume you know, did not survive. Rest assured however it wasn't QUITE as bad as it looked, and I am absolutely fine!!! However I appreciate it was most likely pretty horrid for you to see your childhood home in that context. So I am really sorry about that!

I write with fab tidings! As you also probably know, or may also have read in the newspapers or whatever, we had your Mama's inquest in Todeister last week)-: The police were absolutely super and I must say have been super throughout. They are very helpful individuals for which Eggie and I will be ever grateful!! The verdict from the coroner came through that nothing malicious occurred, despite all the vile rumours, and it was all just an accident (-: Yay!

So now we can 'move on' as it were, and really pull together to make Tode Hall a historic house which is more than just historical! I have lots of plans, which myself and Alice Liddell (who you will remember from your childhood days!) intend to set in motion asap! So watch this space!!

However, on a more serious note, you guys need to start thinking about a funeral, as now the verdict has come in, they can't keep your lovely Mama's remains in the morgue much longer! Brilliant, brilliant Ecgbert is super-concerned about the type of coffin etc, and is very keen to go ahead and order one — I am enclosing a link to his fave, in case you think his choice is a bit OTT (sorry Ecgbert!!). So basically I think you guys should come home and help your bro with this. As you know there is LOTS of room at Tode Hall (-: so please feel welcome to stay at any time, and let's give your Ma a decent send off, as we know she was one amazing, unique lady who, despite being quite difficult in some ways, probably deserves a fabulous send off, just like anyone!!!

Big hugs to you all and REALLY look forward to welcoming you super-gorgeous people home to your super-gorgeous home!

XOXOXOX India

ACKNOWLEDGEMENTS

Thank you Harry Mount for the Latin. Thank you Paola Frankopan for the German. Thank you Nick Howard and Vicky Barnsley for being such amazingly good sports. Thank you to Clara Diaz, Hannah Wann, Gemma Shelley, Bekki Guyatt and especially Anna Boatman – I feel very lucky to be working with you.

Thank you to my mother, Teresa, and my husband, Peter, and my children, Panda, Zebedee and Bashie. Extra thanks to Panda, as always, for her sharp comments and generous encouragement ... And most of all ... thank you, Clare Alexander.

**Read on for an exclusive extract from
Daisy Waugh's new novel**

PHONE FOR
THE FISH KNIVES

When Hollywood wants to do a remake of the film
that made Tode Hall famous, India and Egbert are delighted.
They envisage a summer of free money and star-studded
dinner parties ahead . . .

But the Hall is soon overrun by wardrobe trucks
and catering tents, and lusty, insecure actors squabbling about
nudity clauses. When the movie's producers threaten to sue over
the exact colour of Tode Hall's rolling lawns, India and Egbert
realise that having a film crew on their doorstep isn't such a
breeze after all. With so many egos in one place things were
bound to end badly, but no one would have predicted
quite so literal a backstabbing . . .

Coming in May 2021

THE TODES OF TODE HALL

THE NORTH LAWN
TUESDAY, 8.41 A.M.

The lawns that stretched around Tòde Hall had turned to a drab mustard colour through the summer, making the pale stone of Britain's seventh most recognisable, privately owned stately home appear a tiny bit grubby. But there was nothing to be done. It was mid August and the county of Yorkshire hadn't seen a drop of rain in almost six weeks. On Britain's social media platforms, concern for polar bears and world apocalypse had reached yet more feverish levels. In London, Manchester, Edinburgh – even in York – furious young people were chaining themselves to buses and demanding an end to life as we live it. And in the Old Stables gift shop at the end of the drive, also in the gift shop by the ticket office, and at all three Tode Hall restaurant-cafés, there had been an unprecedented run on individually wrapped frozen lollies. In fact, across the entirety of Tode Hall's retail sector, only lemon-flavoured ice pops remained.

It had been an extraordinary summer: a wonderful summer

for almost everyone, and a useful one for the climate-change campaigners. Nevertheless, this being England, everyone was complaining.

Fifty-two year-old Sir Ecgbert Tode, 12th Baronet, for example, dressed in thick corduroy jacket, polo neck and long trousers, loping across parched lawn, keying security code into private entrance, swatting at imaginary flies, was at that very moment sounding off in a negative way about his body temperature.

'It's only eight-thirty in the morning, Trudy, and I'm already hot,' he moaned. 'I'm literally *boiling*. What is going on? Can you actually believe it?'

He was leaving a voicemail for Alice Liddell, also fifty-two years old, and currently employed as Tode Hall's 'Organisational Coordinator', whatever that meant. Nobody seemed to know – least of all Alice, who'd been in the job for almost a year. But it was a nice job. Very low key. It came with a beautiful cottage, set behind a high hedge, in the heart of Tode Hall's ancient Rose Garden, and a small car with broken seatbelts. Alice was a lifelong Londoner, but she'd spent much of her childhood on the estate staying with her late grandmother, the late Lady Tode's lady's maid. So in a way, the Hall felt a bit like home. Sir Ecgbert was calling her this morning because he loved her. But obviously he wasn't going to tell her that.

'By the way I'm at the house,' he said instead. 'And it's like a frying pan, Trudy. An absolutely massive frying pan ...' Ecgbert's voice echoed as he entered the Great Hall. 'In fact the entire country is like one massive frying pan, I've just realised. There's no escape. I'm quite worried about the badgers in Brendan Wood. God knows how they're coping. Are you awake? Will you come over for breakfast?'

Alice loved Sir Ecgbert as much as Sir Ecgbert loved Alice. But she couldn't have told him that, even if she'd wanted to, because she didn't yet know it herself. In any case, it was far too early for breakfast, especially after such a strange and disagreeable evening. She reached an arm from beneath her thin bed sheet and switched off the phone.

Sir Ecgbert, though its natural heir, didn't live at the Hall, and nor, thankfully, was he responsible for its management. This was a good thing. The Tode estate constituted not only one of the grandest and most beautiful houses in the country, but over 10,000 acres of agricultural land, fifty or sixty small cottages, aforementioned gift shops and restaurant-cafés, a farm shop, a grouse shoot, a luxury campsite, an exhibition centre, a nursery garden, an archery school, a shooting range . . . the list continues . . . It was a very large enterprise and an important local employer: definitely not something to be handed over to a man whom, in more than fifty years, had yet to complete a single day in paid employment. Sir Ecgbert, nicknamed 'Mad Ecgbert' by friends and family, would not have made a good manager.

The estate had long been cocooned in family trusts and clever tax-avoiding wheezes, so no single individual ever really 'owned' it anymore, in any case. But the right to reside in the Hall as king of the castle (not to mention draw an income from its considerable interests) was more fluid. That right would, by tradition, have been Ecgbert's. But shortly before her shocking death, his widowed mother, Lady Tode, had decided to hand the reins to a Tode better suited to the job.

In fact Lady Tode had overlooked all three of her children. She turned instead to Sir Ecgbert's young cousin Egbert (*Mr* Egbert. Also please note the lack of a 'c'). It was generally agreed that Egbert(Mr), together with his beautiful, merry wife, India, were doing a splendid job. There had been a bit of spilled blood in the early months, admittedly, first with Lady Tode herself and then with the other fellow – but luckily no one in the family had been blamed for either death; and better still, ticket sales were up. In the year since young cousin Egbert(Mr) had taken over, visitor numbers to the Hall, already in six figures for the period, were up by 14 per cent. Astonishing. Excellent. Great news all round. Of course, the long hot summer had played its part. Ditto, the newspaper headlines, after all the bloodshed. But therein lies another story (available at all good bookshops).

So.

Ecgbert (*Sir.* Sir E*c*gbert has a 'c') wandered around the house a little aimlessly, as was his wont at this time in the morning. He often arrived too early for breakfast. Since the death of his mother, almost ten months ago, he had grown in confidence and stature, and had moved from a luxury boarding house in the local town of Todeister, into a house of his own on the Tode estate. But as this was the first time he had ever lived alone, and it was early days, and he had yet to master the art of keeping food in the fridge, he tended to eat a lot of his meals at the Hall.

His good-natured cousin Egbert(Mr) would normally be returning to the house around now, mud-spattered and glowing, post twenty-mile pre-breakfast bike-a-thon. But on this Tuesday morning he had chosen to skip the bike ride and had joined his wife, India, in her luxurious daily lie-in.

Ecgbert(Sir) appeared to have the place to himself. The house was full of guests, as he well knew, having been present at the disagreeable dinner the previous night, but at 8.30 a.m.

that morning, the place was disconcertingly quiet.

Mrs Carfizzi ought to have been in the kitchen, preparing breakfast for everyone. Ecgbert sniffed the air, hoping for bacon.

Nothing.

He pricked his ears, hoping for sizzling sounds.

Nothing.

He made his way to the kitchen. But there was no sign of life in there. Last night, at the disagreeable dinner, India had mentioned how oddly the Carfizzis were behaving. And it was true, dinner had been an unusually hotchpotch affair. Mrs Carfizzi (the cook) barely put in an appearance all evening and what food she eventually presented definitely wasn't up to scratch. Her husband Mr Carfizzi (the butler) hadn't been much more visible, and he normally adored throwing his weight around when the Hall put on grand dinners.

Uncertainty shimmied and fizzed through the 12th Baronet's long body. What was going on? Had Mrs Carfizzi, born and raised in Calabria, melted in the English heat? It seemed unlikely. But then what had become of her? Ecgbert loved Mrs Carfizzi better than he had loved his own, dead mother. Since he could be bothered to remember, she had always been there, sizzling bacon in the kitchen. Breakfast and Mrs Carfizzi were (or so Sir Ecgbert felt at that instant) the only true constants in his life. And yet . . . here he was. He breathed deeply. His therapist had provided him with techniques for dealing with exactly these types of situations. He tried to remember how they went:

'The *Being* of "Now": Six Steps for Feeling OK When Life Deals You Surprises':

Breathe deeply.

Don't panic!

Remember, you are beautiful.

Bear in mind that Mrs Carfizzi is probably fine.

Perhaps Mrs Carfizzi's alarm clock has broken?

(Something like that.)

Anyway, it occurred to Ecgbert he might need to forage for his own breakfast this morning. And that was fine. An adventure, almost. It reminded him that at the end of the unsatisfactory dinner last night, India had advised guests who were still feeling peckish to help themselves from the large larder beyond the pantry, where there was 'food galore'. Chocolate cake, she said. He didn't feel like chocolate cake for breakfast. He hoped to find Mrs Carfizzi in there, and some bacon sizzling in a pan.

He wandered through the back of the kitchen, past the boot room (for boots), the gun room (for guns), the stick room (for fishing rods, long bows, cricket bats and croquet mallets), the coat room, the overnight safe, the pantry – and so on. He'd not been back here for years, and yet it still smelled the same! He used to spend hours back here as a child, stealing food, swinging off the shelves, making a nuisance of himself. Perhaps he would fry himself an egg? It couldn't be that hard. Or some sausages? God – wouldn't it be marvellous if he found sausages?

He was deep in thought as he pulled back the larder door, lost in breakfast imaginings, eyes down, shoulders a little stooped, according to habit. If all else failed it probably wouldn't be the end of the world to eat the cake for breakfast, anyway. Might even be delicious. Seriously. When you thought about it, what was so wrong with eating cake at breakfast?

It was a smallish room. Perhaps fourteen by fourteen feet,

with deep shelves from floor to ceiling on every wall, and in the middle of the room, from the ceiling, a line of large metal hooks for hanging game. As he turned on the light, the bulb popped, but he hardly noticed. He knew the room so well.

In the half-light, his head banged softly against something bulky, swinging from the hooks. A massive pheasant, perhaps. A goose. A wild boar. Hanging low. A massive, low-hanging wild boar. Wholly unlikely, of course. But he was hungry and upset about Mrs Carfizzi. His mind was on chocolate cake and sausages, and he thought he might see them both on the shelf behind the . . . the bulky object, which swung gently this way and then back, obscuring his view. Irritably, he pushed it aside. The back of his hand brushed against fabric.

He noticed shoes swinging somewhere round his hips. And then he noticed legs, and a torso, and a dark jacket hoiked awkwardly over a drooping head, and between the shoulder blades, embedded deep enough to hold the bodyweight, a rusty meat hook normally used for hanging pheasant.

A horror show.

Ecgbert reacted instinctively. The hook lodged between the shoulder blades looked agonising, and he felt compelled to do something to relieve it. The body was already stiff and cool, but he lifted it with both arms, held it tight, and *jiggled hard*. The hook stayed put – not embedded in flesh, Ecgbert realised, so much as entangled in cloth. He clambered up onto the shelves, just as he had as a child, and tried again. He leaned in, reached for the hook with one arm and yanked. A ripping sound. The hook came free. Ecgbert lost his footing, the body slipped from his grasp and, together, they tumbled to the floor.

This was all very unexpected.